The Berlin Murders

M. B. Cagin

DEDICATION

For my beloved husband and enabler, Harry Cagin

ACKNOWLEDGMENTS

I am grateful for the work of Susan Baruch as my editor and also for the help of Dennis Ross and Dr. William Fowlkes. Many thanks to Dr. Herbert Hochhauser for his analysis, to Hannah Fowlkes for her cover design and to Hannah Feinberg for providing information on Berlin.

CHAPTER 1 — BERLIN, GERMANY 1930

It was a few days before Christmas when I arrived in this cold, dark city. Snow was falling heavily. I hated coming here.

The taxi driver announced, "The Adlon Hotel, sir," as he pulled up to the curb. And there it was... the hotel where I always stayed in Berlin, now glowing with a thousand Christmas lights.

The Adlon Hotel

The white-walled lobby was filled with red oriental rugs and tall tropical plants. Cushy sofas and lounge chairs were all occupied by an elegantly dressed, over-flowing crowd. Even so, the Concierge rushed to greet me. "Ach... Herr Von Bruener, how wonderful to see you again. You look marvelous. How long will you be staying with us this time?"

"Oh... I don't know. Maybe just a few days." I raced up to my room, cleaned up quickly, and put on my tux. I knew my father would be upset if I was late for his fancy dinner party and I had to have a drink or two first.

The cocktail lounge, with its famous mahogany paneling, buzzed with conversation and the laughter of those whose painted women sparkled with diamonds. I slid onto the nearest barstool. The bartender came over at once. "It's good to see you again," he said with a smile. "Whiskey as usual?" I nodded. As soon as it was served I gulped it down like a condemned man. I ordered another, threw that one down too, and gazed into my empty glass as I considered having a third.

I dreaded going to see my father. Even though my annual Christmas visit was an old tradition, I was considering making this one my last. Suddenly I heard a loud voice. "Erich... Erich Von Bruener... is that you?" I stood up and looked at the man. For a moment I didn't recognize him. Then, I remembered this old school friend. "Karl? Isn't it? Karl Klempner?"

He grinned. "Of course it's me! Just because we haven't seen each other for years doesn't mean you don't know an old friend when you see one." I grinned back at him and we shook hands.

"Well, you've changed." I told him. "You're not as short and skinny as you used to be."

We both laughed. "You haven't changed a bit," he said. "You just got taller and taller, and more blond, and now sun-tanned as well. Where have you been?"

"Oh, mostly in Spain and Italy, where it's sunny and warm."

"And what are you up to these days?" Karl asked. "You left school so suddenly, I didn't even get a chance to say goodbye."

"Yes... well... my life changed. While my father was off fighting the war, my mother died. Didn't you hear?"

Karl shook his head. "No... no... I didn't. I'm sorry. I remember her very well."

"She was English, you know. And I was sent to live with her brother, my Uncle Tony and his family in England."

"In London?"

"No... in a small town called Doncaster. I graduated from Cambridge last year and have been traveling around Europe ever since, trying to decide what to do with my life. I'm lucky though, my mother left me an inheritance that my Uncle invested for me. So I can afford to be idle, at least for now. But what about you, Karl?"

"Ah... me? Well... my father was killed in that war and a few years later my mother remarried. It wasn't a good situation for me. I went to live with my grandfather in Zurich and graduated from the Konservatorium, their wonderful music academy. I was always interested in music, if you remember."

"Sure I remember. The violin? Wasn't it?"

"That's right, and after graduation I played for the Municipal Opera Company here in Berlin, with Bruno Walter conducting. He is unbelievable, a great talent! Then my grandfather died and left me enough money to acquire the bankrupt Berlin Opera Company. Because of the Depression, I was able to get it for a good price. But I still need a financial partner. As a matter of fact, I'm here to meet a potential investor for dinner. And you? What brings you here?"

"I'm visiting my father for the Christmas Holidays. He still lives here, in the old house, you know."

Karl nodded. "Aren't you staying there with him?"

"No… I'm staying here at the hotel. We… ah… that is… I don't get along with him very well. I visit him twice a year, for Christmas and Easter, but I never stay with him."

"I see. But do you always have to wear a tuxedo when you visit your father?"

I laughed. I suddenly remembered why I always liked Karl. "No… my father's having a fancy dinner party. He wants me to meet a lot of important people, including Adolf Hitler. Do you know who he is?"

"Yes and no. I've read about him in the newspapers, but I don't pay much attention to politics. Ask me about music." Karl glanced at his watch. "Oh, sorry, I've got to run. I can't be late."

"I've got to get going too. But listen, these dinners can't last forever. How about meeting me back in the lounge, say around ten thirty or eleven. We'll have more time to catch up."

"Great! I'll see you then," he yelled as he hurried toward the dining room. I tossed on my coat, grabbed a taxi outside the hotel, and headed for Dahlem.

In a short time the car swung into the driveway. It was very dark. I could barely make out the big pond at the front of the estate where Karl and I and other friends used to swim and sail our toy boats in the summertime. The headlights of the taxi illuminated the tall stand of pines that lined the driveway on the right. Then we rounded the bend and I saw the huge house all lit up.

As the taxi drove away I was approached by three men in some sort of uniform. "Your name, sir?" one of them asked in a crisp voice.

"What do you mean MY name? Who are you?"

"Your name?" he shouted, as the other two men drew clubs from their holsters and began to slap them into the palms of their hands. I didn't answer. Slowly they came closer... and closer.

Finally I shouted, "MY NAME... IS ERICH VON BRUENER. AND THIS IS MY HOME!"

"Ach... so sorry, Herr Von Bruener," he purred, "But you're very late. We weren't expecting any more guests." Smiling, he escorted me to the front door and bowed as he opened it for me.

I stood in the front hall seething with anger. What the hell was going on? I paced back and forth a few times to regain my composure. I focused on the childhood memories that always came flooding back whenever I returned to this house. Once again I admired the curved marble staircase and remembered the fun I had sliding down the banister.

Straight ahead was the Salon, now filled with women in silk and satin gowns and men in formal wear or military uniforms. They were seated with drinks in hand, listening to the soft music of a string quartet. On the far wall was the imposing stone fireplace and above it hung the portrait of my beautiful mother, Emily Ambrose Van Bruener. She stood smiling, her fair hair hanging loose, with the dark horse at her side, her favorite steed. The one that had thrown and killed her so long ago.

I stared at it again, as I had so many times, and wondered if it was my father I came to visit twice a year, or this painting of my beloved mother and the memory of those few short years we had together.

Nearby, a soft voice murmured, "May I take your coat, sir?" I turned to see a young girl, maybe twelve or thirteen years old, with yellow braids pinned up on top of her head. She wore a plain black dress and a starched white apron. She waited patiently for my reply. I wiggled out of my coat and handed it to her. She took it with trembling hands, gave me a frightened look and quickly disappeared.

I knew at once she was my father's latest victim. Otto Von Bruener was fond of hiring young, pretty servant girls from the poorest sections of the city, knowing they would be only too grateful to have a warm place to sleep and enough food to eat. The small salary he paid them would be vital to their unemployed parents. The only thing she had to do was satisfy her employer's desires, and maybe the desires of some who visited her employer as well. But in the end it wouldn't matter. My father would tire of her eventually and throw her out into the street. Then he'd find another destitute young girl. There were so many of them.

My father came rushing towards me with outstretched arms. "Erich... Erich... I thought you'd never get here," he shouted as he clasped me in an iron bear hug and kissed me on both cheeks.

"Come in... come in... Let me introduce you around."

First I met Leni Riefenstahl, a slim, young, newly recognized talent in the movie-making business. I found that fascinating. I hoped to get to know her better. But I was dragged off to meet Maria Von Bulow, widow of Hans Von Bulow, the famous pianist and conductor.

My father whispered loudly, "She's the patron saint of every poor musician in Berlin. Isn't that a fact, Cosima?" I was then introduced to Cosima Wagner, widow of the revered composer, Richard Wagner. After a few pleasantries were exchanged with these women, I found myself shaking hands with Adolf Hitler.

CHAPTER 2 — THE DINNER PARTY

"You're a fine looking young man," Hitler said with a smile. "Your father tells me you've graduated from Cambridge University. Are you planning to go into the family business now?"

I had to think fast. I made something up quickly. "No... no... not at all. I really like the academic life. I plan to return to Cambridge for an advanced degree. I hope to become a mathematics professor."

Otto interrupted. "It's just as well that he doesn't come into the business now. I have nothing but trouble at the paint factory. Those damn Jew trade unionists and communists are constantly whining and threatening to strike." He began to shout. "They make all kinds of claims. They say the dyes get into their skin and make them sick. Then they protest that poison vapors get into their lungs and cause insanity... others claim to die from lead poisoning. They are all a bunch of filthy liars!" He was red in the face by now, and spitting with rage. "We've owned the Von Bruener Paint Company for three generations. I know what to do and nobody is going to tell me how to run my business!"

"Otto… Otto… calm yourself," Hitler replied in a soothing voice. "I can handle all of these matters. I've told you that before. But, our Nazi Party has to gain more seats in the Reichstag and elections are expensive. How much can I count on you for?"

My father became subdued. He whispered into Hitler's ear, just as they announced that dinner was being served. Everyone was invited to take their seats in the dining hall.

The glitter of the chandeliers reflected in the mirrored walls and on the gold-rimmed China. The finest linen adorned the table, along with highly polished silver and crystal wine goblets.

I was grateful to find myself seated next to Leni Riefenstahl. I wanted to ask her about the world of movie-making. But before I could say a word… a group of uniformed men, like the ones that accosted me earlier, marched into the room and took up their stations, standing shoulder to shoulder against the walls, surrounding all of us at the table. A hush fell over the room as they filed in. I asked Leni who they were. "Oh, those are Hitler's followers," she said casually. "They're called the Brownshirts."

That was certainly an accurate description. Their uniforms consisted of light brown shirts, buttoned up tight, with riding pants that matched, tucked into highly polished black leather boots. They each had a holster for their truncheons, and a black and red armband, the Swastika. Obviously this was Hitler's personal army.

The dinner was then served… a Christmas goose with all the trimmings and a huge roast pig. Leni leaned toward me and whispered, "Isn't that Fritz Thyssen seated among the army officers?" I murmured I didn't know. But I thought to myself, that was the real German Army. They were resplendent in their uniforms, decorated with campaign ribbons and medals from the Great War.

I spotted the little girl with the blonde braids among the servants. Her hands shook as she doled out the vegetables. Her eyes were downcast to avoid eye contact with anyone. Even so, one of the Army Officers smiled, nodded in her direction and looked at my father, who smiled back and winked. Obviously they had plans for her later. The thought of it sickened me. I couldn't eat. I pushed my food around on the plate and looked toward the front hall, wondering how soon I could escape. They poured champagne and the guests smiled broadly, toasting each other and the holiday season. There was a clatter of dishes as the desserts were set out... strudels, kuchens, fruit tarts with whipped cream. Coffee was being served. I looked around. Maybe now I could slip away. But at that moment my father rose to address his guests.

He thanked them for their friendship and for their presence at this important dinner. "Our Fatherland is in serious trouble," he began. "Unemployment is at half a million here in Berlin. The German mark is declining in value from day to day and our government is not functioning. So I'm proud to announce that we have among us a man who can bring order out of all this chaos. He has pledged to return prosperity to our industrialists, the backbone of our economy, and to restore our military pride. I'd like you now to listen to a man I believe will be the future leader of our nation, Adolf Hitler.

There was loud applause from the Brownshirts and polite

applause from the dinner guests as Hitler rose to speak.

He thanked my father for the excellent dinner, for the fine introduction, and for this opportunity to address civic, business, and military leaders.

"Today Germany is in total decline," he began. "We are burdened with heavy debt from the Great War. On top of that we lost portions of our land, land we need for our economy. You've all heard the statement by our President, Von Hindenberg, that our glorious army was never defeated in the field. We were stabbed in the back by the Jews and their cronies…"

The Army Officers stood up and cheered when they heard these words. Others applauded in agreement. Hitler continued.

"Even though we are now suffering because of the World Depression, and unemployment is approaching two million in our country, still we are making great technological advances. And why? Because the pure German, the Aryan Race, is superior to all others." Again there were loud cheers. This time mostly from the Brownshirts.

"Jews call themselves a religious group." Hitler went on. "But they are the biggest liars. They are a race. A race of inferior beings bent on the preservation of their own kind, to the detriment of all others.

The time has come to take severe steps against the whole treacherous brotherhood of these poisoners of the people. Now is the time to deal with them summarily, without the slightest consideration for any screams and complaints that might arise. We need to rescue our industries from them. But, let me warn you,

Germany has to accustom herself to the idea that someday her attempt to secure her daily bread by means of peaceful economic labor will have to be defended by the sword.

I see clearly what needs to be done and how to do it. I ask for your confidence. I ask for your cooperation. I ask for your contributions, to help me establish a greater Germany for all of us."

The room rang with cheers and applause. Hitler shook hands all around, whispered some parting words to my father, and left with his Brownshirts.

This was my opportunity. I ran to say goodnight to my father. He gave me another bear hug. "So soon? You're leaving so soon? Erich, I want to see more of you. You'll be here Christmas Eve, won't you? Come early. We'll have drinks and dinner together, as always." I promised hurriedly and rushed off.

Back at the hotel, I spotted Karl in the Lounge. "Been waiting long?" I asked as I slid into the booth.

"No… just a few minutes." We ordered drinks. "Well… how did it go?" I asked. "Is the investor going to invest?"

"I don't know. I don't think so. He told me the way the economy looks right now it's not a good time to invest in an opera company. I tried to convince him that even in bad times, there are always people with money. And they want entertainment… they want culture. He said he'd think it over. But how about you? How's your father?"

"My father? Well… I… uh… what can I say. Karl, he's not the way you remember him. The Great War changed him. Both his brothers were killed and, as I mentioned before, then my mother

14

died. I don't think he ever recovered."

"I'm sorry," Karl said. "I'm sorry to hear that."

I didn't say anything more. I couldn't tell him about my father's sick appetite for young girls. It was terrible enough that I knew.

"Well... how was the dinner party?" Karl asked innocently.

"Ach... the dinner party was a disaster. The whole thing was nothing but a grim ordeal."

"An ordeal?" he chuckled. "Why? What did you eat?"

"No... no... it had nothing to do with the food."

Our drinks arrived. Karl raised his glass. "Maybe we should drink to better days, 'cause this one turned out pretty bad, that's for sure!" We clinked our glasses and downed our drinks. Then I told him about Hitler's Brownshirts and how intimidating they were. He was shocked. "You had to tell them your name before they let you into your own house?"

I nodded. "And worse. This dinner was a fundraiser for Hitler. He claims he needs more money for the upcoming elections. But I wouldn't be surprised if he used it to hire more of those thugs. He'll probably be successful too. He's a very effective speaker. He told everybody exactly what they wanted to hear. Didn't matter if it was true or not."

"What do you mean? Like what?"

"Well... some guys from the real German Army were there, medals and all. And Hitler is after their support. So he told them that they were never defeated in the Great War. They all stood up and cheered that stupid lie."

Karl snickered. "Then how did we manage to lose the war?"

"Easy… Hitler claimed we were stabbed in the back… betrayed by the Jews. And that they must be dealt with severely. I don't know what he wants to do with them, but no one objected to any plan he might have, including me. I don't even know any Jews.

"You're joking. There were Jewish kids in school with us. Don't you remember?"

I shrugged. "Maybe so, but I didn't know them. Then I went to live in Doncaster. There were no Jews there. And later when I went on to Cambridge, I didn't meet any there either."

"I'll tell you what," Karl said. Tomorrow morning I'm going to Warsaw. I've arranged an audition for a tenor from Trieste and a Jewish soprano who lives in the city. I've heard that these two are outstanding. If the audition turns out well, I'm going to sign them to a contract and bring them to Berlin. New talent always arouses interest. And with or without an investor, I have to go forward. I've already hired most of the orchestra, and by the way, many of them are Jews. If you don't have any other plans, why not come with me? It'll give you a chance to see beautiful, ancient Warsaw. And you can meet your first Jew!"

I laughed. "I don't have any plans and I'd love to see Warsaw. I've never been there. And I certainly wouldn't mind meeting a Jew, whether she can sing or not."

"Good. The train leaves at six-thirty in the morning. It's a long trip, so we'll probably have to stay overnight." Karl glanced at his watch. "Oh damn, look at what time it is. I have to get home. My wife will be worried."

"Your wife? Karl, you're married?" Karl nodded.

"Unbelievable! You're too young!" I said. "Besides, there are so many beautiful women around. When I was in Italy and Spain I was dazzled. I didn't know which beauty to look at first. They all had that gorgeous long, black hair and flashing dark eyes."

Karl grinned and gave me a wink. "I like being married. See you in the morning."

CHAPTER 3 — WARSAW

The snow was a foot high and it was bitterly cold when we arrived at the Waszava Wiedenski Station in Warsaw. Karl was in a hurry. "We can get something to eat at the hotel and then go on to the Theatre Square," he shouted, as we made our way through the crowds to the taxi stand on Jerzolinski Street.

"The Europejski Hotel," he told the driver, as we slid inside. "Let's have a quick lunch so I'll have time to show you at least a little of Warsaw."

When we arrived at the hotel we were greeted by a giant doorman in a visored cap and a uniform worthy of a Napoleonic Marshall. He took our bags and escorted us into the lavish lobby. This was a hotel in the grand manner, with white marble floors and walls covered in gold satin. The crowd inside was richly dressed. Men and women were smoking, chatting, and looking around to see if anyone important had arrived. No one noticed us.

Our spacious suite had a high ceiling with heavy beams. A fire blazed in the fireplace and beyond was a large marble bath. But time was short. We had to rush down to the dining room. We ordered ham sandwiches and beer.

"You should come here in the summertime," Karl said. "They have the most wonderful outdoor cafes and you can watch the world go by, when the weather is nice and the city is filled with flowers. But now Warsaw is a place of intrigue."

I don't know who decided the new borders after the Great War, but today a million Germans live in Poland and two million Poles live in Germany. There's plenty of bad blood on both sides. Everything here is a bone of contention."

As we finished the last of our beer, Karl began to look worried. "What's wrong?" I asked.

"I'm not sure, but it's my understanding that the soprano auditioning this afternoon is from a religious family and I know religious Jewish girls don't sing on a public stage. Something isn't right."

I laughed. "I'll say! I told you, Herr Hitler doesn't like the Jews in Germany and you want to import one from Poland!" We both laughed as we made our way into the wintry cold.

"Let's take the trolley," Karl said. "It's slow, but it goes right down the Nowy Swiat, the Grand Avenue of Warsaw. So you'll get a good look at the remains of the old castles where the ancient Saxon Kings once lived. We'll even get a glimpse of the Raziwill Mansion where the first Polish Operas were performed."

The streets were crowded with Christmas shoppers. Traffic was slow, with many taxis and Droshkas, those charming horse-drawn carriages that always seemed to get in the way. By the time we had seen the sights and arrived at the Theatre Square, we were late.

We hopped off the trolley directly in front of the magnificent Grand Theatre of Warsaw and I was completely overwhelmed. It covered one entire side of the Square. It was huge! The main building was three stories high with Corinthian columns across the entire front. It looked like the Parthenon in Athens, but bigger.

The Cultural Center of Poland

"Karl, is that the Opera House?"

"Actually it's more than that. It's the cultural center, not only of Warsaw but for all of Poland as well. They don't just have Opera here, there's also Ballet performances and theater productions. The main hall can seat almost two thousand. Our audition is in a small rehearsal hall, over there on the right."

Everyone was waiting for us when we entered the massive lobby. Lech Dombrowski, the Theatre Director, introduced himself. Then we met Leon Carbonne, the tenor from Trieste, a barrel-chested, dark-haired young man in his twenties. Next came the little soprano, Chani Machinski. She seemed excited. Her cheeks were flushed bright pink, and long dark lashes framed her blue-green eyes. They sparkled like jewels. Her dark hair was pinned up in front and hung long in back. And like most girls her age, she had the innocent air of one who doesn't yet know how beautiful she is. But I knew.

She was accompanied by her grandmother, a bosomy, heavyset woman wearing a kerchief on her head and a heavy black knit shawl around her body. She had piercing blue eyes. Her thin pale lips were clamped shut. She looked serious and determined.

The men shook hands all around. But when I extended my hand to the grandmother, she waved me off with a frown and took a step backward. I was surprised. I didn't know what I'd done wrong. There was an awkward silence for a moment then Karl whispered, "I'll explain everything to you later." To the others he shouted, "Let's go into the auditorium. I want to get started.

Leon and Chani, I want to hear you sing these arias from Act I of La Boheme." He handed them the libretto. "On stage, please."

The small auditorium was paneled in dark wood. It was dimly lit except for the stage, which made it seem warm and cozy. I snuggled down into one of the plush seats.

Leon Carbonne, as the destitute poet, Rodolpho, sang the aria to introduce himself to the main character, Mimi. He sings in Italian…

"I'm a poet. What's my employment? Writing! Is that a living? Hardly!

I've wit… tho' wealth be wanting: Ladies of rank and fashion… all inspire me with passion. In dreams and fond illusions, or castles in the air… richer is none on earth than I!"

Leon Carbonne was superb. No question of that. But for some reason my heart was pounding as I waited to hear Chani sing. "She's so young!" I whispered to Karl.

"I know… I know… she's only seventeen. Shh…"

Chani began:

"They call me Mimi, I don't know why. My name is Luci. My story is a short one… Fine satin and silk I embroider at home and outside. I am content and happy. It is my pastime to make lilies and roses. These flowers give me pleasure… they speak to me of love, of beauteous springtime, of dreams and fancies that only poets know. Do you understand me?"

She was marvelous! She was magical! I applauded, and she gave me a shy smile. I was instantly attracted to her, though I didn't know why. Sure, she was beautiful and talented. But I think what made her so exciting is that she's so different from any others that I've met - exotic like a rare flower.

I noticed that Karl was thrilled too. His eyes glistened and he licked his lips as he spoke to the singers, "That was great! I'd like to hear more. Chani, can you sing Un Bel Di from Madame Butterfly? And you, Leon, can you do Cavaradossi's aria from the last act of

Tosca?"

As Chani began her aria and I listened again to her magnificent voice, it was clear that her future was in opera. My mind began to wander. I wondered about my own future. I was never planning to go into the family business, the Von Bruener Paint and Dye Company. So what would I do? I could always return to England, attend Cambridge for graduate studies. Yet somehow mathematics seemed dull and boring. On the other hand, the Berlin Opera Company could be an amazing adventure.

When the audition ended, Karl approached the two singers. "I'm impressed with your talent," he told them. I'd like to discuss a suitable contract with each of you."

Chani's grandmother now stepped forward. "We cannot agree to anything, Herr Klempner. You must speak to Chani's father, Rabbi Saul Machinski. He makes all the decisions concerning his daughter."

Karl, who understood her Yiddish very well, stammered… "Yes… yes… of course." And, turning to me, he asked if I would get the necessary information for him… a telephone number, an address, and a time when her father would be available to speak to us this evening.

I nodded. I was thrilled to have this opportunity to speak to Chani. Karl turned to the Director and asked if he could use his office to discuss the contract issues with Leon. Mr. Dombrowski was glad to oblige and showed them the way.

Of course, I never got the chance to speak to Chani. Her grandmother did all the talking, and in Yiddish, which was difficult for me to understand, even if it is Germanic. Finally, I got the gist of it. We could meet at eight o'clock tonight at the Machinski apartment on Stawki Street. She wrote down the address. There was no telephone. Then she and Chani left.

Alone in the empty theater, I again considered this new opportunity. If I became an investor/partner, I'd be working with Karl. We'd be involved together in the cultural life of Berlin. I liked that idea. Karl had such an easy manner and a great sense of humor. And, of course, I'd get to see Chani Machinski... and often.

My thoughts were interrupted when I heard Karl returning. He was speaking to Leon Carbonne. "I hope you can wind everything up in Trieste and come to Berlin by mid-January. Here's my card. Please contact me and let me know when I can expect you. I'll need time to arrange for a suitable apartment for you." Then he turned to me. "Erich, congratulate me on my new tenor!"

I said, "No... I want to congratulate OUR new tenor on behalf of the Berlin Opera Company." Karl looked at me... surprised. He hesitated... then a smile lit up his face. I shook hands with him and then with Leon, who thanked us both as he left the theater.

"So, explain exactly what it is you're telling me," Karl asked.

"I'm saying that you were looking for an investor and partner, and I think I'm your man. That is, if we can work out equitable terms."

Karl grinned. "I don't think that'll be a problem. And I'm delighted you made this decision." We shook hands again. "And now, down to business, partner. What did you find out about Chani Machinski?"

"Well, there's no telephone, but I do have her address and we can meet with her father at eight o'clock tonight."

Karl looked at his watch. "Eight o'clock? That doesn't give us much time. Listen, I think we'd better get back to the hotel, freshen up a little, have dinner and give some serious thought to our first problem. We need to figure out an approach to Chani's father, to get his permission to bring her to Berlin. It won't be easy, but we want her as our soprano."

I nodded. "Oh... absolutely!"

CHAPTER 4 — CHANI MACHINSKI

It was dark by now… snowy and blustery. Still, the streets were filled with Christmas shoppers and traffic was snarled. The taxi inched its way towards our hotel. When we finally arrived, there were so many guests in the lobby we were afraid we wouldn't get a fast dinner. Karl asked me to get a table in the dining room while he drew up a contract and got all the papers ready for our meeting with Chani's father.

"There will be a forty-five minute wait, sir," the Maitre D' informed me.

I knew that wouldn't work. I told him, "My partner and I have an important business appointment this evening. We cannot be late." I slipped him a large bill.

"I'll see what I can do, sir, he said, glancing casually at the amount. "Perhaps a small booth against the wall will suffice."

As soon as I was seated, I ordered a bottle of wine. By the time it arrived, Karl showed up clutching his briefcase. The first thing we did was to toast our new partnership. Then we ordered something fast –

cold sausage and cheese sandwiches.

Karl again looked troubled. "I still think we're going to have a problem with Chani Machinski... It's true she came to the audition, which is something an observant Jewish girl would NOT do. So I figured maybe she's not so religious after all. But her grandmother came with her, and that's very puzzling." He paused. "You don't know anything about Jewish people, do you?"

I shrugged. "No. Nothing at all. But, even so, I don't understand why she wouldn't be allowed to sing for an Opera Company such as ours. What is it that stands in the way?"

"Jews have their own unique customs. You saw what happened when you offered your hand to the grandmother. Religious women don't touch any man except their husbands."

I didn't believe what I just heard. "Karl, are you trying to tell me... well, even if she is only seventeen... that no one has ever kissed Chani Machinski's luscious, pink lips?"

Karl glared at me. "Listen, Erich, whatever happened to all those dazzling dark-eyed beauties in Italy and Spain that you mentioned?"

"I don't know. I suppose they're still there."

"Well... if you want romance, concentrate on them. This is business. When we get to the Machinski's home, don't even look at Chani. If you're introduced to any females, young or old, just smile, nod, and take a step backward. Shake hands only with men and boys."

Our dinner arrived and we ate hurriedly. "I have some experience with Jewish people," Karl continued. "When I was about twelve years old, we lived around the corner from Dr. Steinmetz and his family. They were observant Jews. My father was one of his patients, and the doctor mentioned to him that he was looking for someone to come to his house on the Sabbath to do a few chores, like turn the lights on and off, keep the fire going in the fireplace, and the stove lit… things like that. Jews are not allowed to do any work on the Sabbath.

My father recommended me for the job. So every Friday after school I went to their home. They taught me to speak Yiddish, which was easy. It's so much like German. And they taught me a little Hebrew. I got to be part of their Sabbath celebration. At sundown they lit candles, sang a few songs, and the children would line up in front of their father who blessed and kissed each one of them before they all sat down to dinner. Then the Steinmetz made a toast to his wife… in Hebrew, if I can remember… it went… 'A woman of valor. Her price is above rubies…' etcetera. Anyway, I got to drink their wine, eat their wonderful food… and they paid me!"

"Karl," I interrupted, "what the hell are you talking about? What does that have to do with anything?"

Karl answered with a sigh, "I'm trying to tell you, partner, that even if we get Chani as our soprano, she will not perform on any Friday night or Saturday. She will only sing on Thursday nights and Sunday matinees. That means we will have to hire another soprano to perform when she doesn't. It's an additional cost."

I said, "I don't care about that. She's worth it. But now I'm worried. Do you think we'll be successful? I mean, if we offer a substantial salary, will it be enough to win her father's consent?"

28

"I don't know. I just don't know. It's complicated. There's something here that's strange. But thanks for reminding me. Here's a copy of the contract and the salary I plan to offer. Do you agree with that figure?"

I read it and nodded.

Karl shrugged. "I'll do my best to convince her father. But don't count on it."

"I am counting on it," I said.

Karl looked at his watch. "We'd better get started."

We finished the last of the wine and went outside. It had stopped snowing. The air was cold and crisp as we climbed into a taxi. "28 Stawki Street," I shouted at the driver.

He sneered. "Stawki Street! Why do you want to go there? The place is filled with nothing but Jews and rats!" We didn't answer. He put the car in gear and joined the traffic on the main road.

Our destination turned out to be an apartment building in a wretched, raggedy section of the city. It was dark and sinister-looking. We could see trash strewn about. As we entered the hallway, we were immediately struck by the sickening smell of garlic, or cabbage, or garbage. The stench was almost overpowering as we climbed up three flights of stairs toward number 305. Before we even knocked on the door, we could hear a child screaming.

"Oh, good god," I whispered. "What are they doing in there?" We looked at each other, paralyzed for a moment. Then Karl banged on the door. The grandmother opened it.

"Oh yes... yes... come in." But she was distracted by a blonde curly-haired little girl writhing on the floor, kicking and screaming. The grandmother scooped her up. "Sarah... Sarah... what's the matter?" she said in a soothing voice. But Sarah was not soothed. She twisted in her grandmother's arms and shrieked even louder.

"Natan... Natan... the grandmother called. "Come and get your little sister." From a dark hallway off the living room, a voice answered. "Coming, Bubbe." A slender, dark-haired boy about twelve years old came forward. He smiled shyly at us, as he took Sarah in his arms.

"You're the only one who can stop her from crying," the grandmother said. "Read her a story... Do something. We have company now." The minute Sarah saw Natan she stopped screaming.

He sat down with her on a worn dark brown sofa, crammed against the wall. The only other furniture in the room was a huge cloth-covered dining table surrounded by many sturdy wooden chairs. The wallpaper was faded and peeling. A heavy brown curtain was closed against the cold and the room was dimly lit.

Sarah was still sobbing, her face red and wet with tears. "Why was she screaming like that?" Karl asked. Natan looked at us with big brown eyes. "Oh... well... we have a NEW baby now," he answered gently. "And it's very hard on her because she's the OLD baby."

Suddenly two blond-haired boys ran into the room. They were playing tag and shouting as they chased each other around. The grandmother stopped them at once and introduced them to us as her twin grandsons, Joshua and Jeremiah. The boys dutifully shook our hands. "They're only eight years old. You know how boys are," she said as she shooed them back to their room. "And don't make so much noise. Can't you see that Sarah has finally fallen asleep?" And sure enough, Sarah had her thumb in her mouth and her eyes were closed, as Natan droned on with his story.

I whispered to Karl, "How many people do you suppose live in this apartment?"

"I don't know," he whispered back. "I'm still counting."

"Ach… here are the girls," the grandma announced. "You've already met Chani. This is her older sister, Fannie."

We turned to see the girls, who apparently came from the kitchen. They were wiping their hands on their aprons. Fannie was tall and slender with dark hair and dark eyes. She was a sweet-looking girl with a charming smile. But she was nothing next to her incandescent sister, Chani.

I remembered Karl's advice. I smiled, nodded, and took a step backward. Chani, seeing my new and improved manners, put her hand to her mouth and tried to suppress a giggle. I smiled back and tried not to stare. But I couldn't take my eyes off her. Then I heard the grandmother say, "And this is my daughter, Rebbetzin Bayla Machinski."

Bayla had entered from the dark hallway, a pale, gaunt woman in a long black dress, holding an infant in her arms. She took a few steps towards us then sat down quickly on the nearest chair.

A kerchief around her head revealed wisps of blonde hair. And her pale blue eyes seemed filled with pain. She gave us a thin smile, but didn't speak. Her mother bent down and whispered in her ear,

"Are you alright?" Bayla tried to answer, but instead broke into a hacking cough and clutched her stomach. Her mother kissed her forehead and slowly helped her back to her room. I wondered what was wrong with her.

As soon as the grandmother returned, she motioned for us to follow her, and led us through a small alcove on the right. She knocked on a heavy oak door before opening it.

Inside was a small, windowless study whose walls were lined with books from floor to ceiling. Nearby was a battered old desk, lit by a small brass lamp. Two wooden chairs faced it.

As we entered, a tall heavyset man with a graying beard and dark hair and eyes rose to meet us. The grandmother made the introductions in Yiddish. "Rabbi Saul Machinski, Herr Klempner und Herr Von Bruener, fun Berlin." After we shook hands and were seated on hard wood chairs, she left us.

Reb Machinski wore a serious look. To me he seemed coldly polite and guarded. Karl cleared his throat and opened the discussion, speaking in Yiddish. The Rabbi looked surprised. His eyes widened as Karl continued.

"As you know, your daughter Chani auditioned for our Berlin Opera Company this afternoon at the Cultural Center. I was very impressed with her. She is remarkably talented for such a young girl. She knows the repertoire, has great stage presence, and a magnificent voice.

Despite Karl's complimentary remarks about Chani, Reb Machinski sat stone-faced.

Karl continued cautiously, "When I was a boy, I was a 'Shabbos goy. So we are aware of the many issues that must be addressed here. And we are prepared to discuss all difficulties. We also want to submit this contract for your consideration. Please notice that we offer a substantial salary which will be paid in Swiss francs rather than Deutschmarks or Zlotys. The contract is written in both German and Polish. But if anything is unclear, I'll be glad to answer any questions." He handed a copy to Reb Machinski, who began to read it.

The grandmother entered with a tray of tea and poppy seed cookies which she distributed to each of us. She acknowledged our thanks with a smile and left.

Within minutes Reb Manchinski rose from his chair, excused himself under his breath and slammed the door on his way out. Karl and I looked at each other in stunned silence. Then Karl bolted to the door and noiselessly opened it a crack, just enough for us to see and hear what was happening.

Chani, Fannie, and their grandmother were seated at the dining room table, also having tea and cookies. The rest of the family apparently had gone to bed. Reb Machinski began to speak quietly to Chani. "I'm only a poor Hebrew teacher in a Yeshiva, but even I knew you had talent and a great love of music. That's why I permitted you to accept the scholarship to the finest music school in Warsaw where you could receive the best training from the best teachers. You wanted to sing... and you can sing, but only for other women or for your family." He raised his voice. "You know it's

absolutely unacceptable for you to perform for men! It leads to
lustfulness and then inappropriate disrespectful behavior on their
part!" He banged his fist on the table and shouted, "And you sang for
those Germans? For those goyim? You're a disgrace! A disgrace to
our family! A disgrace to the whole community!"

Chani burst into tears. Fannie put her arms around her sister, and
she too began to cry.

"And you!" He turned to the grandmother. You who know better.
You went with her?"

The grandmother stood up. "Stop your shouting, Saul. You'll
wake up the children. Chani doesn't disgrace our family. She's the
only one who can save it. We need money! And you... you're not
only poor, you're also deaf! You don't hear little Sarah screaming
because her mother is too sick to pay attention to her? And you're
also blind! You can't see that your wife is struggling to care for a new
infant when she's so sick she can hardly walk? And you don't care
that the doctors here haven't helped her? Saul! Bayla is dying!

The best doctors in the world are in Berlin. We have to get her
there as soon as possible. It's our only hope... our only chance to
save her... And if we don't do it and my Bayla dies... it will be on
your head!"

She and the girls packed up the tea things and went back to the
kitchen. Rabbi Machinski stood there for a few minutes then sank
into the nearest chair, buried his face in his hands and wept. He
didn't see the girls go off to bed with downcast eyes. He didn't notice
that the grandmother had returned and was sitting opposite him, not

until he pulled a handkerchief from his pocket and wiped his eyes. He blew his nose and cleared his throat. Finally he spoke in a quivering voice.

"So you and Chani went to meet these two Germans this afternoon?" She nodded. He said, "They're nice-looking young men, well-dressed and apparently they have money. They seem educated and cultured. They're wonderful representatives of that sparkling, glittering Christian world that looks so desirable, but is so treacherous for a Jew."

He choked back tears. "They want to take Chani to their world in Berlin. And she's so young... so innocent... so beautiful... I'm afraid for her..." And again he wept and wiped his eyes.

For a few moments no one spoke. Then, in a trembling voice, the grandmother answered. "It's only because of our desperate situation that we have to go forward. You have the most important part. You have to work out the best possible arrangements for our Chani... And Saul, I'm also afraid."

Karl quietly pushed the door shut and we went back to our seats. As we drank our cold tea, Reb Machinski returned. He went to his desk without a word and began to read the contract again.

As we waited I looked around at the room full of books, all written in a strange language I'd never seen before... almost like hieroglyphics.

Finally Reb Machinski cleared his throat and coughed a few times. "There are a number of issues here that need to be resolved. First, Chani would have to live in Berlin and she is too young to be separated from her family." He was going to continue, but Karl interrupted.

"Yes, that's true. But the Berlin Opera Company is prepared to provide you with telephone service, at company expense, so that you can contact your daughter whenever you wish."

Reb Machinski considered that. Eventually he nodded in agreement and continued. "The contract calls for a long term commitment and that's not satisfactory."

Karl answered, "My plan is to have Chani come to Berlin by mid-January at the latest, to begin rehearsals. We want to go into production for a mid-February opening. This, of course, is unusual because the opera season is always from October to May. But we are a new opera company and we need to make a big impression quickly. Therefore Chani would only be with us from January to May. She can come home for the summer and return to Berlin the following September, when rehearsals will start for the usual October opening. That season will end in May of 1932 and at that time we can renegotiate the contract."

"I see," Reb Machinski said. Then he added, "It's important that Chani stay with an appropriate Jewish family in Berlin. I will make the necessary arrangements for her. Then I will advise you when she will arrive and where she will be staying. But in order to do it, we will require a month's salary in advance. When and how will you pay it?"

Karl hesitated. "We weren't expecting this requirement," he said. Let me discuss it with my partner."

We both got up and went towards the door. With our backs to

Reb Machinski, Karl whispered, "We've agreed to pay her salary in Swiss francs and since I'm the one with the Swiss bank account, I can give him a cheque for the necessary amount. You can reimburse me for your half later, in British pounds. We'll work it out. Is that agreeable?"

I nodded and we turned around. Karl then advised Reb Machinski that he was prepared to issue a cheque from a Swiss bank for the advance in salary as soon as the contract was signed.

At that point we all signed and the deal was done. We shook hands and the Rabbi showed us to the door. He mentioned that it might be difficult to find a taxi in this neighborhood, but if we went around the corner to the left, we might find a Droshka to take us back to the hotel. He looked doleful and troubled as he said goodnight.

The dark hallway was as dismal and smelly as before, but I didn't care. I was filled with energy. I scrambled down three flights of stairs and pushed the entry door open. A blast of icy air hit me. Karl turned up the collar of his coat and shivered as he clutched his briefcase. I didn't mind the cold or the crisp snow underfoot as we plunged ahead. Chani Machinski was coming to Berlin in just a few weeks. The thought of it kept me warm.

Suddenly Karl shouted, "Isn't that a Droshka up ahead?" He let out a shrill whistle, yelled and waved. And sure enough, a skinny gray nag pulling a carriage appeared out of the gloom. "The Europejski Hotel," he shouted at the driver as we climbed aboard.

It was late and the horse clip-clopped along at such a leisurely pace that we were half-frozen by the time we got there. As we entered the warmth of that majestic lobby, Karl murmured, "Thank god we're here and that damn horse didn't drop dead on the way. How about some hot coffee before we turn in?"

There were still some well-heeled revelers milling around, but far fewer now and much more subdued. The Maitre d' winked at us in recognition and seated us right away.

Karl poured so much cream in his coffee it was practically white. I preferred mine strong, black, with lots of sugar and a dab of cognac. I fairly hummed as I felt that first gulp go all the down to my toes.

"You know, I've been thinking," I said.

Karl smiled. "I noticed. What's on your mind?"

"Well… moving ahead, I was considering the future publicity for our opera company and the excitement we want to generate with the new talent we're bringing to Berlin. We won't have any trouble with Leon Carbonne from Trieste. But what about Chani Machinski from Warsaw? There's so much anti-Jewish and anti-Polish feeling in Berlin now, it won't be good for us."

"You're right. I agree completely," Karl said. "We need to give her a stage name. It's done all the time. Anything come to mind?"

"No… no… not right now. Let's sleep on it. But instead of Warsaw, it might be better if we said she came from Danzig. There's a lot of sympathy for Germans living there. And then, of course, she has to learn to speak good German as soon as possible. I'd be more than glad to teach her," I teased.

Karl's face became grim. "The family she'll be staying with will teach her whatever she needs to know. Listen, Erich, I know you find her attractive, but get over it. She's not for you! Our association with her is strictly business. Anything else can only lead to serious problems. Please listen to me."

We finished our coffee and turned in. I knew Karl was right. Still, it didn't stop me from dreaming about her, with those twinkling blue-green eyes and long dark hair.

I dreamt she was on top of me. I unpinned her hair and all that black silkiness fell across my chest. She smiled and spoke to me. I don't know what she said, but then she brushed those lips, unkissed by any man, against mine and I was consumed in fire!

CHAPTER 5 — CHRISTMAS EVE

Early the next morning we were on the train to Berlin. As we settled into our compartment I told Karl, "I think I have a good stage name for Chani."

"Oh… yeah? What?"

"How about Heidi? That sounds a lot like Chani, doesn't it?"

Karl laughed. "Well… it's a little trite, but okay. Did you have something in mind for her last name?"

"I'm not sure about that. I wanted to use the most common German name I could think of. What do you think of Mueller? Heidi Mueller?"

"Heidi Mueller. Hmm. I think that'll work. I can see it now… THE BERLIN OPERA COMPANY ANNOUNCES THE DISCOVERY OF TWO BRILLIANT NEW TALENTS. TENOR LEON CARBONNE FROM TRIESTE AND SOPRANO HEIDI MUELLER FROM DANZIG. BOTH WILL APPEAR IN LA BOHEME ON FEBRUARY 14TH. TICKETS ARE ON SALE NOW! ETC. ETC. How does that sound for our first publicity?"

"I like it. I think it's good. You know, Karl, I made a pretty quick decision to become your partner in all this, but it looks like I made a good decision. It's going to be exciting!"

"Yes… yes… it is. I'm excited too. And perfect timing. We'll be back in Berlin for Christmas Eve. Are you going to be with your father?"

"Yes… I'm afraid so. Tonight we're having dinner together then we'll exchange gifts. That's been our custom for many years. Of course it's difficult to buy a gift for someone like my father. He has everything. But this year I bought him a special book. It's an autographed, first edition copy of ALL QUIET ON THE WESTERN FRONT, by Erich Remarque. He's French, but he published his book in German just this year. It got excellent reviews. Have you read it?"

"No. Not yet."

"Well… the author tries to show that the most devastating effect of the Great War was the destruction of an entire generation of young men. And not only the ones who died. He claims that those who lived were also destroyed. I believe that's what happened to my father. He's a damaged person now. But I still hold out some hope that he can be restored to his former self. You know, since I was raised in England, we grew apart. I miss the man he used to be. Now I hardly know him. His biggest involvement these days is with his friend Adolf Hitler and the Nazi Party. Anyway, I'm hoping after he reads this book we can discuss it together."

Karl nodded and we sat in silence, listening to the clickety-clack of the train as it sped towards Berlin. I soon fell asleep and dreamed of the time when my mother was alive and we were celebrating Christmas so differently. Then, Christmas took up the whole month of December. She spent all her time in the kitchen, baking cookies and cakes. The entire house smelled delicious. We had a gingerbread house too. And then the excitement of decorating the tree together. And all those presents! I suddenly woke up.

Karl was smiling at me. "We're almost there. Did you have a good sleep?"

I stretched and yawned. "I guess so."

"What are you doing Christmas Day?" he asked. "Are you going to be with your father again?"

"I don't know. I'm not sure. Why?"

"Well… if you don't have any other plans, how about coming to my place? I'd like you to meet my wife Gretchen. Come around noon. We're having an open house. It won't be anything fancy, but Gretchen is a great cook. You can expect sausage, potatoes, beer, and great company. We're having a few friends from our church over. You'll find them interesting. I live on Friedreichstrasse. Here, let me give you my address and phone number, in case you can make it."

"Yes… thank you… that'd be great."

The train pulled into the station. We gathered our things together and then it was time to say goodbye. We shook hands. "Thanks for taking me to Warsaw. Thanks for accepting me as your partner. Thanks for everything," I said, as I gave him a hug.

"Merry Christmas, Erich. Hope I'll see you tomorrow." And he rushed off. I made my way back to the Adlon Hotel. As soon as I got in the door, the Concierge ran up to me.

"Herr Von Bruener, you have five messages waiting for you at the front desk."

"Five messages?" I mumbled to myself. The first one was a cable from Uncle Tony and his family, wishing me a Merry Christmas and asking when I planned to come back to England. They all missed me.

I felt guilty. I hadn't sent them so much as a Christmas card. I made a mental note to write them as soon as possible, explain my new situation and let them know that I won't be returning to England.

All the other messages were from my father. One said, "Call me." The second one said, "Why don't you call me?" The next one read "Where are you?" and the last one said, "Dinner is at 6:00. Don't be late."

Christmas Eve is such a busy time. I had trouble finding a taxi, so of course I was late. He growled when he saw me, but still greeted me with his usual bear hug.

"I'm so glad to see you. I was worried. You didn't answer any of my calls. Where were you?"

"I'll tell you all about it over dinner. Let's have a drink first. Then we can exchange our gifts. I'm really excited for you to see what I brought you."

"All right... all right... whatever you say. Let's sit in the library." He rang for Josef, his old valet, and asked him to bring us some shnaps. Josef was the perfect servant. He had been with us since I was a child. Slender, with a full head of white hair, he saw everything, knew everything, and said nothing.

It was warm and cozy in the library. A fire blazed in the fireplace and Josef soon returned with the whiskey and some pate. "Let's have a toast to the Holidays and to your annual visit," my father said as he raised his glass. "Merry Christmas, Erich."

"Merry Christmas," I echoed, and we downed our drinks. "I've brought you a special gift," I said. "It's an important book that has a lot to say about the Great War and its effect. I'd be most interested in discussing it with you."

My father said nothing as he unwrapped his gift. Then he slid a small box in my direction. "This is for you." He quickly leafed through the book and then frowned. "I don't need anyone to tell me about the War. I was there!" He tossed the book aside.

I was more than disappointed. I was offended. But I didn't say anything. I opened my gift. It was a set of gold cufflinks with large diamond centers. They were fancy and garish. Nothing I would ever wear.

I said, "Thank you. They look expensive."

"I only want the best for you, Erich... only the best."

Suddenly I felt depressed. We were off to such a bad start. He would never read the book and I would never wear those cufflinks.

"Dinner is served," Josef announced and we went into the small dining room. Josef brought us a dark, hot vegetable soup to get us started.

"So where did you disappear to, Erich? I called at the hotel many times. But you were never there."

"I met an old school friend at the hotel. Do you remember Karl Klempner?"

"No... no... I don't think so."

"Well... he is a fine musician now, a graduate of the Konservatorium Swiss. He recently came into an inheritance and with it he purchased the Berlin Opera Company. He had a dinner engagement with a potential partner/investor at the Adlon. That's how we happened to meet. He told me he had an audition in Warsaw to attend and asked if I wanted to go along. And that's where I went."

My father dropped his spoon and looked at me in disgust. "You went to Warsaw? That pig sty? The only people there are ignorant Poles and hook-nosed Kikes," he shouted. "Are you going to bring those god-damned filthy Jews to Berlin? Who did you audition?"

"That is really ugly!" I said. But I was afraid to tell him the truth. "We auditioned Leon Carbonne, a tenor from Trieste, and Heidi Mueller, a soprano from Danzig. The audition was held in the Grand Theatre of Warsaw, a magnificent cultural center. And more... the voices of those two talented young people were so impressive that I decided then and there to become Karl's partner in the Berlin Opera Company. So congratulate me on my new business venture and wish me luck. I'm going to be a part of Berlin's cultural scene."

He didn't answer. He looked stunned. Then in a thoughtful voice he said, "From a business point of view I can tell you this is NOT a good investment. Unemployment is at 20% and the Deutschmark loses value every day. We don't need culture. We need manufacturing, industry, jobs. But the good news for me is that you've come home. Back to the Fatherland where you were born and where you belong. Of course, I'm hoping that all goes well for you. But if you run into a problem, you can always count on me, Erich. You know that."

"And by the way," he continued, "when this Heidi Mueller comes to Berlin, I'd like to meet her."

I suddenly swallowed the wrong way and began coughing and sputtering.

"Danzig is a German city," he continued. "At the end of the War they gave it to Poland. Hitler claims that our German people are constantly abused there. I'd like to ask her about that situation."

I couldn't talk. I immediately realized I could never allow him to meet Chani.

"Erich, this changes everything for me," he said softly. "From now on you'll be here in Berlin. And this is your home too. You can move in anytime you like."

"No... no... Thank you..." I said. "I really need my own place. After the Holidays I'll look for an apartment."

"Well... I'm disappointed." But let it be whatever you say. Meanwhile I'll tell my friends about your new position. Let me know when you schedule your first performance and I'll make sure they all attend."

I broke into a sweat. The last thing I wanted was for my father and his friends to show up. The door opened and Josef came in with the main course, a crisp roast chicken that he served on an elegant silver tray. With him came the little girl with the blonde braids. Her eyes were downcast as before and her hands shook as she gathered up the soup plates and the tableware. When she approached my father he smiled and reached under her dress. She drew away, as if she'd been stung by a bee. The dishes rattled as she ran from the room. She soon returned however. And as Josef sliced up the meat, she doled out the potatoes with trembling little hands.

My father's eyes narrowed as he watched her fumble with the food. "The trouble with you, Erich," he said as he gazed at her," is that you're too serious. You ought to have a little fun sometimes. Now a girl like Sonja here knows how to give a man a good time. Don't you liebshen?" He laughed. "And I taught her everything she knows. Didn't I?" and he slapped her on her rear end... hard. She let out a yelp. Her eyes flew open, filled with pain and fear, like an animal caught in a trap.

I couldn't stand it another minute. I leaped up, ran to the front hall and grabbed my coat and the book I brought. I left the cufflinks behind and slammed out the door.

It was pitch black outside and freezing cold. It was Christmas Eve and I knew I wouldn't find a taxi. I'd have to take the U-bahn back to the hotel. The underground train ran all night and the station wasn't far.

I stuck the book inside my coat to keep it dry. As I raced down the drive, I could see the lights from the main road now. I ran faster. Suddenly my feet slid out from under me and I fell flat on my back, banging my head on the concrete.

Icy sleet began to fall on my face. I didn't care. I didn't move. I just lay there with my eyes closed, thinking about this horrible night. How could I have thought that my father might ever change back to the way he was?

My head hurt. I tried to get up. I felt a shooting pain in my right leg. Oh, damn! Is it broken? What am I going to do now?

I crawled toward the trees that lined the driveway and with enough effort, pulled myself upright. The pain was intense. I couldn't put any weight on that leg. Slowly... very slowly... grasping the tree branches and whatever other support I could find, I managed to hobble down to the station.

Drenched in sweat, I clung to the walls, afraid someone would jostle me or step on my foot. Luckily the train arrived almost at once and some kind soul gave me a seat. The hotel was a couple of stops away. I knew it was just a short walk from the station, but only if you have two good legs. Sleet was falling harder.

I got off the train and held onto any structure... buildings, storefronts, anything to keep from falling. When I got close to the hotel, I began to wave at the doorman. As soon as he saw me, he came running. And with his help I soon found myself inside the warm lobby of the Adlon once more.

There was a roaring fire in the huge fireplace. The Christmas lights blinked happily, and in the back of the lobby a man was playing Christmas Carols on the piano. A crowd had gathered around him, singing to his music.

I breathed easier now. I made it! The Concierge came running, bringing me towels. I dried my hair as best I could, wiped my face, and then I saw him. My father was standing there!

He came closer, scowling and red with rage. "What's the matter with you!" he bellowed. I didn't answer. I swallowed hard. I didn't want to argue. "I fell," I said. "I hurt my leg."

"That's not what I mean and you know it!" he screamed. The music stopped. The crowd came toward us. "Erich," he pleaded. "You're my son. My only child. I have no one else in this world but you. And I love you. Why do you treat me like garbage? Yes, I'm a lonely old man. But I keep myself strong. I still have a young man's appetites. So what? Who are you to judge me? I'm your father! And here's your damn book back! I found it in the driveway." He threw it at my feet and thundered out the door.

The crowd closed in. They glared at me with angry eyes. No one spoke. I didn't move. I waited to see what would happen. Finally, one of them gave me a look of disgust and walked off. The rest followed slowly, muttering under their breath. I felt completely drained. I asked the Concierge to get me an aide to help me to my room. I couldn't help but notice a look of disdain on his face.

As soon as the aide got me to my room I asked him to draw a hot bath for me. He helped me strip off my wet clothes and slip into the tub. Then I asked him to bring me a pot of black coffee and a bottle of cognac. I was more relaxed now. The hot bath made my leg feel a little better. And this dirty, ugly night was finally coming to an end.

CHAPTER 6 — CHRISTMAS DAY

Within an hour, with the help of the aide, I was bathrobed, slippered, and had my leg elevated on a footstool. It was late. I sipped my coffee. It comforted me after such a bitter day. I phoned Karl and told him I was sorry I wouldn't be able to come to his place tomorrow. And it was really too bad. I'd been looking forward to it, and to meeting Gretchen.

Karl asked, "How bad is your leg?"

"Right now it's swollen to almost twice its size and it's throbbing."

"Is it broken?"

"I don't know."

"Don't you think you should see a doctor?"

"Karl, it's Christmas Eve! Where would I find a doctor? They're all celebrating the holiday."

"Listen, Erich, I'll make an appointment for you with a Jewish doctor. They aren't celebrating anything. Maybe he can patch you up. What were you going to do, lie around the hotel all day? I'll call you in the morning with the details." And he hung up before I could even

50

say thank you.

After a long, rough night of increasing pain, by morning I was ready to see a doctor. As a matter of fact I was ready for an amputation! The phone rang at eight o'clock. It was Karl. "We have an appointment to see Dr. Max Leibman at the Jewish Hospital within an hour. I'll pick you up in twenty minutes." And again he hung up before I could say one word.

I rang for the Concierge and asked him to send the aide back. I didn't bother getting dressed. I figured I'd return to the hotel and go back to bed after the doctor's examination. When Karl arrived, he and the aide managed to get me into his car.

"The hospital is on Iranische Strasse. It's not far," Karl said. I looked out at a cold, bleak Christmas Day and thought it was the worst one I'd ever endured. When we arrived at the hospital I was given some medication to dull the pain while the doctor carefully probed my leg. Even so, it was agony. The medication was the only thing that kept me from screaming.

"It looks like your ankle is broken," Dr. Liebman said. "But to be sure, and to set it properly, we need to have it X-rayed." As it turned out, he was right, and I wound up with a heavy cast and a set of crutches. I was given more medication and Karl took me to his apartment where he and Gretchen put me into their bed. I immediately fell into a drugged and dreamless sleep.

I don't know how long I slept, but I woke up because I heard voices and laughter. And I smelled food! I was hungry... very hungry. I looked around at the green flowered wallpaper and the dark furniture. For a moment I didn't know where I was. Then I remembered. This was Karl's place. I tried to get out of bed. What a catastrophe! I forgot about the cast. Now I felt shooting pains in my leg. I couldn't move. I had to close my eyes and wait for the pain to subside. I looked around for my crutches and found them nearby, leaning against a wall.

Slowly I inched my way to the edge of the bed, grasped the bedpost for support and lowered my legs until the good one touched the floor and I could stand on it. Still clutching the bedpost, I tried to straighten my pajamas and bathrobe then struggled to get my crutches and almost dropped them. By this time I was sweating and woozy. Somehow I made it to the bedroom door and opened it.

I saw a room full of people, mostly men, talking, eating, and drinking beer. Karl caught sight of me and helped me get seated at the dining room table, just where I wanted to be, though I was embarrassed by my rumpled and unshaven appearance. Gretchen came running. "Ah…" she smiled "Sleeping Beauty is awake. How about a cup of coffee and some fresh warm rolls?"

"Thanks," I said. "I think that's just what the doctor ordered."

She gave me a wink and rushed off towards the kitchen. I liked her right away, this pretty girl with reddish curly hair and sparkling brown eyes. Her cheeks were bright red too, no doubt from rushing around serving all her guests. To a hungry guy like me, the only thing she didn't have was a halo!

She was back in a few minutes with my breakfast and then ran off to get more refreshments. I looked around at Karl's guests as I scarfed down the rolls and coffee. Most of them were men in their forties or older. I mentioned it to Karl. "We belong to the Lutheran Evangelical Church and these are some of the members," he said. "I think you'll find them interesting."

Meanwhile Gretchen noticed that I'd finished eating and promptly brought me a huge plate piled high with sausage and potatoes. It was steaming hot. I leaned toward Karl. "You know, I can see why you like being married." He grinned and poured me a mug of cold beer.

"Sometimes it gets even better," he whispered. We both laughed.

"Can I get in on this?" one of the guests said as he slipped onto a chair across from me. "Let me introduce you," Karl said. "Reverend Maas, meet Erich Von Bruener, my old school friend and new business partner. Erich, Hermann Maas is one of the great intellectuals of our Church."

"Oh... please..." the Reverend waved aside the compliment. "Don' let me interrupt your lunch. Erich, I wanted to meet you because I heard you're a patient of Dr. Liebman who is a close friend of mine. He's an excellent doctor. So rest assured your leg is in good hands." We all laughed.

"How is it a Lutheran Minister like you is a close friend of a Jew?" I asked.

"I have many Jewish friends. As a matter of fact, years ago I happened to be in Basel, Switzerland when out of curiosity I attended the Zionist Congress that was meeting there at the time. That's where I met Liebman."

"Pardon my ignorance but what's a Zionist?" I asked.

"Hmm... well basically it's a Jewish organization that promotes a return to the Holy Land for the Jewish people because they don't think they have much of a future here in Europe."

"But Dr. Liebman didn't go to the Holy Land. He's still here in Berlin," I said. "So what kind of Zionist is he?"

"Well... that's the thing. They are trying to raise money to buy land. Liebman is involved in that. They want to go back to farming... a new kind of farming... a collective they call a Kibbutz. I heard Theodor Hertzel and Chaim Weitzman give the most impassioned speeches on that subject. They spoke in Yiddish, of course, which is easy enough to follow. It's mostly Germanic, but written in Hebrew letters. I was able to get a better grasp of the discussion because I'm also fluent in Hebrew. As you might guess, it's mostly young people that want to be part of this new experiment. They call themselves Chalutzim, pioneers! It's a bold dream."

He glanced at his watch. "I have another event to attend. Please excuse me. Erich, I was glad to meet you," he said as he shook my hand. "I hope to see you in church sometime."

Karl escorted him to the door and I watched as they said their goodbyes. So I didn't notice that another man sat down almost immediately.

"Mind if I join you?" he asked.

"No. Not at all."

"Even if I am a convict?"

"What?"

"I'm Carl von Ossietzky. And yes, it's true. But let me explain. I'm the editor of a journal called Die Weltbuhne (The World Stage). I published an article by Berthold Jacob that criticized the government for condoning paramilitary organizations. As the editor, I was held responsible. I was tried for libel, found guilty, and sentenced to one month in prison."

"You're not a convict," I said. "You're a hero!"

He paused for a moment. "That's a strange thing for someone like you to say. Isn't Otto Von Bruener your father? It's common knowledge that he raises funds for Hitler and his vile Brownshirts."

My mouth went dry. "My father's politics are his, not mine."

Ossietzky nodded. "You must know that Germany is re-arming. I want everyone to know it and I refuse to be intimidated by the government. This summer I published an article by Walter Kreiser who described his opposition to the secret German re-armament in violation of the Treaty of Versailles. As the editor, I was charged again. This time for the betrayal of military secrets. Can you believe it? And my trial is set for November 1931! They want to give me enough time to run. And if I do, that will confirm my guilt. I refuse to do that. I'm going to defend my right to print the truth. Still, rest assured I'll be found guilty and returned to prison."

I was amazed. I thought about those belligerent menacing Brownshirts and admired this forty year old, broad-shouldered man with the receding hairline and prominent nose. He wasn't afraid of them. He wasn't afraid of anything!

"Not everyone has your courage, Ossietzky," a slender man said as he shook my hand and introduced himself. "I'm Pastor Martin

Neimoller. And I can tell you that times change and opinions change too. I admit that I voted for Adolf Hitler in 1924. I believed his speeches on restoring German pride."

Pastor Martin Neimoller

"What? Martin! You voted for Hitler? I would never have believed it. Oh, excuse me gentlemen, I'm Helga Reinhardt. And I'm going to change the subject for just a moment. I'm leaving shortly and I wanted to meet you, Erich, because Karl told me you're looking for an apartment to rent. I have one on Neukonigstrasse that will be available after the first of the year. My poor tenant lost his job and is relocating to Munich. Here is my telephone number. If you're interested, let me know."

"I can tell you right now that I'm interested. I'll call you and arrange to see the place as soon as possible."

"Very good. And now back to your subject, Martin," Frau

Reinhardt continued. "I just received this letter from my nephew Siegfried. He's a successful business man in Bavaria. And in a meeting he attended at the home of a friend, he met Adolf Hitler. Listen to how he describes him." She took the letter from her purse and read: "A jelly-like slag-gray face, a moon face into which two melancholy jet-black eyes have been set like raisins. So sad, so unutterably insignificant, so basically misbegotten… Eventually Hitler managed to launch into a speech. He talked on and on endlessly. He preached. We did not in the least contradict him or venture to differ in any way. But he began to bellow at us anyway. The servants thought we were being attacked and rushed to defend us. When he was gone there was a feeling of dismay, as when on a train you suddenly realize you are sharing a compartment with a psychotic. It was not that an unclean body had been in the room, but something else, the unclean essence of a monstrosity."

She put the letter away. "Gentlemen, if Adolf Hitler comes to power in Germany, I don't know what will become of our country."

"I agree with you," Neimoller said. "That's why I'm now part of the opposition."

"Well… I'm certainly glad to hear that," she answered as she turned to say her goodbyes.

I wondered if she knew that my father was helping that monstrosity get elected. Suddenly I had a headache. I wanted to go back to the hotel. I mentioned it to those at the table with me.

"I'll be glad to take you," Pastor Neimoller said. Maybe Dietrich can help. Have you met Dietrich Bonhoeffer? He's close to your age and a student at the seminary here." He introduced us and then the two of them helped me into my coat. It was time to say goodbye to Karl and Gretchen. I didn't know how to thank them enough for all they had done for me. And that's what I told them as I gave each of them a farewell hug.

The two men managed to help me into the car. It wasn't easy. Crutches and slippery pavement inspire real fear and I was grateful for all their effort. On the way to the hotel I asked Pastor Niemoller if he had always been interested in a religious life.

"No... no... Actually I was the commander of a U-boat in the Great War," he said. "I was responsible for sinking 55,000 tons of Allied ships in 115 days at sea, killing thousands of sailors in the process. For that I was awarded the Iron Cross First Class. After the war it pressed on my mind. I needed to atone somehow. I wanted God to forgive me for winning that medal." Dietrich Bonhoeffer nodded in agreement.

I said, "It's strange how the same war affects men differently. My father doesn't want forgiveness for anything he did. He wants revenge for the humiliation of defeat! As a matter of fact, he can't even admit that Germany lost that war."

"Yes," Niemoller said as we pulled up to the hotel. "Many feel that way." We're living in a time of confusion and chaos."

Then these two men, strangers really, helped me maneuver on my crutches until I was comfortably settled in my room. I was deeply grateful for their kindness and promised to keep in touch.

After they left I got out some hotel stationary and began a letter to

Uncle Tony. I apologized for my Christmas negligence and promised to make up for it. I wrote about my father's dinner party, Adolf Hitler, and the Brownshirts. Then I told him about the exciting auditions in Warsaw and my decision to become my friend Karl Klempner's partner in the Berlin Opera Company. I continued:

Because of this new business venture, I will NOT be returning to England. I'm going to live in Berlin. I'll send you my new address and phone number as soon as I'm settled.

If you're wondering why I don't live with my father in our family home, the truth is hard for me to admit. But I am disgusted by his shameful exploitation of very young girls. It's deeply disturbing. He involves others in his sexual perversions as well. He even wanted me to participate with him. This whole situation is so grotesque it's beyond description. I want to distance myself from him in every way.

Economically the Depression has taken a terrible toll here and the government is in chaos. My father has become a virulent Nazi and it appears that their solution for all of Germany's problems is rearmament and war. I hope I'm wrong.

There's so much more to tell. I promise to write again soon. But for now let me wish you and the family all the best in the coming year. Let's hope 1931 will be a good year for all of us.

Love,

Erich

P.S. I met a beautiful Jewish girl in Warsaw. More of her later.

I didn't mention anything about my broken leg. It would just worry them needlessly. As I folded up the letter I made a mental note to have it sent in the morning. Meanwhile I phoned the Concierge and again requested an aide. Within a few minutes a husky middle-aged man showed up. He said his name was Wilhelm and he helped me get washed, shaved, and into clean pajamas. I asked him to bring me black coffee.

When he returned he handed me a message from the front desk. It was from my father. It read, CALL ME.

I didn't want to call him. There was nothing to talk about. As I sipped the coffee I thought about this unforgettable Christmas Day. Sure, it started out in pain and agony from my leg. Still, I'd met the most incredible group of intellectuals and idealists. Even the German government couldn't intimidate a man like Ossietzky. Neimoller got it right though when he said, "Not everyone has your courage." Certainly I didn't.

The phone rang. "Why didn't you answer my message?" my father shouted. "When I didn't hear from you I got worried. Listen Erich, we have to find a way to get along. Tell me, how is your leg?"

"My ankle is broken."

"Oh, my god… Did you see a doctor?"

"Yes, Dr. Liebman took care of me."

"Dr. Liebman!" he screamed. "A Jew doctor? You went to see one of those poisoners? Are you crazy?"

"Calm down," I said. "Dr. Liebman is highly recommended. He examined me at the Jewish Hospital, X-rayed my ankle and I wound up with a cast and a pair of crutches. I'm doing as well as possible."

There was silence on the other end of the phone. Then my father said, "You're on crutches then? Who is looking after you? You'll need help getting washed and dressed and things like that. Why don't you come home, Erich? I have everything you need here. I have servants to cook meals and Josef knows you since you were born. He can help you with everything and drive you around to wherever you want to go. We have a car for you."

It was true. He did have everything I needed. It was an enticing trap. "No, thank you. I have everything here. There's an aide to help me, meals can be delivered to my room, and I can take a taxi wherever I want to go."

"So you're planning to stay at that fancy-ass hotel? Is that it? It costs a lot of meney to stay there. And now that you're in business, you might need that money. Come home!"

I hadn't told him my plans to rent an apartment from Frau Rhinehardt. I didn't want him to know where I was or what I was doing.

"Erich, I want to see you tonight. We have to discuss your future. I'll send a car for you."

I didn't want to see him. I said, "No! Absolutely not. I'm exhausted." And I hung up.

I was glad this long day was over. I asked Wilhelm to help me into bed, turn off the lights, and lock up. I was sound asleep when I thought I heard the click of a key in the door. I wasn't sure. Maybe I was dreaming. Then I felt someone try to cover my face with some sweet smelling cloth. It was pitch black in the room and they missed.

I shouted, "Who is it? What do you want?" and as I turned to light the bedside lamp I was grabbed!

I lashed out with my fist. I heard someone groan and fall. But others held my arms and legs and tied me up. I screamed! A gag was stuffed in my mouth. I could feel myself being lifted out of bed and hauled away. I turned my face from side to side to keep from being drugged. It was no use. A cloth was clamped over my nose and I sank into unconsciousness.

CHAPTER 7 — REVELATION

I woke up in a blue room. I was groggy. Everything was a blur. Sunlight poured through the pale curtains on the window. I wondered what time it was. What day it was. Still, as I gazed at those pale blue walls, I knew exactly where I was. This was my childhood bedroom. I noticed the familiar bookshelves at the far end of the room, filled with my old books… the little desk and chair nearby. I could almost feel my mother's presence as she tucked me into bed with a goodnight kiss.

Old memories clogged my mind. I closed my eyes. My head ached. I tried to focus. What happened to me? How did I get here? Slowly it all came back. I was assaulted in my hotel room in the middle of the night. I was tied up and knocked unconscious with some kind of drug. But why? Why would my father do this?

I opened my eyes. I could move now. I was no longer tied up. The gag was gone too. I remembered when they shoved it in my mouth. It still hurt to swallow.

Carefully, I sat up in bed. I felt dizzy. I waited for it to subside. I looked around and saw my suitcases standing in front of the closet door. I stared at them in disbelief. They'd brought my clothes from the hotel! My father probably got some of those strong-armed Brownshirts to attack and kidnap me. He must have checked me out of the hotel, paid the bill, and advised whoever asked that I was ill and required treatment, or some kind of excuse, as they dragged me out of there. It was crazy. He was crazy!

I decided I had to get out of bed and out of here. I looked around for my crutches but didn't see them. They weren't anywhere in the room. Did they leave them in the hotel? Maybe they're inside the closet... I hoped. I had to find them.

It was a problem getting out of bed. But I finally scooched my way to the edge and stood on my good leg. Clinging to the walls and furniture, I hopped on one foot until I reached the closet. I opened the door. It was empty.

I felt a jolt of fear. I was helpless. There was no telephone up here. It was downstairs. I figured if I could make it to the bedroom door, I could get out of here. Then I'd slide down the banister, just like when I was a kid. The thought of it made me smile. But first I had to make it to the bedroom door with only one good leg... clinging to whatever was available. It took all my effort. I was dripping with perspiration by the time I reached the door and turned the doorknob. It was locked!

I closed my eyes, leaned against the wall and rested for a few minutes. I was exhausted and furious. What the hell kind of game is this? I'm a prisoner! How can I get out of here?

I banged on the door and shouted, "Josef... Josef... open this door! I'm hungry and thirsty!"

I waited. Nothing happened. I listened for footsteps. Nothing. I yelled louder, "Open this goddamn door I tell you! Josef, do you hear me?" I waited again. This time I heard a key in the lock. Josef opened the door. "Help me get down to the kitchen," I said. "I need a cup of coffee. And see if you can make me a couple of eggs too. I'm starving! What the hell happened here? I don't know where my crutches are. I'll have to lean on you to get downstairs. Why was the door locked?"

"You don't have to go downstairs, sir," Josef said. I'll be glad to bring your meals up to you... And I have no idea why the door was locked." He lied, we both knew he was aware of everything that happened in this house.

"I have to get downstairs. I don't want to stay up here. And I'm desperate for a cup of coffee." I put one arm around his shoulders and hopped on one foot down the stairs, hanging onto the railing with the other hand.

"Is my father at the factory?"

"I'm right here," he said quietly, as he waited for us at the bottom of the staircase. "It's nice to see you up and around," he smiled.

"How did I get here?" I growled.

He didn't answer. He turned to Josef, "I'll have a cup of coffee too, although it's not a good time for it."

"What time is it?" I asked, as we sat down in the breakfast room.

"It's three o'clock."

"Three o'clock! In the afternoon? What day is it?"

"It's Saturday, December 27th. Why?"

"What happened to December 26th?

"You slept through it."

Josef poured our coffee. I sat there seething and grinding my teeth. I wanted to punch Otto Von Bruener in his smug, smiling face and break his leg for him. But of course I couldn't. I gripped my cup with shaking hands and took a couple sips to calm myself down. Then I placed my cup firmly on the table and whispered, "Why?"

He didn't answer right away. Finally he said, "Because we have to talk. We have to straighten out our relationship, discuss present feelings, and concentrate on your future."

"Listen Erich, you're young and dumb... or let's say naïve. Maybe that's why you make such bad decisions. You reject me! Disrespect me and everyone can see it. That's why you stay at that hotel. You reject our family business where you can succeed me, as I succeeded my father. But no! You don't want that! You want to be a partner in an opera company. Why? What education or expertise do you have for such an enterprise? Erich, that's not a legitimate career. That's a hobby!

I had to do something drastic so you'd listen to me and face reality... the new reality."

"No, you didn't," I yelled. "I didn't have to be subjected to a goddamn assault!"

The bile of our contentious relationship was leaking out. He leaped off the chair and screamed, "We could never discuss anything!

The last time we tried you ran out the door. That's how you broke your damn ankle in the first place! You could never tolerate me or anything that was important to me. You always ran back to England... back to your Uncle Tony. And the final insult! You became a British citizen. What's wrong with you? You're a German! This is your country, the land where you were born. You have a duty to our Fatherland... to be of service, as our family has been for generations. That's why I brought you here. Back to your roots, back to a recognition of who you really are, and more. You need to see our country's present predicament. How did you feel locked up and crippled with no crutches to help you? Well... that's how Germany is now! We are crippled by the Versailles Treaty and the Great Depression... imprisoned by the helplessness of our government. We need the Nazi Party and the leadership of Adolf Hitler. They are our crutches.

My father grew calm. "Germany is on the brink of greatness now. Within the next ten years we will become the strongest nation in Europe. And we'll use that strength to expand our interests. You need to be a part of it. THIS is your future. The military should be your career. Take the first step. Join the Nazi Party. I have a lot of influence. In a short time you could have an excellent position."

I thought... oh my god, I have to find some way to stall for time because I'm never going to join the Nazi Party.

I answered quietly, "I grew up in England. I was educated there. So I became a citizen of my mother's country." Of course what I really wanted to say was: Piss on the Fatherland and Hitler's new

Germany, but I controlled myself.

Then I concentrated on the omelet with cheese and onions that Josef had served. When I finished, Josef came back to clear away the dishes. For some reason, Sonja wasn't helping him as she usually did. I asked where she was.

Always completely impassive, I was shocked at Josef's reaction. He stiffened. His face went white and his hands shook so badly the dishes rattled as he rushed out.

"She had an accident," my father said matter-of-factly. She fell or something. I don't know what happened. But there was a lot of blood. I had to take her to the hospital and then..." he shrugged. "I don't know... I suppose her family came and got her. Why? Does it matter?"

"Does it matter?" I asked, as I looked at my father as if for the first time. Now I saw the person he really was, a strongly built man, not very tall, but with a thick neck and a square jaw. His dark hair was graying. Still, Otto Von Bruener was a handsome man by any standard. Many women no doubt were attracted to him. But he was obsessed with impoverished young girls, the kind he could dominate totally. It wasn't sex. That could always be obtained. No... it was power and control.

Judging by Josef's reaction, something terrible had happened to Sonja. Did she try to escape him? I shuddered. He would never tolerate that.

Suddenly my father leaned forward in his chair. "Erich, you haven't answered me."

"I know… I… I know…" I stammered. "I need time. I have to give it serious consideration. After all, I've made a commitment to Karl. We've signed partnership papers."

The doorbell rang. Josef went to answer it. My father frowned, angry at being interrupted. "So what!" he said. "It's not that difficult to join the Party. I want your answer now!"

I paused. "Well… I can't give you an answer now. There's no sense in my joining anything while I'm in this condition. Let's wait until my leg is healed. I'm not of any value until then anyway."

Josef returned and handed my father a cable. "It's from your Uncle Tony. He hasn't heard from you… was unable to leave a message for you at the hotel… has contacted the British Embassy to locate you. Why didn't you write to him?"

I swallowed hard and coughed. I suddenly remembered the letter I wrote. But where the hell did I put it? Maybe it was still at the hotel.

I said, "I was going to write him as soon as I moved into an apartment. I wanted to give him my new address and telephone number."

The phone rang. Josef answered it and handed it to my father. "It's Herr Hitler's secretary, sir." I couldn't hear their conversation. I just saw that my father looked anxious. He started to perspire. I heard him say, "Yes… yes… he's here. Tell them he's visiting his father. Give them my address if they insist on seeing him. Okay… okay… It's not a problem. I'll take care of everything." And he hung up.

Then he turned to me. "We don't want to worry your uncle, do we? I'll cable him that you're safe here with me."

The telephone rang again. "It's Karl Klempner," Josef announced as he handed the phone to my father. My heart pounded. I heard my father say, "No... it was so long ago. I really don't remember Erich's friends. Yes... yes... he's right here." He handed me the telephone.

Karl sounded worried. "I called the hotel," he said, "to see how you were doing. The clerk told me you left on a stretcher two nights ago and that you were unconscious. I figured you were in some hospital. I called your father to find out which one. What the hell happened? You told me you don't stay with your father, so I'm surprised to find you there. Is everything alright?"

"Not exactly." I avoided meeting my father's steely gaze and continued, trying to keep my voice from quavering. "But you're right. I don't want to stay here. Any chance you could come and pick me up?"

"Sure. Gretchen and I will pick you up tomorrow morning on our way to church."

"Thanks, Karl. I'll see you then." I hung up.

My father looked at me with narrowed eyes. He wasn't happy. "I'm sorry you're leaving so soon."

"Yes, but you know how difficult it is for me to go up and down the stairs with this cast on. I'd be grateful if I could sleep down here in the library tonight. Josef could fix the sofa into a makeshift bed in there. I'll just need a pillow and some blankets. That way, I'd avoid the stairs altogether.

He stared at me. "Before you leave I want you to understand one thing. I fought and my brothers fought and died for this country. And what did we get for it? Nothing! Nothing but humiliation! Still, a new year is coming. 1931 is almost here and the Nazi Party grows more powerful every day. You can be a part of the New Order that's coming. If you choose!"

He half closed his eyes and lowered his voice to a whisper. "Be aware of your present condition. It would be a terrible thing if your other leg was broken." He got up and left the room.

It was like an electric shock. "What?" I screamed after him. "Did you really say that to me?!"

There was no answer.

CHAPTER 8 — DECISIONS

I sat on the sofa in the library. My crutches were now leaning against the wall close at hand. The telephone was nearby and the door didn't lock. I supposed my situation had improved to this extent because the Nazis didn't want the British Embassy to make inquiries or investigations of any kind. Germany was re-arming secretly and wanted to keep it that way. I was grateful to Uncle Tony for applying that kind of pressure. It enabled me to get out of here. But where could I go?

First I needed to go back to the Adlon to find that letter. But I knew I wasn't going to stay there. I didn't know where to go until Frau Rhinehardt's apartment became available. Karl's place was too small. My only hope was that he could recommend a place for me to stay, just for a few days.

Of course I didn't have to remain in Berlin. I could always go back to England, back to Cambridge, and just be a silent partner in the Berlin Opera Company. But I didn't want to do that. I thought about Ossietzky. He knows he's going to be sent back to prison. He could run, but he isn't going to... and I'm not going to either!

There was a tap on the door.

"Come in," I said.

It was Josef. "Can I do something for you, sir? Draw a bath or help you into pajamas?"

"No... thank you... I'm alright. Oh... just a minute. There is something you can do for me. Tell me what happened to Sonja."

He didn't answer. He grew pale and lowered his eyes. "She's dead," he whispered, and left, closing the door behind him.

"Wait!" I shouted. But he was gone. "Dead?" I mumbled. That little girl with the yellow braids is dead? I reached for my crutches, stumbled to the window and pulled back the curtains. It was black outside, icy-cold and stormy. I had a dark and frightening thought. I whispered it to the howling wind. Did he kill her?

There was a knock at the door. I turned to see my father standing there.

"Well..." he said, settling into a lounge chair. "Where do you plan to stay after you leave here? Are you going back to the hotel?"

"No... I'm not sure where I'll stay."

He nodded... and sat there looking at me. The silence between us became uncomfortable. Maybe five minutes went by before he stood up and walked to the door. He said, "I'm looking forward to meeting your business partner tomorrow. Goodnight."

After he left I tried to fall asleep but couldn't. I waited until I felt sure everyone else was asleep then I made my way carefully and quietly to the Salon. This house, once my home, was now a sinister place. Now I couldn't wait to leave but I wanted to see the portrait of my mother for the last time. I gazed at her beautiful face and silently said goodbye. I was never coming back.

In the morning, Josef helped me bathe, shave, and get into fresh clothes. I again asked about Sonja. "I can't discuss it," he said. "And now if you'll excuse me, the cook will see to your breakfast. I have to feed the dogs."

"The dogs? I haven't seen any dogs. I didn't even hear any barking. Where are they?"

"They're out back, sir. We have three German Shepherds. We let them out a few times a day. Otherwise they're kept caged and muzzled. They're guard dogs, you know."

The hair on the back of my neck stood up. "Why do you need guard dogs?" I asked. But he left without answering.

The cook came in, put breakfast down, and poured the coffee. My hands were shaking so badly I had to grip my cup with both hands.

The doorbell rang. I jumped. It was Karl and Gretchen. My heart banged in my chest so hard, I could almost hear it. I grabbed my crutches in time to see my father greet them at the door. He was most cordial. "Come in… come in…" he said. "Karl, now that I see you, I do remember you, although it's been many years." They shook hands. Then he turned his attention to Gretchen and, making a slight bow, he said, "I'm delighted to meet you, Frau Klempner. I hope we'll meet again, and soon." He turned to me. "Goodbye, Erich. Don't forget what I told you."

I glared at him. Karl helped me on with my coat, loaded my

suitcases into his car and then helped me navigate the ice-covered steps. Somehow I managed to get into the back seat. My leg began to ache. I ignored it. I was so glad to be out of that house and away from my father.

Once in the car I said, "Karl, I can't tell you and Gretchen how grateful I am for your help. I was in such a hellish situation. Thanks for being such good friends. I don't know what I would have done without you."

Karl said, "Erich, Dr. Liebman also called your hotel. He's very concerned... doesn't know what might have caused you to become so ill. He wants to see you as soon as possible. So please call him. But first, tell us what happened!"

I didn't know how to tell it. It was so insane. "I'll tell you later. But right now there are a couple of things I need to do and I hope you'll help me. First, I want to go back to the hotel. I must look for an important letter that I left in my room. Of course I'm not going to stay there anymore. I'm looking for another place, just for a few days until Frau Rhinehardt's apartment becomes available. I know you don't have room. But do you know anyone who can accommodate me for a short time?"

The car pulled up in front of a pink mansion.

"Why are we stopping here?" I asked.

The Confessing Church

"That's our church," Gretchen answered. "It's where we always go on Sunday mornings."

That was a jolt! I didn't know it was Sunday. I'd lost all track of time.

"I guess this place doesn't look much like a church," she continued. "But it's where our congregation meets and Reverend Maas is delivering the Sermon today. He's always excellent. Then afterwards we can do whatever you want."

Karl said, "Come to think of it, Hermann Maas has a spacious place. He may be able to put you up for a few days. His wife, Kornelie, is very sweet. And they have three lovely daughters. Who knows? One of them might interest you!"

I ignored that last remark. "When can we speak to him?" I asked.

"Probably after the Service would be best," Karl said as he helped me enter the warm and crowded room. I'd never seen a church like this one. It was so plain, as if it was a temporary meeting place… just a dark wooden floor, lots of folding chairs, and a small table with hymnals. Aside from the podium, there was little else.

I spotted Neimoller at the far end of the room, along with Ossietzky. I waved to them. As much as I wanted to join them, it seemed too difficult to maneuver on crutches among so many people. I found the nearest chair and sat down.

The Service began. It was similar to those I'd attended in England with Uncle Tony's family. Here in Germany I'd been baptized as a Catholic though I was never very religious. Still, for some reason I liked this church.

When the Service ended, the Reverend Maas began his Sermon. He spoke at length of the chaos of our present government, the tragedy of the Depression, and the financial burden of our defeat in the Great War. "But…" he continued, "Can that be an excuse for the violence we see on the streets every day? Adolf Hitler blames the Jews for all our problems. We are bombarded by negative messages about them, fake newsreels, phony documentaries, and fabricated news stories. Jews are being beaten in the streets in broad daylight.

Yet it's Adolf Hitler who proclaims that we must have order! Of course he's speaking of his New Order which proclaims we must focus on restoring German pride and prosperity by maintaining our Aryan Race. He claims the Jews do not belong to our race and therefore are not German citizens. The Jewish people have been

German citizens for more than 700 years.

Even more troubling is Hitler's assertion that Judaism itself must be rejected. The Ten Commandments no longer have any validity and the German people must give their first allegiance to their country and their race, not to God or to our Lord, Jesus Christ! Friends, as true Christians, surely we cannot just stand by. I tell you we must protest publicly against all violence. We must protest theologically against this assault on Christian values. All of us must become like Jesus and bring to our troubled time and place what he brought to his... kindness, compassion, and love."

"Amen," I said silently.

I got up to congratulate him on his fine Sermon. As I made my way in his direction, I heard mumbling and whispers. Others in the congregation didn't agree with him. Someone said, "I'm not going to defend any Jews. I hear Hitler has 100,000 Brownshirts. Those Storm Troopers are a rough bunch. You stick your neck out, they might break it."

"That's right," another chimed in. "Our protest should be solely on a theological level." They weren't talking to me so I didn't answer. But I thought their cowardly position would encourage the Nazis.

As I stumbled through the crowd, I could see that Karl and Gretchen were already talking to Reverend Maas. When I joined them, Maas smiled and said, "Erich, nice to see you again. My wife and I would be delighted for you to stay with us. It's just a small room that we can offer. But we'll do our best to make you feel comfortable and welcome. Please, all of you, join us for lunch. We don't live far."

Gretchen spoke up. "Thank you," she said. "That would be lovely." I shook the Reverend's hand and thanked him for his inspiring Sermon as well as his kindness in taking in a needy stranger. "Count me among your admirers," I enthused.

"Ach... please..." he waved that aside. "I look forward to your company."

So despite my intentions to get back to the hotel as soon as possible, I found myself seated in the dining room of the Maas home. I couldn't protest too much. Besides, I was hungry.

Reverend Hermann Maas

Their Sunday dinner began with hot chicken soup followed by a generous portion of roast chicken with sausage stuffing and potatoes. I licked my lips as we polished it off with cold beer. Still, I was getting a little anxious. I whispered to Karl, asking if we might excuse ourselves now and go over to the hotel. We stood up and thanked our host for the wonderful meal. The Reverend's wife was dismayed that we weren't staying for dessert. But we insisted we were already stuffed. Gretchen chose to stay behind while Karl and I made our way to the Adlon. He drove slowly and cautiously through the snow-covered streets. "So… are you going to tell me what happened to you?"

"It's difficult to discuss because it was so crazy. But the truth is I was unconscious when I left the hotel because I'd been drugged." Karl shot me a startled look. "Yes… and my father was responsible. He's angry about my involvement with the Berlin Opera Company. He told me that it's just a hobby and I should pursue a real career with the German Military. As a first step, he's adamant that I join that goddamn Nazi Party immediately!"

Karl shook his head. "I see. So what are you going to do?"

"I want to go forward with our partnership and our plans. I'm not interested in a German Military career, or any military career for that matter. But my father is a very dangerous man. For the moment I've stalled him because of my broken leg. But that won't last. Eventually I'll have to think of something else."

Karl grinned. "I'm glad you're sticking with our partnership, at least for now. If things get really tough, I guess you can always run back to England. But let me know if you need my help while you're here."

"Thanks, Karl. You're helping me right now. I need to retrieve an important letter I wrote to my Uncle Tony. It was left behind when I was dragged out of the hotel. I don't want my father to get his hands on it."

When we entered the hotel, I went directly to the front desk clerk. He smiled broadly. "Ah, it's so nice to see you again, Herr Von Bruener. "And fully recovered too. What can I do for you?"

"I left something important in my room," I told him. "I'd like to retrieve it now."

"Ach… I'm so sorry, sir. Your room is now registered to another guest. But you can speak to the Concierge. He has the keys to all the rooms. See what he can do for you."

"Thank you," I said as I stepped away from the desk. My mind was racing. So that's how my father got into my room. The Concierge gave him the key and, no doubt, received a big tip in return.

The Concierge frowned as he saw us approaching. "I was taken from my room in such dire circumstances," I told him, "that I left something important behind. I'd like to look for it now."

"That's out of the question, Herr Von Bruener," he answered curtly. "Your old room is taken."

"I understand," I said. "But we can certainly enter with the permission of the current guest, or when the housekeeper is there."

"That is absolutely against the rules here at the Adlon," he snapped. "Tell me what was left behind and I'll search for it myself after the guest has checked out."

I growled at him. "It was also against the Adlon's rules for you to give my room key to an unauthorized person. If you don't allow me to look for my property, I will report that incident to the management and demand that you be fired!"

He turned pale and stammered, "Of course... for a steady client like you, sir... I'll make an exception. Follow me."

He knocked loudly at the door of my former room. When there was no response, he opened it with his key and we all entered. I couldn't remember where I put that letter. I checked the drawer in the nightstand first. No luck. I gave it more thought and opened some desk drawers. And there it was. What a relief! As I slipped it into my coat pocket I saw the Concierge grimace. He'd just missed a big payoff. That letter would have been worth a lot of money to my father, and he knew it.

We quickly left the hotel and headed back to Reverend Maas's house. I figured I'd mail the letter first thing in the morning. It was getting late now. Karl brought my suitcases inside and put them in the small guest bedroom that would be mine for the next few days. I gave him a hug and Gretchen a kiss as we said goodbye. I thanked them again for being such good friends as I walked them to the door. "I promise to call Dr. Liebman at once," I shouted as their car pulled away. "And thanks for everything."

As soon as they left I asked Hermann Maas if I could use his telephone. "Yes, of course. It's in my study. Come this way."

He ushered me into a spacious room with a large desk, a sofa, several lounge chairs and tall bookshelves filled with what looked like thousands of volumes. There were glowing embers in the fireplace and he stoked them into a bit of a blaze. "May I offer you a glass of wine?"

"Oh… yes, that would be nice." After he left I phoned Dr. Liebman. I assured him I was perfectly alright. But he remained unconvinced. "Please come to the hospital at 10:30 tomorrow morning. I want to examine you again and perhaps take another X-ray of your ankle to see if it's healing properly."

There was no sense arguing. "Alright, I'll be there," I told him. After I hung up I scanned the bookshelves and noticed a copy of "All Quiet on the Western Front." I was again impressed with Hermann Maas. Then I saw a number of books with the same kind of writing that I'd seen in Rabbi Machinski's study. When the Reverend returned, I mentioned my visit to that study in Warsaw and asked about the strange writing. "What language is it?"

"It's Hebrew, the language of the Old Testament, the Torah, as they call it. It's a very ancient and somewhat magical language." As we drank our wine, he continued. "All the letters have numerical values as well. So you have both language and mathematics all in one. For example, the letter chai has a numerical value of eighteen. It's considered a lucky number."

"That's fascinating. I'd like to learn it. Could you teach me Hebrew?"

"Are you serious? It's not an easy language to learn."

"I'd like to try."

He smiled warmly. "Then I'd be glad to teach you. Why don't we start after supper?"

It turned out to be a short lesson because the day had been a long one and I was exhausted. We made plans to continue the next night and every night after dinner.

In the morning I took a taxi, first to the post office where I mailed my letter to Uncle Tony, and then to the Jewish Hospital for my appointment with Dr. Liebman.

The hospital was huge. As I made my way to the waiting room I noticed a young woman walking ahead of me down the hallway. She wore a long dark dress and boots. A heavy knitted shawl draped her shoulders. She was small and slender with long black hair almost to her waist. I couldn't see her face, of course. But somehow she looked familiar.

CHAPTER 9 — THE JEWISH HOSPITAL

The waiting room was crowded. I spoke to the receptionist and gave her my name. "I have an appointment with Dr. Liebman at 10:30," I told her.

"The doctor is running a bit late. Please have a seat. We'll call you when he's available."

I didn't want to sit down and wait. I went back to the hallway, hoping I could get another glimpse of that young lady. And there she was! This time, coming towards me holding an infant. My heart leaped! "Chani," I shouted. "Chani Machinski, is that you?"

She came closer. Her jewel-like eyes sparkled wide with amazement. When she saw my cast and crutches, she said, "Oy... Herr Von Bruener, vos hast passeert? (what happened to you)?"

I chuckled. She was so proper... so formal... while I... night after night dreamed of sleeping with her.

"I'm just clumsy," I said. "I slipped on the ice and broke my ankle. I'm waiting to see my doctor. But what about you? What are you doing here?"

"My mother is so sick. We had to bring her to the hospital right away. She's being examined by the doctor now. And the baby got a little cranky and started to cry, so I had to take him out of there. He's asleep now. Poor little Avi" and she kissed him gently. I was hot with envy. I changed the subject.

"Is your grandmother with you?"

"No... no... Bubbe had to stay home with Sarah and the boys. Papa wanted Fannie to come instead. My sister is in medical school, studying to be a nurse. Papa thought she would have a better understanding of whatever the doctor says is Mama's sickness. I was coming to Berlin anyway, to get settled with a suitable family here, you know, before rehearsals start. So Fannie is staying in Berlin with me until Mama can go home. Papa can't stay. He has to get back to work."

"But what about Fannie? Doesn't she have to get back to school?"

Chani hesitated. Her eyelashes fluttered. "No..." she whispered. "My sister wants to continue her studies at Hadassah Hospital in Jerusalem. She's planning to go there as soon as Mama is better." Chani bit her lip. "But it's very far..." her eyes filled with tears. "I don't know if I'll ever see her again."

Oh my god... I couldn't bear for her to cry. I blurted out, "So Fannie is a Zionist then, isn't she?" Chani looked startled. She took a step backward. "What do you know about Zionists?"

"Not much," I answered. "Just that they're a group of Jews who want to leave Europe and return to the Holy Land. Right now I'm staying with the Reverend Maas, just temporarily. And he knows quite a bit about Zionism. He's also fluent in Hebrew and has agreed to teach it to me."

"What?" Chani gasped. Then she smiled. "You want to learn Hebrew? Why?"

"Well... Maas explained what a fascinating language it is, where letters are also numbers. So what we have are letters making words... language, and the same letters also making numbers, which can lead to all kinds of mathematical formulations. I think that's incredible. I believe that language and mathematics are the basis of civilization itself. Of course I'm only at the beginning and having a terrible time with pronunciation. Maybe you can help me with that?"

She smiled again. "And I'm learning to speak good German. Maybe you can help me with that."

A loud voice rang out. "Von Bruener? Erich Von Bruener?"

"Ach... that's my doctor's appointment. I have to go. Listen we'll talk again... and soon."

My mind was still on Chani as I sat down in the doctor's office. Dr. Liebman was the fatherly type. He had a full head of gray hair and greeted me with a concerned look in his dark eyes. "I was told that you were unconscious when you were taken from the Adlon Hotel. Can you tell me what happened to you?"

I sighed... closed my eyes and shook my head. "No, I don't want to talk about it, except to say it had nothing to do with your treatment of my broken ankle, or any medications you prescribed. So... take it from there."

He nodded and said gently, "Apparently you've suffered some

kind of trauma. I want to X-Ray the ankle again, do some blood work, and examine you more thoroughly."

Later, once he had reviewed my test results, he said, "Everything seems to be fine. It may be that you've been too active. You need more rest. Keep your leg elevated as much as possible. Get some good books and spend more time in bed. You'll recover faster. Are you still staying at the Adlon?"

"No… no… I plan to get my own apartment after the first of the year. I'm staying with the Reverend Maas right now."

The doctor broke into a smile that lit up his whole face. "Hermann Maas? He's a dear friend of mine. Please give him my best regards. And by the way, have you seen his library? It's filled with wonderful books. I'm sure he'd loan you something good to read. So take it easy and come back to see me again in three weeks."

I didn't bother to tell him all the things on my busy agenda. No sense in worrying the good doctor. I thanked him for his care and concern. Then I headed back into the hallway to look for Chani. No luck. I went to the Information Desk and inquired about her mother. I was informed that Bayla Machinski had been admitted to the hospital. But no visitors were permitted except for family members. I was asked, "Are you a member of the family?"

"Not yet," I smiled.

As soon as I got back to the house, I called Frau Rhinehardt. We agreed to meet at her apartment on Neukonigstrasse at two o'clock. Then I phoned Karl. "I'm going to need a valet when I get into my own place," I told him. "I need a man who can drive because I'm planning to buy a car and I can't drive with this damn cast on. Can you recommend someone?"

"Let me think about that. There are a lot of guys looking for work now. And by the way, I have a friend in the car business. When do you want to look for a car?"

"How about tomorrow morning, if you're not busy."

"No... that's fine. I'll pick you up around nine."

"Great! Oh, incidentally, I was at the Jewish Hospital this morning to see Dr. Liebman and while I was there I saw Chani."

"Really?"

"Yes... she's here in Berlin. They brought her mother to the hospital for a diagnosis. I hope the doctors can help her. Anyway, I thought you'd want to know that Chani will be on schedule for rehearsals."

"Ach... wonderful! I worried about how things would go with her. Rehearsals start in two weeks and I have a lot of work to do. So far I've found a room for Leon Carbonne. But we still need costumes, scenery and more musicians. We'd better go over the budget. Let's talk about it tomorrow. I'll see you in the morning."

I was glad I didn't tell Karl how exciting it was for me to see Chani again. No sense putting him on edge about that. I'd already heard his objections.

I looked at my watch. I had to hurry. So I grabbed a sandwich from the housekeeper in the Reverend's kitchen and taxied over to Frau Rhinehardt's apartment. The sun was shining, melting the snow into slush, making my progress treacherous. What an inconvenience for an agnostic like me to need crutches in this weather. I had no god to pray to for protection against the terrors of slipping and falling.

I was so intent on getting to the front door safely that I hardly noticed a car passing slowly. Had I seen that car before? Frau Rhinehardt opened the door for me and began to show me around the apartment. There were four rooms all furnished with dark, sturdy furniture. There were rugs on the floor, drapes on the windows, and all was included. My only extra expense would be fuel for the fireplace and telephone service. We agreed on a reasonable rent and I signed a two-year lease. Now I had my own place. I just had to wait a few days to move in.

It had been a successful day. I was smiling when I joined the Maas family for supper and told them all about it. "And tomorrow," I announced, "with luck, I'm going to buy myself a car."

After supper, I took another Hebrew lesson in the library. When we finished, I mentioned that I'd seen Dr. Liebman that morning and that he sends his best regards to you and the family. "All my test results were good. He just wants me to spend more time resting. Would you mind if I borrowed a book or two from your library?"

"Please do. I'm glad you're listening to the doctor's advice. Max Liebman is one of the best doctors in Berlin. If you do what he says, you'll be out of that cast in no time."

I looked around. There were so many great books to choose from… classics, new novels, History, Poetry, Philosophy… I took my time and finally decided on MOBY DICK, a book about the sea. I don't know why. I'd read it many years ago. But somehow I felt compelled to read it again. Maybe the images of the sea reminded me of Chani's blue-green eyes.

It was getting late. I said goodnight and hobbled off to bed, too tired to even open the book. I fell asleep as soon as my head hit the pillow. I dreamed of Chani swimming naked in the ocean like a mermaid, her long dark hair trailing behind her. I swam after her but she was too fast for me. She headed for a rock jutting out of the sea and hoisted herself onto it, swooshing her wet hair back, revealing her beautiful body. There she sat, smiling back at me. I swam closer and watched as she licked one shoulder and then the other. She made a face. "It's salty!" she shouted above the crashing of the waves. I grinned back at her. "Why don't you let me do that!" I yelled.

The telephone in the library rang. "God dammit" I muttered. I didn't want to wake up. I pulled the covers over my head, trying to get back to my dream. But the phone rang and rang until someone finally answered it.

I was awake by then. I didn't know what time it was. I just figured it was probably the middle of the night and that phone call must have been bad news. Good news can always wait until morning. A sliver of fear stabbed me.

The bedroom door opened. Hermann Maas was standing there. "Get up, Erich. Something terrible has happened at the Jewish Hospital."

"What?" I cried. "What's happened?"

"Let's get going. I'll tell you on the way." He helped me into my clothes, threw my coat on me and got me into his car. It was pitch black and bone-chilling cold as we raced through the deserted streets.

"Tell me what's going on," I said.

A tear ran down his face. He wiped it away with his hand. "Max Liebman was attacked and badly beaten. So badly that he's in surgery now. They don't know…"

My brain froze. I remembered my father's ugly reaction when I told him I was being treated by Dr. Liebman at the Jewish Hospital. An evil darkness gripped me, just as it had when I'd heard about Sonja. I felt a stab of fear in the pit of my stomach at the horror of my suspicions.

At the hospital a policeman was waiting to speak to me. "According to Dr. Liebman's appointment book, you saw the doctor this morning. Is that right?"

"Yes."

"Did you notice anyone suspicious-looking in the waiting room?"

"No."

"Do you know anyone who might want to harm the doctor?"

I didn't answer.

"Are you Otto Von Bruener's son?"

"Yes."

"Well… thank you for your cooperation. We are continuing our investigation." And he left.

In the waiting room Maas introduced me to Mrs. Liebman and her two adult sons, Emil and Stephan. She sat wiping her tear-filled eyes as the two young men, white-faced and anguished, paced the floor. "This is Erich Von Bruener, one of your husband's patients. He saw the doctor only this morning and all was well. Ilse, do you know what happened?"

"What happened?" She whispered tearfully... "What happened? Max told me he would come home early. He wanted to spend more time with Emil before he goes back to medical school. But he didn't come home and he didn't call, which wasn't like him. We waited and waited. I became worried and phoned the office. No answer. I called his associate, Dr. Wolfson. He told me Max left the office hours ago. I was frantic when I heard that. Before I could call the Police, the hospital called me. They told me my husband was injured and I should come at once."

Ilse Liebman began to tremble and sob. "When I came here... I was told that the janitor found Max behind the building by the trash cans, unconscious in the snow, his face covered with blood."

"Hermann, this was an anti-Semitic attack! The Nazis have been spreading outrageous lies about Jewish doctors. I think they're responsible for this! But no one heard anything. No one saw anything. There's no evidence. The Police say they're investigating."

She paused, and in a low voice she murmured, "It's painful for me to say this to you. Germany is my country and I love it. We've lived here for generations. But now it seems my country doesn't love me or any Jewish person. As soon as Max is well enough, we have to leave Germany. Hermann, can you help us?"

"It depends. Where do you want to go?"

"I don't know yet. I have to talk it over with my husband."

The door opened and the surgeon came to speak to us. His face was ashen. And in a hesitant voice, he said, "It may be a long and difficult recovery. Dr. Liebman suffered a severe concussion, a badly broken nose and the loss of his left eye."

The room exploded into shrieks and screams.

CHAPTER 10 — 1931

It was still hours before dawn, the darkest time of the night, when we left the hospital. Shocked into silence by the brutality of the attack on Dr. Liebman, we drove slowly through the black, icy streets of Berlin.

I wasn't cold. I was seething with anger... so hot I could have ignited coal. I shouted, "Not a goddamn person saw anything! Nobody heard a scream? And that's it? Nothing can be done?!"

"We KNOW who did this! It was those Nazi bastards. They call themselves Brownshirts? They're brownshits! Even their uniforms are the right color. Like the punch line to that old joke... THEY'RE LOWER THAN WHALE SHIT AND THAT'S AT THE BOTTOM OF THE OCEAN!"

"Erich! Why are you ranting like that? What do you want to do about it? What can be done?"

"I don't know... I just don't know... but somebody should do something!" We rode on in silence. Finally I said, "Do you remember that famous letter Emile Zola published in the French Newspapers?

In huge letters he wrote, J'ACCUSE! He addressed it to the president of France, accusing him of anti-Semitism in the false conviction of the Jew, Alfred Dreyfus, as a spy. Zola's letter caused such a stir that eventually Dreyfus was freed from his life sentence in prison on Devil's Island.

"We can't undo what's happened to Dr. Liebman. But as a prominent Christian Minister, such a letter from you would make all of Berlin aware of this vicious crime. It might even prevent others… It might spur a real investigation… it might do some good!"

"Listen, Erich. I'm glad you know History so well. Do you also remember that Zola was prosecuted and found guilty of libel? That he fled to England to avoid his own imprisonment?"

We pulled up to the house and Maas helped me get inside. He continued, "Of course that was soon straightened out. But it's a very risky proposition you're suggesting. You see how dangerous the Nazis are. Propaganda and violence… that's their job! And they're really good at it."

I shrugged. It was true. I had nothing more to say. He looked at me with grieving eyes. "Nevertheless, I'll do it. I can't sleep anyway. I might as well get started on it." He headed for the library.

Surprised, I murmured, "I'll help you," and followed behind him.

It took longer than I thought it would. We argued over several points. I didn't want it to sound too preachy. By morning we had it finished.

"I think it's good," I told him. "Now all we have to do is get it published. I'm sure Ossietzky would print it in his Journal."

"True. But he doesn't have a large readership. I'll give it to him after I take it to the BERLINER TAGBLATT. That's the largest newspaper. I'd better get going. Aren't you expecting Karl this morning? Didn't you tell me you were going to buy a car?"

"Oh, yes... but that was before all this happened. I'd forgotten all about it. You know it was Karl who took me to see Dr. Liebman when I broke my ankle. I'll have to tell him this terrible news."

Maas shrugged. "Listen," he said wearily. "I've got to get cleaned up and shaved. A strong cup of coffee wouldn't hurt either." And he headed off.

Karl arrived right on time. He was filled with excitement. "My friend at the car dealership has an old Mercedes to show you. He says it's in excellent condition and since the car business is bad now, I think you can get it for a really good price." He stopped talking and looked at me. "What happened to you? Is something wrong?"

I just sat there, exhausted, rumpled and unshaven. Karl pulled a chair over and sat down. "What is it?"

When I told him about Dr. Liebman, the color drained from his face. He shook his head, shocked by the news. He said, "You know, I met Max Liebman and his family years ago. Their son Emil is about our age. Stephan is a few years younger. They used to go skiing at Davos in Switzerland. They were pretty good. We skied together. I was a poor orphan boy back then, living with my grandfather. The Liebmans were very kind to me."

"I hope the doctor's going to be alright." He buried his face in his hands. Then he gave me a puzzled look. "Why? Why him?"

I didn't say anything. But he persisted. "Do you think your father had something to do with it?"

Somehow I managed to whisper, "Yes." He waited for me to explain. Finally I told him, "My father was outraged, furious, calling Dr. Liebman a poisoner when I mentioned that Dr. Liebman was treating my broken ankle at the Jewish Hospital. As far as I know there is no evidence... no witness... no proof of any kind. Still, I believe my father got those Brownshirt brutes to do it. And nothing is going to happen to any of them! They're going to get away with it."

"But isn't there an investigation? An inquiry into the matter?"

"Oh, yes. Yes... a half-assed investigation. But to put more pressure on the authorities Reverend Maas has written a letter, begging government officials to put an end to this violence. Right now he's trying to get it published in the newspapers. He needs support... at least from the Churches."

"I hope it works. Meanwhile, I want to go to the hospital to see Dr. Liebman."

"So do I. If you'll help me get myself together, I'll go with you."

Later, as we entered the hospital room, we saw that a curtain had been drawn around Dr. Liebman's bed. A nurse and Ilse were inside. Karl went over to Emile and Stephan and offered any help they might require. I watched him grimace as he listened to their whispered, desperate news.

Then the curtain opened. What a shocking sight! Max Liebman was bandaged up like a mummy. His entire head and face were covered. Only one eye and his mouth were exposed.

The nurse left. Ilse remained with her husband, holding his hand. She murmured to him, "Max, you're so strong. You can recover from this. And as soon as you're up to it, we're going to leave Germany. Hermann Maas said he'd help. We just need to tell him where we want to go. There are so many places. Switzerland is beautiful. Or we could go further, maybe New York to be near your cousins, or near my family in Toronto. Think about it, sweetheart. We'll relocate to wherever you say."

He was motionless and made no sound. I tried to be consoling. "He's probably heavily sedated to keep him from pain," I offered. I didn't know if they believed me. I hardly believed it myself.

On the way home, Karl stopped for a newspaper. And sure enough, there was the letter on the front page of the BERLINER TAGBLATT. It began:

ICH BESCHULDIGE (I accuse you) and it was addressed to the highest authorities.

YOU WHO ARE PLEDGED TO PROTECT OUR CITIZENS HAVE LISTENED TO THE ANTI-SEMITIC RANTS OF THE NAZI PARTY AND THE RESULTS ARE VIOLENCE AGAINST INNOCENT PEOPLE. ONLY YESTERDAY DR. MAX LIEBMAN, A PROMINENT PHSICIAN AND A KIND AND HONORABLE MAN, WAS VICIOUSLY ATTACKED AND BEATEN SO BADLY HE IS NOW IN CRITICAL CONDITION. AND FOR NO REASON EXCEPT THAT HE IS OF THE JEWISH FAITH.

GERMANY IS A NATION OF CHURCHES. WE ARE A

MORAL COMMUNITY OF CHRISTIANS. IT IS YOUR SWORN DUTY TO PROTECT ALL LAW-ABIDING CITIZENS, REGARDLESS OF RELIGIOUS AFFILIATION. I ACCUSE YOU OF NEGLECTING YOUR DUTY AND CALL UPON YOU TO BRING AN END TO SUCH VIOLENCE BY DISBANDING THE BROWNSHIRTS AND PROSECUTING THE GUILTY.

RESPECTFULLY,

REVEREND HERMANN MAAS, MINISTER

OF THE EVANGELICAL CHURCH OF CHRIST

"That's a great letter," Karl said as he dropped me off at the house. Congratulate the Reverend for me."

I was excited. I thought it was a fantastic letter. I found Maas in the library. He seemed disturbed and downhearted.

"What's the matter?" I asked.

"Some of the members of my congregation came by. They were angry with me. They didn't like my letter at all. They felt I should not have mentioned the church without consulting them. There might be serious repercussions and they were worried for their own safety as well as for the church itself.

Of course they're right! The problem is that if I had taken the time to consult them and formed a proper committee, the timing would have been gone. Nevertheless, I apologized profusely and they finally left.

After that, a group of Jewish Community leaders came to thank me for my courageous letter. They knew nothing of the attack on Dr.

Liebman and were now concerned for him and his family, and frightened for their own. I don't blame them. Now we have to be alert for the Nazis' reaction."

The following morning, we found out exactly what that was. We got a copy of DER SHTURMER, the Nazi newspaper. They published an article on their front page by Julius Streicher. Over breakfast we read it. The title was DEUTSCHE VOLKSGESUNDHEIT (The German People's Health).

"IN THE HEALING ARTS, BEHIND THE MASK OF A 'FRIEND OF HUMANITY' THE JEW UNDERSTANDS HOW TO SNEAK AMONG THE GERMAN PEOPLE AS A DOCTOR, A BRINGER OF HEALTH. BUT HE HAS NEVER HAD THE DESIRE TO HEAL NON-JEWS. HIS GOAL IS TO RUIN THEIR HEALTH!

THE PROBLEM IS THAT THE GERMAN PEOPLE HAVE LOST THEIR RACIAL INSTINCTS. THEY SEE THE JEW AS A 'PERSON' AND AS A GERMAN CITIZEN. THE JEW IS NOT A GERMAN, BUT RATHER A DECEIVER. HE IS NOT A CITIZEN, BUT RATHER A BUTCHER... A MEMBER OF A RACE OF FOREIGNERS IN BLOOD AND NATURE. HE TRAINS HIS CHILDREN AS DOCTORS AND APOTHECARIES SO THAT THEY WILL BE ABLE TO TAKE THE LIVES OF CHRISTIANS. THE JEW IS THE DEADLY ENEMY!"

I was furious! Those goddamn Nazis tell the most outrageous lies. They turn the victim into the villain, and in such a way that people believe it. The bastards are so good at it. They make the most barbaric acts seem acceptable!

Suddenly I had an idea. What if I wrote a letter to the newspaper, explaining my excellent care as a Christian patient of a Jewish doctor. The most important part of that kind of publicity would be my signature, Erich Von Bruener. What would the Nazis make of that?!

The phone rang. Maas answered it. "Yes… thank you for calling." A tear ran down his face as he hung up the phone. "Max Liebman died," he said quietly.

CHAPTER 11 — THE FUNERAL

It was because of this heart-wrenching tragedy that we lost all sense of time. The New Year -- 1931 tiptoed into existence without our knowledge or celebration. It was an ugly day, dark, cold and raining sleet, as we made our way to the funeral of Max Liebman. Reverend Maas was taking his whole family and didn't have enough room for me. So Karl picked me up.

"Gretchen couldn't come," he explained as he helped me into the car. She's keeping things going at the office. We'll make a condolence call together later."

"Okay," I said, although I didn't know what he was talking about. I peered out the window at all that grayness and recalled the only other funeral I'd ever attended... my mother's. That one took place on a sunny day, when I was eight years old.

I thought my mother looked like 'Sleeping Beauty' surrounded by all that white satin inside her casket. I slipped a smiling photo of the two of us next to her. My grandfather told me to kiss her goodbye. I didn't really understand what 'dead' meant at that time. So even though she felt cold and waxy when I kissed her, I expected her to wake up.

But she didn't and when they closed the coffin and lowered it into the ground, I became terrified. "Don't!" I shrieked. "Don't do it! She's going to wake up soon!"

My grandfather quickly hushed me up. He whispered in my ear, "No, she won't. She's an angel in heaven now." That explanation didn't help. I had bad dreams for many years.

Karl brought the car to a stop in front of an imposing entrance, part of an arcaded yellow brick complex of buildings. The sign in front read, WEISSENSEE JEWISH CEMETERY.

Interior of the Weissensee Jewish Cemetery

Inside was a cavernous columned hall with vaulted ceilings, all in the same yellow brick. The mean weather hadn't kept anyone from attending. The place was filled to overflowing. I spotted Hermann Maas and his wife waving from across the room. They had saved seats for us. As we moved towards them I whispered to Reverend Maas, "I've never been to a Jewish funeral. Tell me what to do."

Maas said, "Ilse and her family are seated in the front row. Why don't you go to them and offer sympathy. It's customary."

I looked toward the front of the room. The coffin, resting on a raised base, was made of plain dark wood, nicely finished, with a large star on the side facing us. It was closed, of course, so no one could see that Dr. Liebman had been beaten beyond recognition. I knew this tragedy happened because a Jewish doctor treated ME, his

Christian patient. What a wretched feeling I had as I staggered to my feet and followed Karl to speak to the widow and her sons.

As we returned to our seats a man approached the podium. "That's Rabbi Berger," Hermann Maas murmured. "I know him. He's quite good."

The Rabbi began, "We're here today to honor the memory of a wonderful man, Dr. Max Liebman. Let me begin by reading a few lines from the Psalms of David.

"THE WICKED WALK ON EVERY SIDE,

WHEN VILENESS IS EXALTED AMONG THE SONS OF MEN

WHY STANDEST THOU AFAR OFF, O LORD,

WHY HIDEST THOU THYSELF IN TIMES OF TROUBLE?

FOR THE WICKED BOASTETH OF HIS HEART'S DESIRE,

ALL HIS THOUGHTS ARE: THERE IS NO GOD.

HIS MOUTH IS FULL OF CURSING AND DECEIT AND OPPRESSION;

IN SECRET PLACES DOTH HE SLAY THE INNOCENT;"

The Rabbi continued, "Max Liebman was a righteous man, devoted to his wife and family, his profession, his patients, and his country."

He asked that we recite the 23rd Psalm together. Then Rabbi Berger told personal stories about Dr. Liebman to round out the picture of a kind and loving man, after which he returned to the Psalms of David.

THE WICKED AND HIM THAT LOVETH VIOLENCE THE LORD HATETH.

UPON THE WICKED HE WILL CAUSE TO RAIN COALS;

FIRE AND BRIMSTONE AND BURNING WIND SHALL BE THE PORTION OF THEIR CUP.

THE LORD LOVETH RIGHTEOUSNESS;

THE UPRIGHT, SUCH AS MAX LIEBMAN, SHALL BEHOLD HIS FACE."

"Please rise for the Kaddish."

I lurched to my feet and threw a questioning glance at Reverend Maas. "This is the mourners' prayer," he whispered. "It's an affirmation of faith in God in the face of terror and death." He handed me a slim prayer book and pointed to the text... YISGADAL V' YISGADASH... EXALTED AND SANCTIFIED BE THE NAME OF THE LORD IN THE WORLD WHICH HE CREATED. BLESSED, PRAISED, GLORIFIED AND EXTOLLED, HONORED ADORED AND LAUDED BE THE NAME OF THE HOLY ONE, ABOVE AND BEYOND ALL THE BLESSINGS, HYMNS, PRAISES, AND CONSOLATIONS THAT ARE UTTERED IN THIS WORLD. AND LET US SAY, AMEN.

After that we all followed the coffin, as the pallbearers carried it outside to the gravesite. The wind blew sleet in our faces. It rolled down our cheeks like icy tears as we lowered him into the frozen ground.

From the cemetery we drove to the Liebman's home. Hermann Maas explained that it was the beginning of what is called THE SHIVA, the seven days of mourning when family and friends gather to comfort the mourners. "I'll meet you there," he said as he headed toward his car to join his wife and daughters. I rode with Karl and tried to get warm as we drove across the frozen city to Tiergarten Strasse and pulled up in front of a large brick house with a spacious front porch.

"I'll drop you off here and park the car wherever I can find a spot. See you inside."

As he pulled away, I found myself at the end of a line of people waiting to get inside. They each stopped at a small outdoor table where a woman ladled water from a pail onto their hands. Then they dried their hands on nearby towels. Are they crazy? I thought. It's freezing cold out here! Then I noticed Reverend Maas waiting for me on the porch. I smiled. Surely he must be the kindliest man I'd ever met.

When it was my turn, he stepped forward. "It's a tradition to symbolically wash death off your hands when you've come from a burial into a house of mourning," he told me. We went inside together. In the elegant foyer someone helped us off with our coats and we entered an inviting but crowded living room. A fire crackled warmly in a huge stone fireplace. A hushed crowd milled around. To the left was a large dining room. The mourners were seated there and a meal was being presented to them. Maas whispered, "Friends and neighbors usually provide sufficient food for the SHIVA. It's important that they eat something. After the family leaves the table, anyone here can get something to eat."

I wasn't hungry. A hot cup of coffee was all I wanted. "Is there anything else I should know?" I asked.

"Well, for the seven days of mourning a minyan is gathered to say the Kaddish twice a day."

"I know about the Kaddish prayer. We just recited it. But what's a minyan?"

Hermann Maas hesitated. "Hmm... I believe it stands for ten righteous men. I'm not sure, but I think it comes from the Book of Genesis. When Abraham has a conversation with God concerning the destruction of Sodom and Gomorrah, a bit of bargaining goes on and finally it comes down to God's promise that he will not cause their destruction for the sake of as few as ten righteous men.

"So they need at least ten righteous men to recite the prayer? Do they have to be Jewish men?" I asked.

"No, no. I don't think so."

"Because that's what I'd like to do," I said. "I'd like to say Kaddish for Dr. Liebman along with the mourners."

As soon as I said it, I realized I couldn't do it. I didn't have a car or a driver. On top of that I'd already overstayed my guest-hood at Hermann Maas's place and I still hadn't moved into my apartment. I needed to get things going.

The mourners left the dining room. Maas excused himself and

went to say a few words to Ilse Liebman. I watched as he then joined his family in the dining room for a bite to eat. I couldn't eat anything. Instead I found a seat near the fire and tried to think.

Karl appeared and handed me a cup of black coffee. "Sorry, I couldn't find any cognac."

I grinned. "A friend in need..." I quoted, as he took a seat next to mine.

"I can't stay too long," Karl said. "What do you want to do?"

I took that first sip of coffee. "I'll go with you," I said. "And if you can spare the time, I'd like to look at that car your friend recommended. But I have to be back here by seven o'clock."

"I'll see what's waiting for me at the theater. But I think we can do it. I'm coming back here with Gretchen later anyway. But why are you coming back?"

"That's when they have the minyan to say KADDISH. I've decided I want to be among the righteous."

Karl raised an eyebrow.

As it happened, there wasn't too much going on at the theater. Karl just had to sign a few papers. So there was time to look at that old Mercedes. The guy assured me that it was in excellent shape and offered his guarantee. He was anxious to sell it to me because he heard I would pay in British Pounds, rather than Deutschmarks which were fast becoming worthless. I got the car at a bargain price.

We returned to the Liebman house by seven for the KADDISH. By then I was already planning to return the next morning by taxi, U-bahn, or a ride from a friend. I still needed to hire a driver. Karl had recommended several men for the job.

He picked me up the next day, after KADDISH was said, and I went to interview them. I settled on Hugo Volpe, a sturdy-looking man in his fifties. He'd recently lost his position as the manager of a grocery chain and, like so many others, was desperate for any paying job, even a temporary one.

I told him, "As soon as the cast comes off and my ankle is healed so I can drive myself. That's the end of the job." He wanted it anyway.

I realized as I said those words that I had to find another doctor, although not right away, and certainly not a Jewish one. I was not going to endanger another Jewish doctor. It galled me beyond words to admit that my father, with his filthy tactics, had won.

The arrangements for the car and driver didn't take long and I managed to be part of the minyan twice a day, every day for the entire week. At the end, Hermann Maas and I said our goodbyes to the Liebmans. Ilse thanked us for staying so close to the family during this painful time. She added, "I'm selling the house and everything in it. We have no life here anymore. We're moving to Toronto. Emil wants to go to Palestine. But he's agreed to stay with me and finish medical school in Canada first."

Tears filled her eyes. "But... in the end..." she whispered, "I'm coming back. I want to be buried next to Max." We kissed her goodbye.

On the way home I had a long talk with Reverend Maas. I wanted to thank him and his wife for their hospitality and kindness to a desperate stranger like me.

"I had nowhere else to go," I told him. "I'll always be grateful to you. And I'm sorry I kind of overstayed my visit. But now that I finally have a car and a driver, I'll be moving into my apartment right away. I just have to pack up my toothbrush and grab my suitcase. But I don't want to say goodbye. I value your friendship and plan on stopping by often. And if you're willing, I'd love to continue my Hebrew lessons."

"Ach... Erich... It's been a pleasure having you with us. And of course we'll go forward with your lessons. Hebrew is a difficult language. We'll work out a schedule." We shook hands and parted.

We were now more than a week into January. Rehearsals at the Opera Company would start in a few days. Thoughts of seeing Chani again were my only happy moments. With Hugo's help I soon moved into my own place on Neukonigstrasse. As soon as I got settled, I made good on my original plan. I wrote a letter to every newspaper in Berlin, including the Nazi paper DER SHTURMER. That one I sent to the attention of its editor, Julius Streicher.

In my letter I stated that the accusations against the Jewish doctors were ugly lies meant to inflame hatred and justify violence.

"AS A CHRISTIAN PATIENT OF A JEWISH PHYSICIAN, I CAN PERSONALLY TESTIFY THAT I RECEIVED THE BEST POSSIBLE CARE. YET THIS FINE DOCTOR WAS VICIOUSLY BEATEN TO DEATH. HE WAS MURDERED BECAUSE HE WAS A JEW! I ASK ALL CHRISTIANS OF GOOD CONSCIENCE TO PROTEST THIS VILE

PROPAGANDA AGAINST JEWS. AND I CALL UPON ALL THOSE IN AUTHORITY TO RID US OF THOSE RESPONSIBLE FOR THIS SAVAGERY... RESPECTFULLY, ERICH VON BRUENER"

Nothing happened. Except for Ossietzky's Journal, not one damn newspaper published my letter. I was shattered. Were the Nazis able to block the publication of a letter like mine? Or was my father that powerful?

Filled with gloom, I headed over to our office. The Berlin Opera Company was in a very old building near Kurfurstendamn... a good location, but the place required considerable repair and renovation. The theater part and the offices were now finished. Still, more work was needed in the building and apparently Gretchen was in charge. Karl had told me that she could recommend a new doctor for me. So I went looking for her.

Finally I spotted her and she came running to meet me, pink-cheeked with excitement. "There you are," she shouted. "I'm so glad you're here. Listen, I've been busy getting publicity lined up for us. I've had posters plastered all over town and now a reporter is coming to do an article about you and Karl, the new building owners, the ones responsible for this big restoration. You have to get back to your office. He'll be here any minute."

She was bubbling over with enthusiasm. I could barely get a word in. Finally I managed to ask her about a new doctor. "I'll have to get back to you on that," she said. "Now hurry. Don't miss the interview."

I was just in time to meet the newspaper guy and the photographer he'd brought along. Karl took charge and showed them around the facility. Of course, on the way he gave them all the details of our new and brilliant performers, the smooth tenor, Leon Carbonne, from Trieste and our young soprano, Heidi Mueller, from Danzig.

"Both of them will appear for the first time here in Berlin, starring in our opening production of LA BOHEME on February 14th," he told them. "The Box Office is open and tickets are on sale now." They took photos of us and the renovations. Karl handed them four free tickets to our Opening Night.

As soon as they left we got down to business. "Let's go back over the budget carefully," Karl said. "I think we'll have to rent costumes and stage sets for now. At this point I don't see how we can afford to buy them. Can you give me a financial picture as soon as possible?"

I started looking at our biggest expenses, the salaries of our employees: the stagehands, musicians, and performers. When I got to Chani's name I saw her Berlin address listed. She was staying with Rabbi Eli Lowenthal on Pestalozzistrasse which wasn't far from the theater. On a good day it would be a nice walk. I made a note of it, as well as the phone number, though I knew I couldn't call her.

It was dark by the time I finished and headed for home. We hadn't driven far when I thought we were being followed. I mentioned it to Hugo and asked him to zip around a few corners, heading in the wrong direction, and then slow up. Sure enough, there was a silver Mercedes tailing us. I knew it could only be my father's thugs. I thought, if they meant to intimidate me, they succeeded. I started to think I might be safer if I carried a gun.

Hugo got me settled for the night and then took the car to his house, as was our routine. "Watch to see if you're followed," I told him.

When he picked me up the next morning he told me he'd also been followed. I was rattled. My father now knew where we both lived. I poured some extra cognac in my coffee to calm my nerves as I considered installing a deadbolt lock on my door as a precaution.

I scanned the morning paper and found the article on our Berlin Opera Company with a flattering photo of Karl and me. This was great publicity. Gretchen did a terrific job and I planned to tell her so. But when I arrived at the office, she approached me with a troubled look.

"What's the matter?" I asked.

"There's some people here to see you. They must have walked a long way. Their faces are red from the cold and their clothes are thin and raggedy. They have no gloves in this kind of weather and their hands are raw."

"Who are they?"

"They said their name is Snyder."

I shook my head. "I don't know anyone by that name, but show them in anyway."

The Snyders were a middle-aged couple and were indeed shabby-looking. They were rubbing their hands to together for warmth as they entered the office. The man spoke. "I saw your picture in the paper. Are you Otto Von Bruener's son?"

I hesitated. "Why, yes," I stammered. "What can I do for you?"

"Our daughter works for Herr Von Bruener. We used to hear from her often. But now we haven't heard anything for a long time. Her name is Sonja," he said softly.

CHAPTER 12 — DARKNESS

"Sonja!" The name ricocheted off the walls... the little servant girl with the blonde braids, always trembling, always afraid. I looked closely at these poor parents. Had she ever confided in them? Did they have any idea what their daughter was subjected to by her employer?

A chill ran down my spine. I remembered when she suddenly disappeared. I'd asked about her. My father told me she had a bad accident of some kind... he didn't know... there was a lot of blood and he took her to the hospital, and then... he didn't know... he supposed her family came and got her.

I didn't believe him even then. I pressed Josef for an answer but he stalled and stalled. Finally, he told me, "SHE'S DEAD!" But he wouldn't say any more. Now, what can I say to these poor helpless parents? They were standing there waiting patiently for my reply.

"Did you speak to my father about her?" I asked gently.

"Oh, yes. Certainly we did," the father replied. "Herr Von Bruener told us she'd run off and he didn't know where she was. We couldn't believe that. I said our Sonja is so young, not yet thirteen. Where could she go in this freezing weather? She would have come home to us.

Then Herr Von Bruener got very angry… red in the face… he screamed ARE YOU CALLING ME A LIAR? GET OFF MY LAND OR I'LL SET MY DOGS ON YOU!

"We were afraid. We went straight to the police and reported our daughter missing. We told them everything. They said they would look into it. But we haven't heard from them. When was the last time you saw our Sonja?"

Oh… my god… my heart sank. I couldn't tell them it was on that ugly night when my father fondled her and invited me to join him in some sexual activity with her.

I stammered… "I … I believe it was on Christmas Eve."

The father turned pale and murmured, "Christmas Eve? But that was weeks ago."

A tear slid down the mother's face. She hadn't spoken a word. She looked at her husband. They both knew something bad had happened to their little girl. But they didn't know where to turn next. I couldn't tell them she was dead! They would want to know how, when, where… I would have to explain where I got my information and that would endanger Josef.

They stood there for a few more minutes, stunned and silent. I saw the desperation in their faces. Then the father said, "Thank you." He took his wife's hand and they turned to leave.

"I'm sorry," I whispered. "I wish I could be more helpful. I'll have someone drive you home. And since it's likely your daughter hadn't received her salary, let me take care of that too." I pressed some money into his hand and summoned Hugo to get the car for them. As I watched them drive away I noticed they were being followed. It was the same silver Mercedes I'd seen before. I tensed up. Were they in danger for asking too many questions? On the way back to my office, I thought about that. No... I said to myself. My father knows where they live. It looks like he's having my car followed, whether I'm in it or not.

Yet what happened to Sonja is still a mystery. The only thing I know is that my father is responsible somehow. And I've been a simple-minded fool to think that he was a fallen, damaged hero of the Great War. Maybe delusion is a form of self-defense.

I sat down, brooding over my stupid attempt to change him back into the father he once was. Karl came in. "Erich, don't you want to take a look at our first rehearsal?"

"Sure. I'd forgotten all about it." I followed him to the back of the theater.

"I like to stand here," he told me. "That way I can hear how the voices project and view all the action."

It was Act I and, of course, I focused on Chani. The sight of her always made me smile. Karl interrupted the singers now and then to give them stage directions. He had more expertise than I anticipated.

As soon as the rehearsal ended, I went to speak to Chani. "How's your mother?" I asked. "Is she back in Warsaw?"

"Oh... no... she's still in the hospital. The doctors say she has pneumonia and that has to be cleared up before she can have the necessary surgery."

"And your sister, Fannie?" Is she still with you?"

"Oh, yes. Fanny will be here until she can take Mama home."

"You know, your German is quite good."

She smiled, "I'm staying with Rabbi Lowenthal and his family. They're teaching me."

Karl came running over. "Heidi, I think everything went very well today. I'll see you at rehearsal tomorrow... same time." Then he turned to me with fire in his eyes. "May I see you in your office, Erich?"

As we watched Chani leave, he whispered through clenched teeth, "Are you out of your mind?"

I knew all his objections. I'd heard them before. But I followed him to my office anyway. He ran ahead of me and was pacing the floor by the time I shuffled in, parked my crutches and sat down.

He slammed the office door shut and locked it. "As you well know," he began loudly, "things are tense in Berlin now and dangerous for Jews. We brought Chani here, and... as previously agreed, we don't want anyone to know she's a Jewish girl from Warsaw. I made it clear to her that she is not to speak to anyone. She is now Heidi Mueller from Danzig! And then you come along!"

Karl sat down on a lounge chair opposite me at my desk. He rubbed his hand over his eyes and became a little calmer. "She's only seventeen, Erich. And you're her employer. She has to answer you. But she's just being polite. And you're talking where you can be overheard. We have to be very careful. If anyone asks why she doesn't perform on weekends, our answer is that she has a contract with another opera company in another city. She performs for them on weekends. We're privileged to have her at all."

He got up and went to the door. Then he turned around. "And one more thing. As far as any romantic interest you may have in her, consider the situation from her point of view. To her you're just a middle-aged German gentile! Erich, the city is full of beautiful women. Pick one out! You can have anybody!"

"I don't want anybody! I don't have a problem getting women. They're easy. Not like Chani Machinski, with those long dark clothes that cover her from her chin to her toes and with long sleeves to hide those soft round arms. Inside those ugly clothes is a beautiful virgin body that no man has ever seen. Not to mention those luscious pink lips that have never been kissed. Karl, you're my best friend and you know about Jewish things. Tell me what I have to do to marry her!"

Karl froze. Then he laughed. "Erich, why are you so goddamn crazy? You have nothing in common with her. We're talking about a religious Jewish girl. She's going to marry a religious Jewish man some day and if you are considering becoming that Jewish man, let me tell you it's not easy! They don't exactly sprinkle you with Holy Water, you know! Listen to me. As your best friend, here is my advice. Go to Warsaw. Speak to her father. Tell him you want to marry his daughter and ask HIM what you have to do."

Again Karl started to leave. He unlocked the door. Then he turned again and said, "I have one more question. You want to marry her. But does she want to marry you?"

As he left I murmured... "Not yet... not yet."

CHAPTER 13 — TURNING POINT

The cast was removed. I finally got to see my leg. The hair was matted, the leg smelled bad. My skin was scaly and itchy. I was sickened at the sight of it. But Gretchen had recommended Dr. Ernst Schumbacher at the Klinikum Rudolf-Virchow in Charlottenburg. He smiled as he gently examined my ankle.

"You've healed up very nicely. Your previous physician did a fine job. How is it you didn't go back to him?"

For a moment a vision of Dr. Liebman filled my mind. "He died," I said.

"Ohhh, I'm sorry to hear that. Well, now… we have to go forward. Let's see you stand on both legs."

"What!"

"Yes… yes… I'll help you. You have to start putting weight on that leg. You'll still need your crutches or a cane for the next four to six weeks because your muscles have atrophied. But it's important that you walk to get them back in shape."

Clinging to his arm, I took a few tentative steps, perspiring heavily the whole time because of the pain. "That's fine. You're doing well." He handed me back my crutches. "Call me if you have any problems. Otherwise, come back to see me in three weeks."

I was exhausted by the time we left. My leg was still hurting. I peered out the window at the icy streets... a bad time to recover from a broken leg. Then I noticed we were being followed again. Obviously my father wants me to know I'm being watched. He likes to be intimidating. I tried to ignore it, but I couldn't.

I was feeling anxious by the time we got back to the apartment. I had some black coffee and cognac while I tried to think of what to do about Otto Von Bruener. I barely finished my coffee when the phone rang.

"How are you feeling?" my father said.

"I could be better... why?"

"You promised me you'd join the Nazi Party as soon as you were well."

"Yes, that's true. But I'm not well yet. I'll still be on crutches for a while before I'm healed up."

"I'm disappointed in the delay," he said. "But at least you learned to get treatment from the right kind of doctor. Didn't you?" And he laughed.

I hung up. The phone rang again. I knew it was him, the filthy bastard! I asked Hugo to bring the car around. "I want to visit Reverend Maas."

Hugo looked at me. "Do you want ME to answer the telephone?"

"No... let it ring."

It wasn't snowing as we made our way to Dahlem, just cold and dark. Even so, that same car followed us until we pulled into the Reverend's driveway.

As we entered the house I was greeted by the family with wide-eyed looks. "I'm sorry I didn't call first," I explained. "I'm having a problem with my telephone." We exchanged the usual pleasantries and then I asked if I could speak to the Reverend privately. Hugo was diverted to the kitchen for some refreshments and I was ushered into the library.

Hermann Maas stoked the fire in the fireplace as I settled into one of his comfortable lounge chairs. I gazed up at the shelves filled with the greatest books ever written. This was a place of intellect, and, I hoped, of understanding.

As the fire blazed, the Reverend also settled down comfortably and waited for me to speak.

"Remember when I first met you? You told me not only was Dr. Liebman a friend of yours, but that you had many Jewish friends, that in fact you were a Zionist, fluent in Hebrew. I thought you were the most amazing Christian Minister I'd ever met, and I believe, the only person who can help me now."

He leaned forward. "What is it you have in mind?"

I hesitated to try to get my words together. "It's complicated," I said. "A number of issues have come together and, considering them, I've decided to convert to Judaism."

The room filled with silence. The crackle of the fire was the only sound. Reverend Maas stared at me intently. "May I ask what brought you to this decision?"

"Well… the catalyst for my thinking in this direction is the fact that I'm in love with a religious Jewish girl. I want to marry her. She's the reason I began to study Hebrew with you. But more compelling is the fact that the vicious, violent Nazis are all Baptized Christians. I started reading the History of the Jews and found that they've faced the most ferocious enemies the world has ever seen. Yet those enemies are gone. Of all the miracles in the Bible, the greatest miracle is that the Jewish people and their God survived. They are still here! Now in our time the Jewish people are facing the Nazis.

The brutal murder of Dr. Liebman has left me deeply scarred. I can't forget him. I can't replace him. I can only stand in his place."

Hermann Maas got up slowly. He filled a couple of glasses with wine and handed one to me.

"Will you help me?" I asked.

He didn't answer. We sipped our wine in silence until he finally said, "Erich, as a Christian Minister I'm well aware that Jesus was a Jew and that everything he taught was Judaism. What else did he know? But I believe in HIM as our lord and savior, and that's the point of departure."

He paced the floor for several minutes, deep in thought. Then he looked at me and said, "I've always wanted to establish an association of Christians and Jews based on mutual respect. Therefore, I respect your decision. However, in these grim political times, and knowing who you are…" He stopped and shook his head. "Such a conversion would be ominous!"

"Of course you're right," I said as I gazed at the fire. "But I'm not afraid." Then I looked at him. "I'll risk it! We both know the Jews in Germany are already in great danger. I'm asking you to arrange for me to meet with an Orthodox Rabbi. I need him to accept me as a convert and tell me what I have to do. I want him to guide me through the process. And because of the danger, it must be done in utmost secrecy.

I know it's presumptuous of me, but for the sake of safety, I'm hoping a meeting can be arranged on any Sunday after Church, here in your home. As a well-known Minister, you're not likely to arouse suspicion. What do you think?"

Again he didn't answer. Apparently he was considering his answer carefully. I think it's too perilous," he said. "And I seriously doubt any Rabbi would be willing to meet with you." He fell silent again. "But... I know several Rabbis quite well and I'm willing to approach them on your behalf. However, I don't think you realize the difficulties involved in converting to Judaism. I'll let the Rabbi explain it to you. As for me..." he raised his glass. "I wish you every success."

I thanked him sincerely. It was late by the time we said our goodbyes and I hurried back to my apartment. This time I noticed no one following us. I told Hugo he could take the car home. "Pick me up early tomorrow. I need to get back to the office and do some work."

After he left I struggled up the stairs to the front hall, thinking about tomorrow. Chani will be at the theater for the dress rehearsal. I could see her in my mind's eye, on stage in costume, singing that beautiful aria from the first act. Despite Karl's objections, I intended to speak to her after rehearsal. I was thinking of what to say and not paying attention as I fumbled for my keys. I hadn't even turned them in the lock when the door began to swing open slowly.

Damn! I thought. Did I forget to lock up? Then my heart stopped. I saw my father sitting there waiting for me!

I didn't move. I looked around to see if he brought any of his Brownshirt cronies with him. I didn't see anyone. But I was ready to bolt to the neighbor if I had to.

"Why are you standing there?" he shouted. "Come in and close the damn door!" I still didn't move.

"How did you get in here?"

"Easy… I know a good locksmith!"

"Why are you here? Are you going to kidnap me again?"

He laughed. "No… I don't have to. I already proved my point, didn't I?" and he laughed again. I just want to talk to you. Last time I tried you hung up on me. Not very respectful, is it? So sit down. Stop mourning that goddamn Jew and listen to me."

I left the door ajar, stumbled over to a hardwood chair in the corner and sat with my back to the wall. I didn't want anyone sneaking up behind me. I placed my crutches across my lap and clutched them tightly, just in case. After all, they were my only weapons.

As I faced my father, I made up my mind that I would not interrupt him or argue or discuss anything. I would let him have his rant and then maybe he'd get the hell out here and leave me alone.

"In hopes of your speedy recovery," he began, "I've brought you a gift. On Christmas Eve you gave me ALL QUIET ON THE WESTERN FRONT, a book on the horrors of war. I bring you an autographed copy of Adolf Hitler's book, MEIN KAMPF, which speaks to the glories of war. It will give you an outline of the Nazi Party goals. There are really only two important ones. The first is that for the sake of our country and our economy we must have 'Liebensraum' (living space). But how can we get it? It's occupied by others. Hitler writes, and I quote, 'The soil of Europe exists for the people who possess the force to take it.'

The second goal is to perfect the Master Race, the German people. That will give us the power that will enable us to make the necessary conquests. To do that, first we must get rid of all the non-Germans… the Jews, the gypsies and such Germans as homosexuals and others who are impaired, either mentally or physically, although they may be put to good use through important experiments. I want you to understand that every German has to make a contribution to the Fatherland, according to their capacity to do so."

Despite my intention not to interrupt, I said, "You mean someone like little Sonja? What kind of contribution could she make?"

My father leaped up red-faced and spitting. He screamed, "Why do you always bring up Sonja? She's none of your goddamn business! I'm trying to have a serious discussion with you about your contribution… your future!"

I shuddered, but stayed calm. "Her parents came to see me.

They're looking for her. You told me you took Sonja to the hospital and that they probably came and got her. Obviously that's not true! So... where is she?"

He glared at me with such intensity I thought he was going to punch me. I tightened my grip on the crutches. Then he snarled, "Read the book!" and he slammed out the door.

I couldn't get out of the chair. I was shaking so badly. That lying son of a bitch... what had he done with her? Josef said she was dead. Did they bury her in the yard?

I made my way to the kitchen and fixed myself a stiff drink. He'd become such a despicable bastard... and he was mine! My father! I had another drink. I thought, what would he say if he knew I planned to become a Jew?

I slept badly. My dreams were filled with questions and one of them was where could I get a weapon. I was groggy when Hugo picked me up early the next morning. When I got to the Opera Building I saw the silver Mercedes out of the corner of my eye. It was parked in an alley behind the theater. I told Hugo to stop.

"I'll meet you inside the theater later," I told him. Then I got out of the car. I wanted to know who was following me. As soon as Hugo was gone, I hobbled into the alley and over to the driver's side of the car. It was Josef!

I went round to the passenger side and got in. "I need to talk to you," I said. "Sonja's mother and father came to see me. They're looking for her. You told me she was dead and I believe you. But I couldn't tell them that. They would want to have a funeral for their little girl. What happened to her? Where did you bury her?"

Josef, always tight-lipped and impassive, broke down and began to sob. Huge tears ran down his cheeks. He mopped his face with a large handkerchief then, choking on his words he said, "We didn't have to bury her. There was nothing left... not a bone... just a little blonde hair."

His words made me turn ice cold. He struggled to regain his composure. Finally he whispered, "Before I tell you what happened to Sonja, swear that you will tell no one what I said, until after I'm gone."

"But if my father is responsible for what happened to her, don't you want him prosecuted? You're an eyewitness. Josef, you have to go to the police!"

His lips trembled. He shook his head. "It's no use. Your father would make up some lie and it would be my word against his. The Nazis have begun to organize the police and Otto Von Bruener is too well-connected. He would never be prosecuted. If I go to them it's more likely that I'll be put in what they call 'protective custody' and never heard from again. Erich, I've worked for your family all my life. I'm old now. I have nowhere to go. I have to stay with your father and do as I'm told."

"I understand. Josef, you can trust me. I swear I'll never betray you."

He thought it over for a while then took a deep breath. "Your father is involved in a program that trains dogs to kill human beings on signal. When Sonja ran away, your father was furious. You know how he is. No one leaves him. You can go when he lets you go.

She didn't get far. He had her caught and brought to the training pit…" Josef's voice trailed off. He couldn't speak for a few minutes. Then he lowered his eyes and murmured, as if he didn't believe it himself, "He set the dogs on her! She was so small… just a child…" Josef again began to sob. "The dogs ripped her to pieces and devoured her! I saw the terror in her eyes! I heard every scream!

Herr Von Bruener stood right next to me and watched everything with great interest. When it was over he explained that this was a very important experiment. 'These kinds of trained dogs are necessary for future political activity' he told me. 'And Sonja has made a valuable contribution to our country.'"

Josef's whole body began to shake. "Erich, if your father found out I told you all of this, I too might have to make such a contribution."

This grizzly tale overtook my mind. I was filled with grief, terror, anger… there aren't enough words… Tears rolled down my face… Sonja… Sonja… the little girl with the yellow braids… She was more than killed! More than murdered! She was terrorized! Tortured! And then, she was erased, as if she never existed. And I had sworn that I would never speak of this unspeakable crime.

We sat in silence. Then Josef spoke up softly. "Following you everywhere is my newest assignment. But don't worry. I don't report everything. Still, be VERY careful. Herr Von Bruener can always get someone else to watch you."

I looked at this old man I'd known all my life, his sparse white hair, his face lined with worry. He glanced at me. "I have to be careful too. I know too much."

"Josef, if I can help you in any way, count on me." We shook hands and I climbed out of the car. I was trembling badly and it was slippery in the alley. Slowly I made my way to the theater and locked myself in my office. I was no use to anyone. The image before my eyes was the look of terror on Sonja's face when they released those dogs. I could hear her screams! I closed my eyes. How is it possible that my father has managed to shrug off all his humanness and become worse than a beast?

I wrote a letter to Uncle Tony. I asked if he could give me the name of anyone at the British Embassy in Berlin whom I might contact if necessary, and also, if it was possible for me to obtain a gun. Then I picked up the telephone and called Reverend Maas. I asked if he could arrange for me to meet Rabbi Eli Lowenthal as soon as possible.

CHAPTER 14 — THE INTERVIEW

Rabbi Lowenthal was a tall, thin, scholarly-looking gentleman with a full head of graying hair. His beard was somewhat darker. Modestly dressed in a black suit with a black skull cap on his head, he looked at me with piercing blue eyes as we were introduced. Then comfortably seated in the library, he said, "Reverend Maas is a special friend of the Jewish people. And in these troubled times, we need every friend we can find. It's for his sake that I am here. He has advised me that you want to convert to Judaism. Can you tell me why?"

"It's difficult and complicated." I paused to figure out how to explain myself. The only sound was a clock ticking as the Rabbi waited patiently. "Until recently I'd never met a Jew. I knew nothing about Judaism. But Karl Klempner, an old school friend and present business partner, has a lot of knowledge about Jewish people. As a kid he even stayed with them on their Sabbath. He explained their customs to me. And it was through him that I met Reverend Maas, who is both a Zionist and a Hebraist."

The Rabbi smiled and nodded as I continued. "So when I met and fell in love with a beautiful Jewish girl, I wanted to find something we could have in common. I began taking Hebrew lessons with the Reverend. And to my surprise I found it a fascinating language. Then I started reading the History of the Jews. But all this is remote."

Rabbi Lowenthal nodded in agreement and, I thought, a look of disdain. But I persisted. "The turning point for me was when my Jewish doctor, Max Liebman, was brutally beaten to death... And it was because of me! Because a Jewish doctor treated a Christian patient. That a man should die as a result of such twisted thinking is insane. But the Nazis are spreading such outrageous lies about Jewish doctor, the murder of Dr Liebman is the result.

I was among the most intense mourners for him. I felt I had to be a part of the daily minyan and say Kaddish for him."

The Rabbi sat up straight and stared at me. I continued, "Another reason occurred because of a crime, this one... so barbaric... so savage... words fail. I believe Christianity is flawed. These vicious acts were committed by Nazis and every Nazi... each and every one of them is a baptized Christian! Yes... I want to convert to Judaism. I want to return to the religion of Jesus!"

Rabbi Lowenthal said nothing. He stroked his beard and appeared to be considering my words carefully. Then he leaned forward and whispered, "And what does your father say about all this?"

"My father? What do you know about my father?" The Rabbi shrugged.

I said, "Otto Von Bruener is a violent man. A powerful Nazi and a determined and dedicated anti-Semite. I want to be the opposite of everything he is. If he found out I converted to Judaism I don't know if he would kill himself or kill me and everyone connected with my conversion. That's why it must be done in absolute secrecy."

The Rabbi shook his head. "Ach... Erich... it's not possible! Let me explain what needs to be done. You must continue your Hebrew lessons. You'll be required to spend at least a year in learning about Judaism. After a year, you'll be asked to appear at a Bet Din, a sort of court of Law, where three Rabbis will ask you questions about what you know. When they are satisfied you've gained enough knowledge, the next step will be circumcision. It's a painful process. Have you considered that carefully? Then you'll acquire a Hebrew name which will be followed by a new baptism... immersion in water at the Mikvah. After that you'll be a Jewish man, accepted and welcomed into the Covenant. Do you really think you can accomplish all that without your father knowing? He'll find out! And when he does, what do you think will happen? Especially to all those involved in your conversion."

I nodded. "Yes... yes... I know. Let's think this over. First I want to thank you for your great courage in coming here to speak to me." Then I turned to Hermann Maas and asked. "Would you be willing to allow me to study here in your home?"

He smiled. "Of course you can study here. It will be a great learning experience for both of us. But before you go forward, remember the person you will endanger most is you... and be afraid."

"I'm not afraid for myself. I just don't want to endanger anyone else. Rabbi Lowenthal, could you outline for me what I have to study… what books I need to read, and send it all here to Reverend Maas through the mail? No one would know about it and that would end your involvement.

The rest would have to be done elsewhere. The Bet Din could be held in Warsaw. I go there on business sometimes. As for the rest of it, the Circumcision and the Mikvah… that might have to be done in London. I have family in England, so that's a possibility. What do you think?"

The Rabbi was wide-eyed. "I think you're the most determined convert I've ever met. Count on me. I'll be glad to provide what you'll need to study."

The telephone rang. Reverend Maas answered it. "Yes… yes… he's here. Just a moment. Rabbi, it's for you."

With trembling hands Rabbi Lowenthal took the phone. We watched as he turned pale. "I see… yes… I'll be home soon… I'm leaving right now… don't worry… I'll… I'll take care of everything."

He hung up, shook his head, mumbled something in Hebrew and said, "Chani Machinski's mother died."

CHAPTER 15 — WARSAW

We were shocked. Although we shouldn't have been. We knew she was very sick. Yet somehow it was unexpected. The Rabbi left at once. And as soon as I got back to my apartment, I phoned Karl with the grim news.

"Listen, don't you think we should leave for Warsaw at once? So we can pay our respects at the funeral?"

"No... no... we shouldn't be there at all! Erich, you know that Reb Machinski only allowed Chani to be our soprano because her mother was so sick and he needed money to try to save her. Religious Jewish girls do not sing or entertain in front of men. It's not allowed. I don't know what Reb Machinski told everyone, but I'd guess he said his daughters were in Berlin to look after their mother while she was in the hospital. So how would it look if we showed up at the funeral?"

"Yes... yes... you're right of course. But now that her mother's gone... maybe Chani won't come back."

"Erich, she has to come back. We have signed a contract! We

open in a few weeks. I'm waiting to hear from her."

The week of mourning went by, and then a few more days. Still no sign of Chani. Karl got nervous. "I've phoned her father every day since the Shiva ended. He doesn't answer. No one answers. I'm afraid we'll have to go to Warsaw after all. We're running out of time. I'm going to take the train tonight. Can you make it?"

I hesitated. I was still being followed everywhere. But Josef was in the driver's seat. "Sure. I'll meet you at the station."

The snow was still high, but the sun was shining when we arrived in Warsaw early Sunday morning. Again we took a taxi to the Europejski Hotel. And again we were greeted by the same huge doorman in his resplendent uniform. The crush of the holidays was over so we were seated in the restaurant immediately. I ordered breakfast for us while Karl went to call Reb Machinski one more time. We didn't want to be unexpected. Still there was no answer. We polished off our breakfast quickly and made our way to Stawli Street.

It was strangely quiet as we climbed up to apartment 305 and knocked at the door. Chani opened it and stepped back in amazement when she saw us. We were just as shocked to see her. Dressed all in black for mourning, she looked almost skeletal. Gone were the pink cheeks and sparkling eyes. She was ashen.

"I'm... I'm... surprised to see you," she murmured. "We... we... weren't expecting you."

Karl spoke up. "I've telephoned many times. But no one ever answered. May we come in?"

"Oh... yes... yes... of course. We were just sitting down to breakfast. Will you join us?"

"No, thank you." When we stepped inside we saw the whole family gathered around the table. Everyone... except Rabbi Machinski. There was Natan, the twin boys, little Sarah, and the grandmother holding baby Avi. All of them stared at us.

"I'm sorry for your loss," I said. "Please accept our sympathy." No one responded except Chani. She nodded with downcast eyes.

"We'd like to speak to your father," Karl continued. "Is he in?"

"Yes," she whispered. "Come this way." We followed her feather-slim figure to the familiar library door. She rapped lightly and opened it. Nothing had changed. Inside her father was at his desk, which was still piled high with papers and books.

"Yes... what is it?" he asked without looking up. Then he saw us. He stood up. "You can leave us now, Chani."

"No, Papa. This is about me and I want to stay." The Rabbi sat down and turned to us. "Have a seat, gentlemen. Tell me what's on your mind."

"We didn't mean to come here unannounced," Karl said stiffly. "I phoned you a number of times. No one ever answered and we therefore had no choice. First, let me offer our sympathy on the loss of your wife. We realize you're still in mourning. However, our opera company will open in less than two weeks and we received no word on when Chani would be returning for rehearsals."

"Thank you for your condolences," the Rabbi answered coldly. "Chani will not be returning. It was only because her mother was so gravely ill, and in our effort to save her Chani became your employee.

However, since that is no longer the case, she will not be performing for your opera company.

Karl stood up and said in a loud and angry voice, "I have a contract signed by you that clearly states your daughter, Chani Machinski, WILL perform for the Berlin Opera Company at specified times until May of 1932. If I have to I'll go to the necessary authorities to enforce this contract."

The Rabbi jumped up and shouted back, "I don't care if I have to go to jail! My daughter is not going to sing on any stage in Berlin!" Chani burst into tears.

The Rabbi lowered his voice, "Chani, don't cry. We have to think of your future. What proper Jewish man would want you for his wife… a young woman who entertains in a theater? What family would accept you? No! I can't allow it!"

Chani sobbed. "Papa… I know you want the best for me, but you can't go to prison. Who will support our family? How will we have what to eat?

Then she faced us. "And you… would you really do such a terrible thing… drag my poor father into a German court?"

I said, "No… no… we don't want to do that." I thought, making ominous threats is my father's way of dealing with tough situations. I don't want to be like him. I knew what would happen to a rabbi from Warsaw in a Berlin courtroom. I said, "Please… everyone… let's sit down and talk this over.

Rabbi Machinski, your daughter is our star. That's why we've made every possible concession for her. After all, the Berlin Opera

Company is our livelihood. But the final decision has to be made by Chani. We can't force her to sing and be a member of our opera cast."

The room was quiet as we waited for Chani to speak. The minutes ticked by slowly. Then she looked at her father and said, "It was Mama who felt I had musical ability. She encouraged me to learn the opera repertoire and saw how much I loved it. So, in her memory, I ask that you honor the commitment that you signed that permits me to continue with the Berlin Opera Company."

The Rabbi's eyes filled with tears. They rolled down his face into his beard as he looked at his daughter. He didn't say another word.

CHAPTER 16 — THE NAZI PARTY

We went back to Berlin… back to rehearsals… and I was back to seeing Chani every day and sleeping with her every night… in my dreams. We went directly to the theater. Gretchen greeted us with smiles and hugs as we went in our different directions. Chani, with a little twinkle restored to her eyes, raced to the dressing room to get into costume. Karl began working with the stage hands to set up the scenery. And Gretchen informed me that my father was waiting for me in my office.

I was grinding my teeth as I muttered under my breath, god damn it! Every time things take a turn for the better, HE shows up! Then I remembered that rehearsals would start in a few minutes. I panicked. I didn't want him to see Chani or hear her at this time. I pulled myself together and calmed down. Then I opened my office door and saw my father standing at my desk reading my papers.

"What the hell are you doing?" I shouted. He didn't even look up.

"I just want to keep informed. I can tell by these names that you have Jews working here."

"So what?" I yelled as I grabbed the papers from him and put them away.

"It's Germans who need jobs. It's the Depression! Who gives a shit about the Jews!"

"They are Germans. They're German Jews!"

His face got red. "There's no such thing!"

I lowered my voice, "Why are you here? What is it you want?"

He calmed down. "I have important things to discuss with you," he said quietly.

I could hear Leon singing his aria. I knew Chani would be singing next. "Let's not talk here. There's a restaurant around the corner and I haven't had anything to eat yet. It's early. It won't be crowded."

I nudged him to leave as Chani began her aria. He stopped. "What a beautiful voice! Who is singing?"

"That's our soprano, Heidi Mueller," I told him as I pushed him out the door.

Seated in a secluded corner at the restaurant, I ordered black coffee and cognac. I needed it to fortify myself for the conversation that I knew was coming. I asked the waiter to bring my usual breakfast later.

"Just black coffee for me," my father growled. Then he stared at me intently. I waited, fearing the worst. Finally he began, "I see you're walking without crutches now. That must mean you're leg is pretty well healed and it's time for you to make good on your promise to join the Nazi Party."

"Well... wait a minute," I said. "I promised under the threat of extinction or something close to it. So that really doesn't count."

He smiled. "I'm glad I was able to teach you something of value. Ominous threats can be extremely effective. Sometimes that's all it takes to get you what you want. I'm holding you to your promise."

This conversation was making me sick.

"You're such a strong supporter of the Party... you're not only a fundraiser for them, but you contribute substantial sums of money yourself. Why isn't that enough? What do you need me for?"

"Listen, Erich. I told you this before. Your partnership in this Berlin Opera Company is just a hobby. Great changes in Germany are coming and you need to be part of it. For a genuine career, you need to affiliate with the National Socialists... politically now and militarily later. The Party is our only hope to build a greater Germany, didn't you read Hitler's book?"

"Oh... I... no... not yet."

"Well... we can't accomplish all our goals with just my generation. We need yours and the generation after yours. We are only at the beginning. First we need to purify our Race... our Superior Aryan Race. Of course, in order to do it we need to get rid of the undesirable elements among us. It's the only way we can go forward."

"The undesirable elements," I repeated. "Are you talking about people? Exactly what is it you want to do with them?"

He nodded... hesitated for a few moments. "Yes, that's the real problem for us. BUT we're working on it. We have highly educated and intelligent men in the Party who are considering that question very carefully. They'll come up with a solution. But back to the point. I'm asking you to take your place at my side and join the Nazi Party NOW! TODAY! Erich, you're the last of the Von Brueners. For my sake and for the sake of my brothers who died for this country, you have to take their place in Germany's future. It's your duty!"

My breakfast arrived and got cold as I pushed it around on the plate.

Finally I said, "Okay... alright... I'll join! I just have one requirement."

"A requirement? What is it?"

"The Nazi Party has to stop their anti-Semitic rhetoric and rantings... and all that violence against our Jewish citizens."

He pounded his fist on the table. "What?" he screamed. "Are you crazy! They're not citizens. They're parasites... making a fat living off us Germans. They are not of our Race. They have their own Race, which is all they care about. We need to get rid of ever damn one of them!"

I shook my head. He glared at me. "I'm going to enroll you in the Party today. I'm going to pay your dues. But mark my words. This will cost you far more than you ever wanted to pay." Then he got up and stomped out the door.

Slowly I returned to the theater, still worried about this meeting and afraid of what might come next. I found Karl standing in the back of the darkened theater, directing the rehearsal of La Boheme. He whispered to me, "They're just terrific! We're going to have a great Opening Night. All we need is a full house." Then he glanced at me.

"So how did it go with your father?"

"He wants me to join the Nazi Party NOW!"

"Well… are you going to make him happy and join?"

"Yes and no. I'm not joining. He's going to enroll me in the Party and pay my dues for me, all the while threatening me with dire consequences.

Karl, aren't you worried about what will happen to us and to this country if the Nazis ever come to power?"

"Ach… Erich. They have plenty of opposition." I wanted to believe him. But he didn't know what I knew.

I waited for Chani to change out of her costume and when I saw her coming toward me, I swallowed hard and forgot everything but her.

"How are you feeling? Now that you're back in the theater?"

She answered softly, "I'm doing okay."

"I'm glad you spoke up and got everything settled with your father. I think soon your cheeks will be pink again and your old sparkle will return."

She nodded. "Please understand… my father is the most kindly and pious man. He knows there is evil all around us and he wants to save me from heartache and protect me from all badness. My father loves me."

"So do I," I said, and immediately regretted it. "I didn't mean to say that," I murmured. "It just kind of slipped out." I could feel myself getting red as she looked at me wide-eyed.

"I realize we don't know each other very well yet. And I hope you're not offended. There are so many things I want to tell you. Will you let me?"

She shrugged… and smiled… and walked away.

I thought… what an ass I made of myself! But she didn't say no. Maybe I have a chance.

CHAPTER 17 — OPENING NIGHT

The theater tingled and crackled with excitement. We were expecting a pretty good crowd. Gretchen was in charge of publicity and she'd done a great job... even called everyone she knew.

All of us were at the door to greet our first audience. Hermann Maas and his family were among the first to arrive. I had to give them each a hug. I spotted Martin Neimoler and his wife Else. They came with Dietrich Bonhoffer and his twin sister Sabine.

Gretchen was so delighted to see them she told everyone within earshot how wonderful it was to have such talented musicians among us. As I showed them to their seats I said, "Maybe you'll give us a critique after you've seen our production." They nodded and smiled warmly.

I saw von Ossietzky and his English wife, Maude Woods. I waved and started in their direction. I wanted to ask her of any news from England. But then I heard Karl say, "Good evening Herr Von Bruener." That stopped me. I thought, damn it! He had to show up! I turned to face him with a frozen smile as he introduced Karl and

Gretchen to Maria Von Bulow and Cosima Wagner. There were several burly Brownshirts with him, armed with their clubs. Gretchen showed them to their seats and Karl whispered, "Stay calm. There are a lot of people here. Nothing bad can happen."

"Listen, Karl, whenever my father shows up he sucks the air right out of the room and I can't breathe. If he talks to Chani it will be a disaster. He'll ask her questions about the Germans in Danzig and she won't know what he's talking about."

"Relax… relax," Karl said. "We have to appear welcoming and businesslike, as if there's no possible problem. But as soon as the last act is over, I'll have Gretchen grab Chani and get her back to the Lowenthal's house. Your father won't have a chance to speak to her."

"Okay," I said. But my heart was pounding as I watched the musicians enter and start tuning up. In a few minutes the lights dimmed and the curtain went up.

It was a thrilling performance. Both Chani and Leon got rousing applause for their arias and a standing ovation at the end. It was everything we could have hoped for. True… it wasn't a sold-out house and I told Karl we're not in the black yet. A lot depends on what the critics have to say. We stopped to congratulate the cast and crew. As Gretchen made her way backstage, Karl and I went to distract my father and his group.

"Well… what did you think of it, Herr Von Bruener?" Karl asked.

"Ach… it was wonderful. I loved it! Especially that soprano… she's a beautfy! Heidi Mueller from Danzig, eh…? I'm interested in her."

"So am I!" I said.

"Well… well… all the better," he laughed. "Why don't you bring her around to the house? I'll make a big dinner party and she can be our guest of honor. Who knows? Maybe she'll even sing for her supper." He winked and let out a guttural, dirty laugh. Everyone with him laughed too.

I whispered to Karl, "If they don't leave soon I'm going to vomit!" Karl smiled amiably and gently pushed them toward the exit.

Within a few minutes the theater was empty. We locked up together. Karl said, "How about a drink."

"Can I have more than one?" I answered as I followed him to his office.

He poured us each a shot and raised his glass. "Here's to us and to our success!"

We clinked glasses together and downed a fiery shot. "Wow!" What is this stuff?"

"I keep it for special occasions" Karl mumbled. "It's a Hungarian whiskey called Shlibovitz. What do you think of it?"

"I think it just burned a hole in my stomach." He grinned and poured us each another shot, and then another until we polished off the whole bottle. Then he began to sing one of the arias. I joined in. We were having a terrific time until Gretchen showed up.

"Stop all the screeching," she yelled. "You sound like howling wolves! C'mon, guys… time to say goodnight."

Hugo got me home and up those few icy steps. In front of my

apartment door we spotted several strange-looking packages. Hugo hauled everything inside before he left. But I was too drunk to do anything but fall into bed.

In the morning, although I was still headachy and groggy, I checked out those packages. Inside the smallest one was a letter from Uncle Tony. He wrote:

The British Ambassador in Berlin is Sir Horace Rumbold, in case you require his services. But what is happening in Germany? Why do you need a gun? We're all alarmed. Please explain in your next letter.

I've sent you two different weapons, and there's a special gift from your Aunt Jane. Of course the news that you're in love with a beautiful Jewish girl came as a bit of a shock, but plan to come home soon and bring her along. We'd like to meet her. Although we wish you great success with your opera company, all of us miss you dearly. Jane and the girls send hugs and kisses. I send my best regards.

As always,

Uncle Tony

A wave of homesickness washed over me. I told myself, I'm so lucky to have this warm, wonderful family. I unwrapped the smallest package. It was a Derringer… just the right size to fit in the palm of my hand, or hide easily in a jacket pocket. There was plenty of ammo too. I loaded it and slipped it into my desk drawer along with Uncle Tony's letter.

The next package was much larger. I was thrilled to see that it was a shortwave radio. A note was enclosed:

Dear Erich,

This gift is for your new apartment. Now you'll be able to hear the latest news from England as well as the world's most beautiful music.

Love,

Aunt Jane

"I love you too," I murmured, and made a mental note to thank her. Then I opened the last package. It was long and slim, perhaps a rifle of some kind. When I opened it I was surprised to find a wooden cane. The note read: "I hope your leg is healed sufficiently so you no longer require a cane. But this one is special. Notice there is a small mechanism under the handle. When pushed forward it releases a thin poisoned blade at the bottom. Just a pin prick, like an insect bite, makes it as lethal as the Derringer, though not as immediate. Push the mechanism back and the blade retracts. I sincerely hope you never have to use it."

The telephone rang. I jumped. It was Reverend Maas. "Your course of study and a lot of books arrived from Rabbi Lowenthal. When would you like to get started?"

"How about tomorrow night? Is eight o'clock okay?"

"Perfect! I'll see you then."

As soon as he hung up I examined the cane more carefully. I pushed the mechanism forward and watched the small blade emerge, pushed it back and it retracted. What a clever weapon! Even though my leg was completely healed, I intended to use it daily so everyone would get used to seeing me with it.

I took it along when I went to the theater on Sunday. Chani was performing at the matinee. She probably didn't know the newspapers had raved about her and Leon in their Opening Night debut. I cut out the articles and bought some flowers. While I waited for her to get out of her costume after the performance, I thought about how I would tell her about my father. It was important that she know how dangerous he is.

She smiled when she saw me. Her eyes sparkled as she read the newspaper reviews. And she was delighted with the bouquet.

"I... I... I... have some important news to tell you," I whispered. "But it must be in the strictest confidence." I paused and took a deep breath. I wanted to tell her about my father, what a violent, dangerous man he is. But I was ashamed to admit I was his son. Instead I told her, "I've decided to convert to Judaism. Rabbi Lowenthal is guiding me in this process."

"What?" She looked shocked. "Why would you do that?"

"It's complicated... and difficult to explain. But I have good reasons for my decision." I didn't tell her she was one of them.

She smiled and shook her head. "What does your family say? Will they accept you as a Jew?"

"I think some of them will. But they don't live in Germany. Here in Berlin, anti-Semitism is so intense that it's best if no one knows you're a Jewish girl from Warsaw. That's why Karl insists you speak to as few people as possible in the theater, and then only in your best German. As for me, my future as a Jew is probably more dangerous than yours."

She grew serious. "There's plenty of anti-Semitism in Poland. We have to deal with it. What else can we do? Trust me, YOUR secret is safe with me. But there's a violinist in your orchestra who is also a Jew from Warsaw. He knows me and my whole family."

Fear gripped me. "I'd... uh... I'd like to speak to him. What's his name?"

"Well... I think he's gone for the day. But he'll be back tomorrow. We're starting rehearsals for La Traviata. His name is Michal Kaplansky."

CHAPTER 18 — MICHAL KAPLANSKI

Somehow I thought he'd be an older man. But Michal Kaplansky was about my age... tall, slim... a handsome man with very dark skin. He had a thick head of black hair and shiny dark eyes. He smiled broadly when we shook hands. He had the whitest teeth I'd ever seen.

"Oh, sure. Chani and I grew up in the same neighborhood. Although she's much younger than I, I knew her and, of course, everyone in Warsaw knows Rabbi Machinski. He's a Biblical scholar... highly regarded."

"Is that right?" I felt a pang of envy. "But what brought you to Berlin?"

"I came to study music here at the Conservatory. After graduation I played for the Berlin Symphony Orchestra for a while, but not on a regular basis. I needed a steady job. So when Herr Klempner held auditions, I tried out..." He shrugged and smiled... "and I was lucky! He hired me."

I grinned back. "I hear you're very talented. But there is a serious matter… You've been in Berlin long enough to know how difficult the situation is for Jews now. We feel we need to protect Chani. We don't want anyone to know her background."

"I knew that the minute I heard her stage name. There's nothing to worry about. I would never say or do anything that might cause her harm."

"Thanks. It's good to know we can rely on you." He smiled and waved as he returned to his place in the orchestra pit. But he worried me.

The rehearsal for La Traviata began. I joined Karl at the back of the theater as the scene unfolded. The sets were lavish, the costumes magnificent. Chani, as Violetta, wore a red velvet gown. Her silky black hair was done up with diamond-like pins. She was breathtaking. I was transfixed at the sight of her.

This time on Opening Night it looked like a much larger crowd. I told Karl we could have a full house and it's probably because of the flattering reviews we received for La Boheme. Again there was trembling excitement. And then my father arrived again and my anxiety level went up. This time he brought Leni Reifenstahl and several men in formal black uniforms. These weren't the Brownshirts. I didn't know who they were.

Leni gave me a warm, friendly smile and remarked about what a great job we'd done in restoring the old theater. Then she excused herself and got busy taking photos of the renovations. The musicians filed in and started to tune up. That got her attention and she began to take pictures of them. I noticed she focused on Michal Kaplansky.

That was frightening. I wanted to get her away from him but my father interrupted.

"Erich, let me introduce you to a dear friend visiting from Bavaria. This is Heinrich Himmler!" He said it as if the man was important. But he certainly didn't look it. He seemed like a mediocre school master to me. He was pasty-faced, with a weak chin and Pince-Nez glasses. He was also wearing a black uniform like the others, but more ornate.

My father continued, "Herr Himmler has a degree in agronomy from the Munich Technishe Hochshule. But with great confidence in Hitler's vision of the new Germany, he has abandoned his lucrative poultry business and changed careers. Now he is active on behalf of the Party. He's gradually building up the Elite Schutz Staffel like these men. We call them the SS."

Then my father jabbed me in the ribs. "You see! Any man can change his career... and at any time." He lowered his voice. "And with a little interest on your part, Herr Himmler can secure a good position in the elite corps for you."

I couldn't laugh out loud. I didn't want to cause a scene. So I put on a somber and thoughtful face and thanked my father for all that information. "At this time I have other interests," I said. And I was glad to see Leni Reifenstahl rejoin the group. "I hope you enjoy the opera," I said as I showed them to their seats. Then I ran to join Karl at the back of the theater. I whispered, "Is there any of that Shlibovitz left? I need it!"

He looked at me. "What's wrong now?! Oh, wait... never mind...

we're starting." The lights dimmed. The orchestra played the overture. The curtain went up.

The opening scene is an ornate nineteenth century Parisian Salon where Violetta (Chani) is receiving her friends for a Soiree. At the back of the stage a door is opened to another drawing room. It's filled with revelers. The women are adorned with jewels and dressed in the crinolines of the 1850's.

The audience is transported back in time to the elegant lifestyle of a successful French Courtesan. Beneath sparkling chandeliers, groups of the assembly dance to joyous music while others sing in praise of pleasure. I thought it was a stunning opening scene!

Of course Violetta meets the handsome nobleman who falls in love with her the minute he sees her. And, as usual, it ends tragically. But the whole opera is dazzling, the music melodic and memorable.

At the end there was wild applause and a standing ovation with many shouts of 'Bravo!' for Chani, Leon, and the whole company.

Gretchen rushed on stage with a huge bouquet of red and white roses for Chani while many more bows were taken. When they made their final curtain call, the crowd began to thin.

Karl and I made our way toward the stage. It was then that my father, Leni Reifenstahl and Heinlich Himmler came to us, insisting they be introduced to the stars of this performance.

"Leni's going to take a photograph of all of us together," my father announced. "And then afterward let's all have a few drinks. Of course Karl and his charming wife are also included. Let's make a night of it and celebrate this marvelous production."

Terrified!! I responded, "No... no... it's out of the question." I tried to stay calm. I didn't want him to notice I was shaking.

My father shouted, "Erich... what the hell is the matter with you? Why can't we all have a good time together? Let's have some fun!"

Karl stepped forward. "Thank you so much for your kind invitation, Herr Von Bruener. That sounds like a wonderful idea. But Heidi and Leon have several more performances and must save their stamina and their voices. No drinking for them. However, we have a large cast and you're welcome to invite any of them to join you. As for Erich and me, we have a lot to do in closing for the night. But again, thank you for thinking of us."

My father growled. "I'm so disappointed. But at least let's get a picture of us. Leni, get everyone lined up." She swung into action, ran to grab Gretchen, Chani and Leon and dragged them over to the group. I broke into a cold sweat. I didn't know how we could get out of this.

Leni put Chani and Leon in the middle and we immediately closed in. Gretchen and Karl were on one side of Chani. I stood next to Leon and we put my father at one end and Heinrich Himmler at the other, with one of the SS next to each of them.

It was a nightmare, but we nagged Leni to take the photo as quickly as possible. As soon as she was finished, I focused on getting Chani away from them so Gretchen could get her safely back to the Lowenthal's.

Finally my father and his group were leaving. By this time I was drenched in sweat. Then I noticed Leni Reifenstahl wasn't with them.

I saw her walking arm in arm with Michal Kaplansky. She was smiling into his face as she whisked him out the door.

CHAPTER 19 — NEW DIRECTIONS

Anxiety kept me awake all night. I have to speak to Kaplansky. I need to warn him. Snow was falling heavily and there were blustery winds as I made my way to the theater. Maybe it was this damn winter that wouldn't let go that made everything seem more and more ominous.

I got there early and looked for Kaplansky. He wasn't around. I waited and waited, getting more worried by the minute. I asked the other musicians. They were surprised he was so late. It was unusual for him. I went to my office to look up his address and see if there was a phone number. No. Nothing. I asked Karl.

"He picks up his paycheck at my office. I think he rents a room somewhere." That's all Karl could tell me. Then I spotted him coming through the door. He looked like he'd slept in his clothes. He was unshaven… uncombed. I had no time to talk to him. The lights dimmed, the Overture started, and the curtain went up.

This was the Friday night performance. Chani was not singing tonight or tomorrow night, as per our agreement with her father. She was observing the Sabbath at the Lowenthals'. Her understudy, Marlene Schiller, was taking her place. She had a fine voice. But she was older, and quite heavy. She had a large mole on the left side of her nose. It was a stretch to think some handsome nobleman would fall in love with her at first sight. But in opera, one is expected to suspend disbelief.

I paced back and forth at the back of the theater, impatient for the final curtain, so I could speak to Kaplansky before he left. I got my chance.

"I saw you were with Leni Reifenstahl last night. How'd that go?"

"Oh… we had a terrific time. She's very exciting… and really talented. She makes movies, you know. I guess I overdid it and drank too much. But we're going to get together again tonight. I just need to get cleaned up."

"Did you tell her anything about yourself?"

"No… you know how it is. She did most of the talking. But I don't mind." He smiled and winked.

I told him, "I think it's important for you to know that although I'm not sure she's a member of the National Socialist Party, I AM SURE that she is very well connected with the top Nazi officials. And they're so brutally anti-Semitic, she could be dangerous. Does she know that you're a Jew from Poland? If not… be smart… don't tell her!"

He frowned at me and curled his lip. "Listen… I can handle my own affairs." And he left. I was afraid for him. I thought, poor dumb Jew. He just wants to be accepted. He doesn't realize it won't happen.

He'll be targeted instead. And through him other Jews may be targeted. They're being beaten in the streets in broad daylight now. Why isn't he afraid?

I again lost sleep that night. I went to the theater early again the next day. I wanted to know how things went with him and Leni this time.

Today he was prompt. He looked cleaned and pressed. But he averted his eyes. He didn't want to look at me. He didn't want to talk to me. It was obvious he didn't follow my advice. He seemed disappointed and depressed. That could only mean he'd told her he was a Jew. Now what? Would she tell others? And if she did, what would happen to him? He shouldn't take a chance. If he was smart he'd give up this job and go back to Warsaw where he'd be safe.

At the closing Sunday Matinee I went to speak to Chani after the performance. I didn't say anything about Kaplansky. Instead I talked to her about my Judaic studies. She was interested and encouraging. But she told me, "If you're really serious about converting, reading books is not enough. You need to study with a Rabbi. They can give you more information and answer all your questions. I knew she was right. But here in Berlin that was impossible for me. She didn't know anything about my father. And I didn't want to tell her, at least not now. I just mentioned, "Here in Berlin there are strong objections to my conversion. It would be best if I could study somewhere else."

As soon as I said that, an idea flashed through my mind.

I said, "The Opera Season will end in May and you'll be going back to Warsaw for the summer. I'd like to study there. As a matter of fact, I'd like to study with your father, if he'd accept me."

Her eyes opened wide and she gasped. "You want to study with my father?"

"Yes... I understand he's an outstanding scholar and teacher."

She beamed. "Yes... yes... that's true... but..."

I said, "Would you speak to Rabbi Lowenthal and ask if he would be willing to make the necessary arrangements for me?"

She paused, blinked her eyes a few times. Then she nodded. "Yes... I'll speak to him right away."

CHAPTER 20 — GOODBYE

'Traviata' was over and the theater was filled with the clanging and banging of the crew as they dismantled the ornate sets and carefully packed them for shipment back to the rental agency. We'd already received the sets for Madame 'Butterfly' which would be our last production of the season. Those sets now had to be assembled.

Gretchen and I were assigned the job of seeing that all of that got done quickly and efficiently so rehearsals could start. Meanwhile Karl was busy with talent agencies. He needed to find a five-year-old boy for a brief, non-speaking, non-singing part. By the time we got everything done, the weather had softened. The snow melted with the spring rains. There were more sunny days and it lifted everyone's spirits. We were ready.

As soon as rehearsals began, I noticed that Kaplansky showed up and took his place among the musicians right on time. I had nothing more to say to him. But I was relieved to see him. Maybe everything would be alright after all.

Then Chani came in and waved as she rushed backstage to wardrobe and makeup. Of course I was impatient to know if I'd be spending the summer in Warsaw with her. But I had to wait for

Rabbi Lowenthal's decision. Still, it was such an exciting prospect, I couldn't concentrate on anything else. Then Chani came on stage in yellow makeup with her eyes painted so they looked slanted for her role as Cio Cio San, the Japanese Geisha. Her silken black hair was done up and pierced with what looked like sticks that had beads of some kind dangling from them. In her white satin kimono costume she looked so exotic. She took little mincing steps, as the Orientals do... a little Geisha with sparkling blue-green eyes, I thought. What a beauty she is!

I didn't know much about this opera. Karl was the expert. So I read the libretto during the rehearsal. The story is simple enough... A young Geisha girl falls madly in love with an American Naval officer named Pinkerton who is stationed in Japan. She abandons her religion and adopts his. But they have a traditional Japanese wedding. After a brief honeymoon, he tells her he has to return to his ship. But he'll be back. And that ends Act I.

Rehearsals continued for the next few days and I was so preoccupied with the production as well as the anticipation of spending the summer in Warsaw, I pushed all thoughts of my father and the Nazis out of my mind. But on Thursday, Opening Night, I began to worry. What calamity would my father cause this time?

As the audience filed in and took their seats, I became increasingly anxious. I couldn't find my father at all. I asked Karl and Gretchen if they'd spotted him. They hadn't. The lights dimmed. The curtain went up and still no sign of him. Fear began to gnaw at me.

I looked around cautiously to make sure no one saw me as I

sneaked out to the alley behind the theater. Sure enough, the silver Mercedes was there and Josef was behind the wheel. I slid onto the passenger seat and locked the door. In the darkness I whispered, "Is something going on? My father came to the last two Opening Nights, but not this one. Where is he?"

Josef said, "Oh… didn't he mention it to you? He's in Nuremberg."

"What? No… no… What's happening in Nuremberg? How long will he be gone?"

"Well… he still has a business to run. So he'll be in and out of town. And of course I only hear bits and pieces, but your father told me it's absolutely imperative that the National Socialist Party gain a significant number of seats in the Reichstag in the next election. It's so important that the campaign is under way now, even though the election won't be held until next April.

Your father is deeply involved. If the Nazi Party is successful, he expects to be appointed to one of those seats. Again, I only hear whispers. But it seems the Nazis are planning to crisscross the country with all kinds of assemblies and rallies. They want to bring their message to every little town and village."

Josef paused and shook his head. "I've been to some of those meetings. Here's how they work. The Brownshirts break up every opposition meeting with a brawl. But at their own events… anyone opens his mouth, he's hauled outside and beaten half to death. Those Brownshirts are armed with steel clubs and they don't hesitate to use them. They're absolutely ruthless. Erich, be very careful."

"Be careful yourself," I warned, as I said goodbye. Again I looked around to make sure no one saw me. And for a moment I thought I saw the gleam of a cigarette way back in the alley. A cold stab of fear gripped me. Is someone back there? Have we been seen? I had to find out! I walked quickly toward the back of the alley. No one was there. The alley opened onto a busy street filled with people walking and heavy traffic.

I was sweating now… my nerves coiled tight. I walked back to the Mercedes. Had I really seen something? Should I tell Josef? I decided not to worry him and slipped back into the theater.

The first Act was coming to an end. I tried to calm myself after that scare in the alley. I read the libretto for Act II with difficulty. My hands were shaking. In this Act, Pinkerton returns and brings with him his American wife. Five long years have gone by. He's come to get the son he's heard of and persuade Cio Cio San the boy will have a better life with him in America. He was successful and the opera ends with Cio Cio San committing suicide. Another tragic ending but wild applause for the performers.

I waited with Karl for the crowd to thin so we could start getting the theater locked up for the night. Chani was out of her costume and makeup when she came running toward me. She whispered, "Rabbi Lowenthal has agreed. He'll speak to my father tomorrow and I'll tell you everything on Sunday after the matinee performance." She smiled and waved as she went to find Gretchen to get her home.

I didn't move! I was mesmerized by the nearness of her. I could smell her perfume. I forgot about my fear in the alley. I forgot everything. I didn't even thank her. Then it began to sink in. I was pretty sure that if Rabbi Lowenthal spoke to Chani's father and asked him to accept me as his student... he wouldn't refuse. My prospects were good. A wave of gratitude washed over me for Rabbi Lowenthal and his involvement on my behalf. I couldn't think of how or when I'd get a chance to thank him.

The weekend dragged by. The Friday and Saturday night performances went well, with the understudy in fine voice. But I could barely wait for Sunday when I'd know if Rabbi Machinski had accepted me as his student.

We had a full house on Sunday. It looked like we might finish the Season in the black. But I was impatient for the final curtain and for the applause and Bravos to subside. I waited and waited and waited... Finally Chani came toward me and handed me a letter from Rabbi Lowenthal. I tore it open and read it fast. Then I looked into those blue-green eyes and whispered, "It's all set! Your father has accepted me!"

She said, "Isn't that great!"

I wanted to grab her and kiss her and twirl her around. But I knew that would have to wait for another time... in another dream! Instead I followed Karl's previous advice. I smiled, took a step back and said, "Thank you... thank you... I really appreciate your help."

She smiled back. "I'm packing tonight," she said. "I leave for home tomorrow." And she rushed off, leaving me hot with excitement and anticipation. I was going to spend the whole summer in Warsaw with Chani. This calls for a celebration, I told myself.

Maybe I'll go to the Tauentzien Strasse again. It's not as great as the Red Light district in Amsterdam, but... what the hell!

I was hung over the next morning. The telephone woke me. It was Karl. "It's Monday. Aren't you coming into the office? You have to do the payroll. We have invoices to pay. You have to balance the books. We're closing for the season. Why aren't you here?!"

"OH... sorry... I didn't feel good this morning. I'll be in later." I made myself a pot of black coffee, without the cognac, and sat down to consider how to get to Warsaw without arousing suspicion about why I'm there and what I'm doing. For everyone's safety, I figured it would be best if no one knew what I was up to. As I sipped my coffee, it came to me. I'd tell everyone I was going back to England to spend the summer with my Uncle and his family. Yes... yes... that might work!

I sat down at my desk at once and wrote to my Uncle. In strictest confidence I told him where I was going and why. I advised him of where I would be staying in Warsaw, according to the address Rabbi Lowenthal had assigned me. I asked him to forward any mail sent to me and cautioned that if anyone inquired, he should tell them I'm with him and the family.

Next I wrote to Frau Rhinehardt explaining I would be away for the summer and enclosing a check for the rent on my apartment that would cover those months. I mailed those letters on my way to the theater. As soon as I got there I told Karl and Gretchen I'd finish up all my work and then leave for England where I planned to spend the summer. I promised I'd be back before the Opera Season started and to write me at my Uncle's place if anything important came up. They protested. They wanted to go out for dinner and drinks before I left. But I told them I had too much to do. "We'll catch up when I come back," I assured them as I gave them each a hug.

I worked late and got everything done. Then I phoned Hermann Maas and asked if I could stop by that evening. I counted him among my closest friends and wanted to thank him for helping me with my studies and everything else he'd done for me. I assured him that I would resume my studies when I returned from England in the fall and we said a warm goodbye.

Hermann Maas was the only one who could connect me with Rabbi Lowenthal, a dangerous piece of information, but I was confident my secret was safe with him. I couldn't imagine what would happen if my father discovered my intentions. He was the greatest danger and I left him for last. I wanted to say goodbye over the phone but decided against it. He, more than anyone else, had to be convinced that I was going to England. Ever since I'd refused to join the Nazi Party, he was suspicious of every move I made.

I phoned and told him I wanted to stop by to see him first thing in the morning. Then I called Hugo and asked him to go with me. I always felt endangered when I was with my father. I planned to take the gun with me.

It felt weird... almost eerie, going back to that house the next morning. I was uneasy from the start. And then a heavyset rough-looking Brownshirt opened the door when I rang. What a shock! I stammered... I'm... eh... I'm... Erich Von Bruener. I'm here to see

172

my father. He's expecting me.

He nodded and looked at Hugo. "Who's he?"

"He's my driver. He'll wait for me in the foyer. We won't be long."

The Brownshirt looked him over… seemed to size him up… and nodded. "Come in."

I found my father in the dining room. "Have a seat. I'm going to have some cake and coffee… Join me."

"No, thank you."

"Well, then… to what do I owe the honor of this visit? Do you have any good news for me?"

I ignored this obvious reference to joining the Nazi Party. "The Opera Season is over. And I'm planning to return to England to spend the summer with my Uncle and his family. I came to say goodbye."

His eyes narrowed. He stared at me and I regretted my decision to come here. "Uh huh. Is that right? Well… be sure to give them my regards and write me… let's keep in touch."

He didn't believe me and I began to feel threatened.

"Why do you have one of those Brownshirts answering the door?"

"I need protection for some of my projects. That's why!" he said. Did I dare ask him what those projects were?

I stood up. "I'd like to say goodbye to Josef too. Where is he?"

"Josef? Josef's dead!"

CHAPTER 21 — THE JOURNEY

"Dead! What do you mean, dead?" I shouted. "What the hell happened to him?" My father didn't even look up. He continued eating his cake and sipping his coffee. I was furious. But I couldn't tell him I'd just seen Josef a few days ago and he was perfectly alright. My voice was hoarse and rasping when I whispered, "Was he sick? Did he get sick?"

Now my father looked at me and shrugged. "Ohhh… I don't know. He was an old man and that's what old men do… they die!"

I glared at him. Sure, a man could look good one day and die of a heart attack the next. But in my gut I knew that Josef didn't just die. He was killed! Was it because he knew too much? Then I remembered the gleam of light in the alley. Is it possible we were seen together? My stomach was churning. But I spoke calmly.

"I've known Josef since I was born. I'd like to pay my last respects. Where is he buried?"

My father put his coffee cup down. "Ohhh… well… he isn't buried. He was cremated and I had his ashes strewn around the estate. After all, he worked here for many years."

He spoke as if he'd done the right thing. My head was spinning. I closed my eyes and put my face in my hands. How could I have been so stupid? When I first came to Berlin I wanted to change him back to the man he was before the war. I didn't want to believe he'd evolved into a brute with a malignant heart. First Max Liebman, beaten to death, then Sonja devoured by dogs! And now Josef... turned into smoke and ashes... erased completely!

It was chilling... yet I was hot! I wiped my sweaty face on my sleeve and leaped up. I had to get away from him... away from this house... this city... this country! I grabbed Hugo on the way out and left without another word.

Once in the car, I decided. I had to leave for Warsaw tonight. But how? Josef wouldn't be watching me... following me everywhere. It would be someone else. And then I paused. I had an idea. I asked Hugo to drive me to the theater. It was closed, of course. But I had the keys. I went backstage to the costume and makeup departments. I picked up a blond moustache and beard, a hat, eyeglasses and a light coat along with some cosmetics, and stuffed them into a briefcase. If I was being watched I hoped it would look like I'd picked up some business papers.

Before I came to Berlin and became Karl's partner, I'd been traveling all over Europe. So my papers were in order. But I wouldn't look like the photo on my passport. I decided when they checked my papers, I'd tell them I'd been in a bad accident and grew a beard and moustache to cover my scars.

Then I went to the office and got my papers and a wad of bills out of the safe for expenses in Warsaw, plus some extra in case I needed it for bribes.

When we got to my apartment I paid Hugo and said goodbye. I told him I'd be away for the summer and gave him the keys to my Mercedes. Take good care of it while I'm gone," I cautioned. "I'll be in touch with you as soon as I get back." He grinned, evidently thrilled to have the use of the car for the whole summer. I watched as he pulled away. No one seemed to be following him, but I wasn't sure of anything. I'd have to be very careful to pull this off.

As soon as I entered my apartment I pulled the shades down and closed the drapes. I poured myself a glass of whiskey and swallowed it in one gulp. Then I sat down to think about my father... who he was and what he'd done. I felt such intense pain that I considered lying about him in Warsaw. I could tell everyone he died in the Great War. I gulped down another whiskey and convinced myself it really wasn't such a big lie. He was a different person now, not the one I remembered. I thought about Justice, and what it is, or if there ever was such a thing... and drifted off.

I don't know how long I slept but it was time to get going. I packed a few essentials in a suitcase and got started on my disguise. I pasted the beard and moustache on, used the make up to put dark circles under my eyes. I wore glasses, got into the light coat and slipped the gun in my pocket. Then I put on the hat and grabbed my special cane. I practice walking with a limp and hoped my disguise would be effective.

The train was leaving at nine o'clock. I wanted to be there early so I could get a ticket for a first class compartment and make sure I had it all to myself, even if I had to buy more than one ticket.

I phoned for a taxi. As we made our way to the train station, I looked around to see if I was being followed. I was! The silver Mercedes was right behind us. But why? Had they seen through my disguise? Or did they mean to follow any man who came out of my apartment? By the time we reached the station I was filled with anxiety. Still, I couldn't rush! I walked slowly, leaning heavily on my cane as I made my way to the ticket office. I had to buy four tickets in order to have the compartment to myself. As soon as I got them, I found a dark corner where I couldn't be seen easily... but I could watch!

The station was crowded and noisy. Many people brought bouquets of flowers as they said goodbye to family. The hiss of steam engines and the smoke mixed with the clanging of the train and the din of conversations. There was no way for me to know who was following me unless it was one of those Brownshirts in uniform.

Then I saw him. God damn it! It was my father and he was slowly coming toward me... looking around. What if he saw through my disguise? What then? My heart pounded in my ears. Nothing was going to stop me. As he came closer I decided if there was any problem I would use the poisoned cane on him.

Suddenly he frowned, turned, and started walking in the other direction, looking all around. The train was boarding. There was a rush of passengers. I forced myself not to panic. I carefully blotted the sweat from my face, making sure my beard and moustache remained in place. Then I walked slowly, limping... just as I'd rehearsed. I showed my papers. The conductor stared at me and said, "You don't look like this photograph."

I explained it's because I was in an automobile accident. I grew a beard and moustache to cover the scars. He accepted that explanation and I made my way to my compartment. As soon as I entered I locked the door. I didn't want to talk to anyone. The damn disguise might slip. I had to keep it in place at least until we came to the Polish border. Then I could take it off.

I was tired... hungry too. But I didn't do anything about that. I leaned against the wall and listened to the rattle of the train. I think I heard it say... you're almost there! Almost there! Almost there!

CHAPTER 22 — WARSAW AGAIN

It was early morning when the train arrived in Warsaw. I'd already stowed my disguise and got cleaned up. According to the instructions I received from Rabbi Lowenthal, I was to rent a room from a woman named Bertha Kessler on Niska Street. I thought it might disturb her to arrive at this hour, so when I hired a Droshka at the taxi stand on Jerszolinski Street, I asked the driver to take me on a tour of the palaces and mansions of the old Saxon Kings. I wanted another look at them. I'd only glimpsed them briefly the last time I was in Warsaw.

In the open carriage the brisk spring air and the bright sunshine mingled with the smell of woodlands and gardens that were part of these elegant, ancient homes.

The memories of Sonja and Josef, along with all the dark tensions of Berlin began to fade as we clip-clopped through this beautiful area of the city. As we made our way to the address on Niska Street, the neighborhood gradually changed until we finally stopped in a poor, rundown section of the city.

Bertha Kessler lived on the first floor of a tenement-like building. When she answered my knock, I saw a pair of pale blue eyes sunk in a dark, wrinkled face. She was pulling her gray hair into a bun at the back of her head as I introduced myself. She smiled as she mumbled a welcome and I couldn't help but notice the poor woman had only one or two teeth in her mouth.

She led me into her kitchen which consisted of a stove, a sink with cupboards above it, a table with three chairs, and a small bed against the wall, piled high with tattered covers. I thought, Why does she have to live in such poverty? Then I silently laughed to myself. This must be the way for me to start a new life… at the bottom! No more posh Adlon Hotel or Deluxe Europejski hotel for me. Now I'm going to share in the life of the poor.

"Let me show you to your room," she said in Yiddish. I answered in German but somehow we understood each other. She opened a door near the stove and motioned for me to enter. Inside was a low feather bed, a battered and scratched desk, and a bureau with a cracked mirror above it. The window had a torn shade. I realized that Rabbi Lowenthal had sent me here as an act of charity. The rent I was to pay was desperately needed. I put my suitcase down.

"Du vilt essen?" (Are you hungry?) I nodded. "Well, get unpacked and I'll put something on the table for you." (Ichl bald gebn.)

I was hungry. I didn't remember the last time I ate. Within a few minutes I was seated at the kitchen table looking into a bowl of hot potato soup. There were onions and carrots in it. It came with brown bread still warm from the oven, and freshly made butter. It was delicious.

She joined me. We finished up with tea and raisin cookies. "Do you have family nearby?" I asked.

She shook her head. "My husband and our two oldest sons were killed in the Great War. My youngest son didn't want to live in Poland anymore. He's in New York. He wanted me to go with him, but I don't want to go. He used to send me money but now he writes things are bad in America. There's no work."

I nodded. "That's how it is everywhere." I said as I started stacking up the dishes. "Thank you for a wonderful meal, Frau Kessler."

"Call me Bertha," she said with another toothless smile. "And don't bother with the dishes. You'll get them mixed up." I didn't know what she meant but I did as I was told.

I looked at my watch. "I'm running late… I'm here to study with Rabbi Saul Machinski. Do you know where he lives?"

"Yah… vu den," she told me as she cleared off the table. "I'll show you in a minute." While she busied herself with the dishes, I put the month's rent on the table. I paid in British Pounds, not German Marks or Polish Zlotys. Her eyes lit up when she saw that. Then she led me outside and pointed the way to Stawki Street.

It wasn't far. Once I got there I remembered which apartment it was. I again climbed the three flights of stairs and was delighted when Chani opened the door.

"Oh… there you are!" she said. Come in. My father's expecting you." I didn't know who else was in the room. I only saw Chani, looking like the first time I saw her, with pink cheeks and sparkling blue-green eyes. I thought, Are you always this beautiful first thing in the morning?

She motioned for me to follow her. Then she rapped on the door of the Rabbi's study and opened it. "Papa, Herr Von Bruener is here." She gave me a shy smile and left, closing the door behind her.

The Rabbi stood up and motioned for me to have a seat on one of those hardwood chairs I'd sat on before. He didn't smile. It was obvious that he'd accepted me as his student only because he couldn't refuse Rabbi Lowenthal.

He cleared his throat. "Rabbi Lowenthal tells me you want to convert to Judaism. Is that right?" I nodded. He looked me in the eye. "Well… I think it's a bad idea and I advise against it. We are a people discriminated against by all kinds of laws and government decrees. You see how we live! As a Christian, you have all the advantages. So why would you want to become a Jew?"

I didn't answer right away. I wanted to put my words together carefully. I needed his understanding. "Perhaps you heard that my father is a devoted Nazi and a violent anti-Semite. He's responsible for three murders. But there's no evidence or any witnesses… who lived! So there were no trials. He got away with it and found reasons to take pride in these evil accomplishments."

When I came to Berlin this past December, I had it in my mind to try to change him back to how he used to be. I found out I can't change him. I can only change me.

So yes, I learned Hebrew, learned about some Jewish customs and traditions and read all the books Rabbi Lowenthal sent me. But the truth is I've never even been inside a synagogue. I don't know anything! I've come to you to teach me how to live a Jewish life. Will you help me?"

There was no answer. The clock ticked. Then the Rabbi shook his head. "Erich, have you really thought this thing through? You're talking about a very dangerous path. How could you live in Berlin as a Jew? What if your father found out? What would happen?"

"In Berlin I'd have to be a secret Jew, like the Spanish Maranos. I don't know what my father would do if he found out. But it doesn't matter. I can't help who my father is, how he thinks or what he does. I have to be my own man and live my own life. Rabbi Machinski, will you help me find that life?"

More silence. Then he sighed and nodded. "You'll need a tutor to teach you the basic tenets of Judaism while you catch up with the Yeshiva students. But since you're so determined to learn Judaism, I'll make every effort to teach you. Come back tomorrow and we'll get started.

CHAPTER 23 — GENESIS

The next morning the first thing he said to me was, "Call me Reb Saul. Everyone does." It was a bright sunny day and I was as excited as a kid on the first day of school. We walked together for several blocks as Reb Saul explained how important it was to learn the laws of Kashruth and Shabbos as well as the Talmud (the body of Jewish civil and religious law). "Plan to be with us every Sabbath. Come on Friday before sundown."

Students at the Yeshiva

When we got to the school he introduced me to the other

students… all young men close to my age. He read a tractate (section) of the Talmud and then all the students joined in with opinions, quotations from past sages, question and answers, all in Yiddish. I'd never been in a class like this. It was a real struggle to understand what was going on. Afterwards Reb Saul tutored me privately for an hour and gave me extra books to read. He said, "Learn Yiddish. You can pick it up quickly."

The week went by in a frenzy… and then it was Friday. Bertha Kessler told me to get scrubbed up and put on my best clothes in honor of Shabbos. I was a little worried. This would be my first Sabbath experience. I tried to recall what Karl told me about it. But I couldn't remember. When I arrived at the apartment it seemed like the walls of the building were permeated with the smell of chicken soup.

The Machinski apartment was dominated by a huge table covered with a white cloth. Candles were lit. Reb Saul rounded up his boys and together we left for what they called the "Shul." It turned out to be a large room, sparsely furnished, mostly with desks. It was part of the local Hebrew School and was crowded with other men and boys… no women. And everyone seemed to know one another. There were shouts of "Gut Shabbos" from all sides. The service was short… a few blessings, songs welcoming the Sabbath, and we were soon back at the apartment, seated around the table.

The grandmother was called Bubbe and she now told the children, "Go to your father." Reb Saul sat at the head of the table. The kids dutifully lined up… little Sarah first, then the twins, Natan, and lastly

Chani in a long pink dress that matched her cheeks and made her eyes shine. She was holding little Avi. The Rabbi went to each of his children, put his hands on their heads and blessed and kissed them. As I watched I realized that was where I wanted to be... at the head of the table with Chani, my wife, seated at my right and our children standing in a row waiting for my blessing. It was a powerful image. The evening was filled with blessings for the wine we drank and the bread called CHALLAH... then more singing about peace in the world, followed by a wonderful dinner. It made me think about my father and our relationship. No blessings in the past and only fear now and in the future.

It was late when I made my way back to Bertha's place and got into bed. I fell asleep thinking about the Rabbi's children growing up knowing that every Friday night their father will bless and kiss them.

The Great Synagogue of Warsaw

The next day, Saturday, I'd been asked to meet Reb Saul at his home and go to the Synagogue with the family. I'd never been in a Synagogue. I was nervous. I didn't want to do the wrong thing or be conspicuous. But I didn't have to worry. As it turned out, the place was huge. It was called THE GREAT SYNAGOGUE OF WARSAW, or Tlomackie Synagogue, because it was on Tlomackie Square. The building was sort of Greek-like, with four pillars in the front. I was told it could seat two thousand people. Inside I was given a skull cap and a prayer shawl as I joined the other men. What a disappointment! I thought I'd be able to sit next to Chani. I learned all the women were seated in the balcony. I made a mental note to ask about it later.

As for the Service, a part of the Bible was read. It was called the PARSHA or Portion of the week. What was most startling was the Cantor, Moshe Koussevitsky, who sang the prayers with such a magnificent tenor voice. He was perfect for the Opera. "He's world famous," Reb Saul whispered. I didn't doubt it.

Stylized Picture of Cantor Moshe Koussevitsky

Services ended around noon with a Kiddish (wine, whiskey and cake). Then we all went home for a huge hot meal right in the middle of the day. They ate a dish called CHOLENT. I don't know what was in it... meat, potatoes, and other stuff. Then we had more wine. It was very tasty. During the meal there was a discussion of the Parsha, what it might mean and how it pertains to us now. This was followed by more singing. Afterwards Reb Saul retired to his study. Bubbe, Avi, and Sarah took a nap. And the boys ran outside to play with their friends. Chani and I went for a walk.

She led the way in her pink Shabbos dress. And even though it was a hot day, her dress had long sleeves and was up to her neck and down to her toes. We passed elderly neighbors sitting outside enjoying the summer sunshine, as well as gangs of kids running around playing games.

This was the first chance I had to talk to her alone. I wanted to get to know her. But she was silent. We left the Jewish area and came to another neighborhood where there were large, sturdy-looking houses with trees, grass and flowers around them.

Polish Mansion

View from Piękna Street

Polish Mansion

Just to get a conversation started I asked, "Are you glad to be home for the summer?" She stopped and turned to me. "No... not at all. I'm not glad. Everything's changed. It's different for me now. You only saw my mother when she was sick. But she was a beautiful, happy person. She loved to laugh and sing. She had a wonderful voice. The three of us, Fannie, my mother and I did everything together. Now they're both gone, Fannie's in Jerusalem and my beloved mother is in the cemetery."

Her eyes filled with tears and one of them ran down her cheek. I thought, no... no... don't cry! I murmured, "I'm sorry. I'm so sorry." She quickly wiped the tear away.

I wanted to say something soothing so I told her, "No one can change that situation, but what is it that would make you happy?" She didn't answer. We walked down Dluga Street, past some magnificent mansions. I could smell the river nearby. That's when Chani stopped and faced me again. "The only thing that makes me happy now is the Berlin Opera Company."

I was shocked by her answer and must have looked it.

"You don't understand. I miss all the excitement of rehearsals, the costumes, and then the performance with the thrill of the audience... their applause, their bravos! It's all so incredible! I love it! But it's not allowed."

"But why?" I asked. "Why isn't it allowed?"

She shrugged. "In our tradition, it's not respectable. My father says young girls that perform on stage promote lustful feelings in men, or worse... sinful or criminal thoughts."

I couldn't tell her that lustful, sinful, and criminal described my father perfectly. And the young girls he used so brutally didn't need any talent at all. I said nothing. I waited for her to go on.

"My Papa told me that every man has to protect his daughters. It's a father's job. So how can I argue about that?"

She turned away. "Come on. We can cut through the woods here. It's much cooler. And then we'll come to the river."

The Vistula River

She was right. Under the shade of the tall trees it was much cooler and then we were on an embankment of the beautiful Vistula River. If Chani weren't around, I'd have taken my clothes off and jumped in. But as it was, I just loosened my collar, rolled up my pants legs and waded in.

Chani was more delicate. She just took off her shoes and dipped her hot toes in the cool river for a moment. Then she put her shoes back on and sat down on the grass. I soon joined her and as we looked out at the shimmering river. I told her, "You still have another year to go on your contract. So you have time to face that issue."

"I know," she said. "But I also know that my father will never sign another contract. So my singing career will be over and I don't want it to be over until I don't have a voice anymore and can only croak like a frog."

I laughed. But it wasn't a laughing matter. I asked, "What will your father expect you to do when the contract is up?"

"He will want me to meet eligible young men, whom he approves of, for me to make a marriage choice from among them."

"I see," I said. And suddenly I realized I had a time frame if I wanted to marry her.

Then Chani stood up. "What time is it?" she asked. "We've walked a long way. We better be getting back. We have to be home for Havdala."

"Who's he?" I said.

She laughed so hard we were almost halfway home by the time she answered. I was glad to be so amusing, even if I did make an ass of myself. Finally she told me, "Havdala is not a HE, it's a ceremony to end the Sabbath. You'll see. Come on."

CHAPTER 24 — FORWARD

Havdala was a brief ceremony... a light supper, a few prayers, a special braided candle, a sniff of incense... and it was over... Shabbos was over. I hated to see it end. I didn't mind going back to my studies but it meant I wouldn't get to be with Chani until the next Sabbath. And that's how it went for the next few weeks.

After that, as I walked back to Bertha Kessler's place in the cool darkness, I looked up at the star-filled sky and wondered how to go forward more quickly. That night I slept badly, if at all, as I devised a plan.

The next morning after class I asked Reb Saul, "Is it possible for you to tutor me for more than an hour a day? Rabbi Lowenthal outlined the steps I need to take for Conversion and the next step is to appear before the Bais Din (House of Judgment) where I'll be questioned on my knowledge of Judaism. Can you get me ready for that? I want to go forward as quickly as possible."

"Yes, I can devote more time to you. But why are you in such a hurry?"

I hesitated. "I hope you won't be shocked when I tell you this, but I've come to Warsaw purposely and deliberately to study with you. I need your help to become the kind of Jewish man you would allow your daughter to marry."

He stared at me. Finally he shouted, "I see! And have you discussed marriage with my daughter?"

"No... no... I want your blessing first, Reb Saul."

He nodded. "That's good. I'm grateful for that."

By this time I had mastered what Bertha Kessler called "the King's Yiddish." On top of that I was much more prolific in Hebrew as we began more intensive study. By the time Friday rolled around, I was exhausted and grateful that Shabbos had finally arrived.

On Saturday afternoon Chani and I went for our usual walk. This time, as we passed some elegant mansions on Ujazdowskie Avenue, out of the corner of my eye I spotted Chani's twin brothers following us. Evidently Reb Saul had asked them to watch us and report back to him about our behavior. I smiled and paid no attention to them.

I asked Chani, "When your father introduces you to the young men he approves of, what kind of man will you choose to marry?"

She looked at me and smiled. "Believe it or not, I want to marry a man like my Papa. He's a devoted family man. I know he wants what he thinks is best for me. He wants what's best for all his children. He's a pious, kind and loving man... educated and intelligent."

"What a coincidence." I said. "That's exactly the kind of man I plan to be!" We both laughed. "Look at these beautiful homes," I said. "If you could have one of them, which one would you pick?"

She looked at them, at their huge magnificence, then back at me. "I don't want any of them! I'm not going to live in Warsaw. I want to go to Jerusalem and be with my sister. I'm very lonely without her. And besides, after I'm married I don't want to raise my children in Poland among all these Jew-haters. I want them to grow up in the Holy Land"

I was surprised by that answer. Well, I thought, she's a determined young woman with dreams of her own. I wondered if I could fit into them somehow.

Again we cut through the woods and headed for the river. It was another hot summer day and we cooled off as usual. I looked around to see if the twins were watching. They were, but at a distance. When we sat down on the embankment and looked out at the serenely beautiful river, she said, "I'm glad you've come to Warsaw to study. It gives you a chance to get to know my family. Of course you haven't met everyone. Papa has four brothers and two sisters. All of them are married and have lots of kids. My mother has five brothers. They're also married and have many children. So I have all these cousins. But they don't live in Warsaw. They're mostly in Vilna, some in Riga and Cracow. Others live in different small towns and villages. Maybe you'll meet them someday. I'll show you pictures of them on a rainy Shabbos when we can't take a walk. But what about your family? I've seen your father and his companions. What will he say when he finds out you're a Jew?"

Suddenly I felt hot. I started to sweat. I took a deep breath and told her, "I was born in Berlin, the only child of Emily and Otto Von

Bruener. My mother died in an accident when I was eight years old. At that time my father was in France fighting in the Great War, so I was sent to England to live with my mother's older brother, my Uncle Tony, and his wife Jane and their two daughters, Elizabeth and Joanne. They are my only cousins. I grew up with them in a little town called Doncaster. When the War was over I stayed on and was educated there, eventually graduating from Cambridge University. In those days I only came to Berlin to visit my father twice a year, at Christmas and Easter."

Now that I live in Berlin, he's glad, although he thinks my association with the Berlin Opera Company is ridiculous. He wants me to have a military career in the New Germany the Nazis plan to create. He's furious that I've refused and has me followed constantly. He's trying to intimidate me and I can't say he's failed."

There was perspiration on my forehead as I whispered, "My father wasn't always the way he is now." I wiped my face on my sleeve and looked her in the eye. "It's painful for me to admit it, but today my father is deeply involved with the Nazis. He's a close friend of Adolf Hitler, and an outspoken anti-Semite."

Chani listened intently. "You haven't answered my question. What will happen when he finds out you're a Jew?"

"He mustn't find out! He's a violent man. I'll have to be a secret Jew in Berlin, like the Marranos in Spain. That means I won't be able to go to synagogue, or observe Shabbos like I do here. I'll have to be very careful."

"But why? Why live like that?" she asked.

"Because I'm like you. The Berlin Opera Company is also my happiness, although in a different way from you. But you're right. To live as a Jew I'll have to go somewhere else. Still, the 1932 elections are scheduled for sometime in April. If the Nazis are defeated, the newly elected government could finally control Hitler and disband his bloody Brownshirts. That will make things much easier. I'm planning to stay in Berlin until after those elections. Your contract ends in May. So I'll be there as long as you are."

"But... what if the Nazis win? What then?"

Then I have to leave Germany immediately. I'm not sure where to go... I could return to England or come back here to Warsaw."

She nodded. I looked at my watch. "It's getting late. We'd better be going if we want to be back for Havdala."

She smiled, but we didn't say another word. We walked all the way home in silence with the twins following far behind.

CHAPTER 25 — THE NEXT STEP

Three old men with long beards sat at the dais conferring with each other and occasionally glancing at me with what I thought to be curiosity. This was the Bais Din The House of Judgement) and I looked exactly as my name implied... blond, suntanned and ruddy from studying outside all summer... like an Erich Von Bruener from Berlin would look. I was on edge. This was the next step! I had to win!

It was a long session. Reb Saul sat on the side as the three Rabbis asked me Biblical questions and interpretations of Biblical events by various Sages. Then they went over the Laws of Family Purity, Kashruth and the Sabbath.

After the questioning we were asked to wait in an adjacent room where we would be advised of their verdict. Reb Saul relaxed in a comfortable chair and seemed calm and confident. I was in a cold sweat... pacing back and forth until at last we were re-admitted.

The Rabbis were still whispering with each other. Then we got the news. The Bais Din recommended additional study but pronounced me suitable for Conversion.

Whew! I wanted to leap in the air, but I didn't. I nodded solemnly and said "Thank you."

Once out the door, Reb Saul clapped me on the back. "Mahzel Tov! You were really good in there."

He seemed proud of me... and that meant everything to me. I told him, "I'm ready for the next step now."

He smiled. "Well... that calls for a spiritual journey and a slight change in your anatomy. Circumcision is next and it constitutes your entry into the Covenant with the G-d of Israel and its people, together with its Laws, delivered by Yad Moshe, the hand of Moses."

"I'm ready. I was told that it isn't any more painful than what women suffer when they have babies. But it was also mentioned that I didn't have to worry because they also have very good drugs. However, if I need extra time to recover, I have family in England and they could be helpful. So I'd like to have it done in London and as soon as possible. Can you help me make a connection?"

"First you'll need a letter from the Warsaw Bais Din and then... I know Rabbi Solomon Shaposhnick in England. He's associated with a synagogue in the East End of London. I'll contact him and ask if he can make arrangements for you at the London Jewish Hospital.

Of course with Circumcision you will receive a new name... your Hebrew name."

I repeated, "A Hebrew name? I hadn't given that any thought. What do you suggest?"

Reb Saul gave it some consideration. Then he said, "I'd suggest

Daniel because when you return to Berlin, you'll be back in the lions' den."

Berlin seemed far away to me but I agreed. "Yes, I accept that name."

"You'll also get a new father."

I smiled. "I could use a new father."

"Converts are usually called Ben Avram... the son of Abraham. So your new name will be Daniel Ben Avram."

I laughed. "You know, when Chani came to Berlin we gave her a stage name to protect her from that poisonous anti-Semitism. There her name is Heidi Mueller from Danzig. But here she's Chani Machinski. In Berlin I'll have to be Erich Von Bruener to protect me from the Nazis. But here and in every Jewish community, I can be Daniel Ben Avram. Thank you."

Within the month, Reb Saul told me that all arrangements for London had been made and I could stay with Rabbi Shaposhnik whenever necessary. I wrote to Uncle Tony at once and gave him the date.

A week after surgery he and Aunt Jane came to visit me at the hospital. Those who told me it wasn't too painful lied. But I managed to recover anyway. Uncle Tony was somewhat accepting but Aunt Jane was rueful about this entire procedure. She said, "Erich, you know, we send Missionaries all over the world to convert people to Christianity. What are you doing?"

I told her I believed that the only true Christians were Jews, and that I was following in the footsteps of Jesus. I didn't know if she accepted that explanation, but she didn't say anything more.

While in the hospital I decided to send postcards to Karl and Reverend Maas as well as to my father, in order to confirm that I was indeed in England.

As soon as I was fully recovered, Rabbi Shaposhnik took me to the Mikvah, a communal bath (men and women separately, of course). The water has to be from a natural stream. It was icy cold and I was dipped in over my head. I felt as if I'd been re-baptized. The following month I returned to Warsaw.

It was wonderful to be back. Everyone at the Yeshiva now called me Daniel and I was anticipating Shabbos with Chani and the family. As it happened, when we left the synagogue on Saturday the sky was overcast and it began to rain. I hoped it would clear up so Chani and I could go for our usual walk down to the river. Instead it got worse. By the time we swallowed our Cholent at our Shabbos lunch, it thundered, lightninged and poured rain. Everyone had to stay inside.

As soon as the dishes were cleared away, Bubbe sat in her rocking chair and closed her eyes. Reb Saul got engrossed in a large book at the dining room table while Natan snuggled into a corner of the sofa with little Avi on his lap and Sarah at his elbow. He droned on and on with a storybook. The twins sat on the floor playing chess while Chani brought out a huge box filled with photographs.

"I want to show you pictures of my family," she said as she pulled one out of the pile. "Now, on the right are Leah and Rachel Machinski. They are two of my Uncle Moishe's children. His wife is Tante Esther. I have pictures of them too, but I'm not really organized. On the left in this photo are Shaindal and Leo Bernstein. They're cousins. I have pictures of their parents too."

Family Picture

I interrupted. "Do you know that Albert Einstein lectures at Humboldt University in Berlin?"

She wrinkled up her nose and gave me a puzzled look. "What does that have to do with anything?"

I said, "I think I can pass one of his tests on relativity much easier than I can learn the names of all your relatives. Don't you think it would be best if I could meet them in person?"

"Well sure... but they live in all different places. So how can you do that?"

I said, "Why don't we get married and invite them all to the wedding?"

A hush fell over the room. Bubbe's eyes opened. Reb Saul closed his book. Natan stopped reading and the twins abandoned their game. It was so quiet I could hear the clock ticking... or was it my heart? Chani didn't answer.

I said, "I want to be your husband... Please say yes."

CHAPTER 26 — THE WEDDING

September 1st, 1931 was our wedding date. Chani and Bubbe were intense about gown and veil, food and whiskey… on and on. Reb Saul instructed me on my part and how the ceremony would go.

I sent out one invitation to Uncle Tony and his family. Chani invited all of her relatives, friends and neighbors. As far as I knew everyone she invited was coming, including the Lowenthals from Berlin. Uncle Tony wrote that Aunt Jane wouldn't attend, and that meant the girls too. He didn't want to leave them alone while he was in Warsaw, so he wouldn't be coming to the wedding either. As it was, my friends in Berlin had been told I was spending the summer in England, so I couldn't invite them. It was disappointing. But starting a new life means a separation from the old one. I accepted it.

On the following Shabbos, when things quieted down, Chani and I took our usual walk down to the river. I needed to talk to her about how we would live in Berlin. When we settled down under the coolness of the trees, I told her, "My father absolutely must be prevented from finding out about us. I've been giving this a lot of thought and here's my plan: I'll go to Berlin first and alone. You'll follow the next day. We can only be together during the week. I'll leave for the theater first thing in the morning, since I'm the one being followed. I'll ask Gretchen to pick you up for rehearsals later. Then Gretchen will drive you back to the apartment immediately after rehearsals. I'll leave the theater much later. Just be careful no one sees you entering my apartment. That's crucial!"

She nodded and agreed to everything, but not happily. "What about Shabbos" she asked.

"We'll have to be apart," I said. "And that's the worst of it. But it can't be helped. You'll have to spend Shabbos with the Lowenthals, just as you did before. But it's only for a short time. If the Nazis are defeated in the elections, we'll be safe in Berlin. If not, we'll come back to Warsaw.

She grimaced. "That means we won't have Shabbos together for a long time."

"It's the best I can do. The most important thing is for you to be safe." I looked at my watch. "We better start back." We walked home sadly and without another word.

When Havdala was over, we got the bad news. Everyone in the family was coming to the wedding except the most important person... Chani's sister, Fannie. Reb Saul was adamant. He said, "Fannie went to Palestine with a group of Zionists, mostly young men. Travel is much safer in a group. But for the wedding she'd have to come back to Warsaw from Jerusalem alone! And then return alone! No... no... it's too dangerous for a young girl to take such a long journey by herself."

Chani burst into tears. It meant so much to her to see Fannie again. I wanted to console her somehow. So I told her, "When the Opera season ends in May, why don't we go to Jerusalem together? That way we'll have plenty of time to spend with Fannie. She can show us around, and we can find out if there is such a thing as a Jerusalem Opera Company. If not... maybe we can start one!"

She wiped her tears away and looked at me with big eyes. "That's a great idea! I love it! That could be really exciting!"

Reb Saul nodded. "Yes... yes... that's sounds wonderful. I wish I could go with you." Then he turned a grim face to me. "I'd like to talk to you in my study now, if you wouldn't mind."

After I followed him inside, he locked the door. I sat down on that same hard chair and waited nervously to hear what was on his mind. He sat behind his desk and said, "Listen, the world is changing too fast for me... and not for the better. Everything seems upside-down and old traditions are shoved aside. Fannie is the oldest. She should be getting married first. But I could not arrange it because she insisted that there is no future for Jews in Poland. She wants to live in the Holy Land.

And now Chani... much as I tried, I came to realize that she would never choose to marry a Biblical Scholar, a banker or an industrialist. That wouldn't fit in with her ambitions. So I wasn't surprised that she accepted you. I know you love her dearly. But a young Jewish girl in Berlin with a Nazi father-in-law? How are you going to protect her? I've been waiting to hear from you because I can't protect her in Germany."

"I understand your concern," I said. "And I'm sorry it took me so long. I gave it a lot of thought and I've made my plan. But you're right. My father must be prevented from finding out that I'm now a Jew and Chani is my Jewish wife. No one in Berlin will know that, except the Lowenthals.

I've had extra keys to my apartment made. One is for Chani and the other is for Mrs. Lowenthal who has agreed to kosher our kitchen in advance of our arrival. I'll advise my partner Karl and his wife about our situation when I get back. I plan to leave for Berlin first and alone. Chani will follow the next day. We've worked out the details and although I admit it'll be complicated and difficult, it's only temporary. We can do it.

A lot depends on the political situation. There are many calls for the government to disband Hitler's Brownshirts as well as the newly formed SS. But the government is not functioning. There's going to be an election in April and I'm hoping the German people will reject the rightwing Nazis as well as the leftwing Communists and continue their Democratic Republic. That will make things much easier for us."

Reb Saul shook his head. "I hope you're right. But what if you're wrong?"

I said, "At the first hint of a problem, Chani and I will leave Germany immediately. We'll come back here or go to England, anyplace that she'll be safe. I love her very much.

He sighed. "Yes, so do I."

Two weeks later our wedding day dawned. The sun shone brightly through the magnificent stained glass windows of the Great Synagogue of Warsaw. I walked slowly down the aisle to the Chupah (the marriage canopy), symbol of our first home together. My heart was like a drum beat. At last I was starting my new life. Chani and I would make a home filled with music and blessings.

Then came Chani in her veil and white satin gown… my bride! She took my breath away.

Rabbi Moses Schorr officiated. He read the Ketubah (the marriage contract) that advised me, under Jewish Law, of what I must provide for my wife. Then a number of Rabbinical dignitaries, including Rabbi Lowenthal, pronounced blessings on our marriage. I gave my bride her wedding ring, we drank wine from the same glass, and then, as tradition demands, I stomped on the wine glass in memory of the destruction of the Temple in Jerusalem. Everyone shouted Mazel Tov! And the festivities began.

Now Chani and I had a few minutes alone together. We'd been fasting all day to mark the solemnity of our marriage. We were served a light snack and given time alone to hold hands and enjoy a tender kiss. As was the custom on this occasion, I gave my new wife a special gift, a diamond ring, another kiss, and then we joined our guests, while the photographers took photos of everyone.

Men and women celebrated, but separately. A curtain divided them. And to my surprise, the guests provided the entertainment. Chani went to the women's section and I to the men's, where the guys from the Yeshiva, in wild wigs and disguises, performed acrobatics and unbelievable dances. All the other men, including me, soon joined in. It was exuberant and wild!

The band played loud and lively Klezmer music. They were great and everyone applauded. But when I glanced at the musicians I suddenly felt as if a knife pierced my heart! Michal Kaplansky was the violinist! What a shock! Oh my G-d! Now he knew everything. I had to talk to him right away and swear him to secrecy! But the band struck up another fast number and I was swept up and pushed onto a chair that was hoisted up in the air by four strong men.

Then four other guys brought Chani in, also seated on a chair, and lifted high in the air. We were both danced around in the center of the room while everyone laughed and clapped to the music.

Finally they put us down and many of the guests came to congratulate us and wish us well. The party was winding down and the musicians were packing up. As soon as I could, I rushed over to them, but Kaplansky was gone. I asked where I could find him. Nobody knew for sure. Someone said, "He's a single guy, you know. He probably had a date." And they left, leaving me shaking as I remembered Kaplansky had also gone on a date with Leni Reifenstahl, and she was well connected to the Nazis… I had to find him.

Reb Saul and the Yeshiva guys came to get me. I tried to swallow my fear and put on a good face. This was my wedding day… my long-awaited wedding day. I smiled at everyone and hid my anxiety.

By midnight the festivities were over and Chani and I went to the Bridal Suite of the Europjeski Hotel. For the moment, all thoughts of

Kaplansky faded away.

As Chani left the room to get out of her wedding dress, I turned on some romantic music. An orchestra was playing and someone was singing... "You are the angel glow that lights a star, the dearest things I know are what you are. Someday my happy arms will hold you. And someday I'll know that moment divine, when all the things you are, are mine."

Then Chani came toward me and I was transported back to the beginning of time... back to the Garden of Eden and that first incredible moment when Adam first saw Eve.

CHAPTER 27 — BACK TO BERLIN

Weeks before our wedding, Chani told me about the old tradition of the Sheva Brochas (the seven blessings). This was an arrangement for us to be entertained by seven different relatives at their homes, in our case, in seven different cities and towns. In each place we'd be wined and dined and receive the blessings for newlyweds, which are: Mirth, Song, Delight, Love, Harmony, Peace and Companionship. It was thought that the presence of newly-wedded couples in your home brought special blessings to you and your family.

So, the morning after our wedding, my beautiful bride was all smiles and excitement as she explained our schedule. "First we're going to Uncle Moshe. He lives in Lodz. Then to Tante Rifka in Poznan, and after that we go to Uncle Dovid in Lublin…"

I hated to interrupt all this happy anticipation, but I had no choice.

I said, "No… no… we can't leave Warsaw now. We have a serious problem. Did you notice that Michal Kaplansky played with the band at our wedding? He left before I could speak to him and I must find him. He's aware of everything! He knows that I'm a convert and that we're married. We can't afford for him to tell that to anyone in Berlin. Do you realize how important this is? How can I find him? Do you know where he lives?"

She turned pale. Her lips trembled and I could see she was holding back tears, which only made me feel worse. She shook her head. Then she whispered, "My father hired the musicians. He might know."

I rushed to phone Reb Saul. He said, "Yeah, sure." And he gave me Kaplansky's address, adding, "He lives just two apartments past Bertha Kessler's place... on the second floor. Why? Is anything wrong?"

I didn't want to alarm him. I said, "No... no... I think everything will be fine. I'll talk to you later" and I hung up. Chani and I grabbed a taxi and got to Kaplansky's place as fast as we could. We raced up to the second floor and I rapped on the door. No one answered. I got a sinking feeling. Maybe he wasn't home. I banged on the door again... harder and louder. It opened.

There stood Kaplansky, still fully dressed, with one bloodshot eye opened and the other one closed. He was surprised to see us. "Ahh... what luck!" he said. "The bride and broom! Ha!" He swayed slightly as he stepped aside. "Come in, come in, come in, come in. Push all that stuff aside and have a seat."

The stuff was sheets of music and piles of dirty clothes. He looked at Chani. "The wedding was beautiful! You were gorgeous, as usual. But I was disappointed. I thought I'd see Fannie, but she wasn't there."

A tear rolled down Chani's cheek, but that didn't stop him. Kaplansky went on, "Do you hear from her? Is she happy in that wilderness? I wanted to go with her, but I'm a violinist. How would I make a living in that desert?"

He opened his other eye and looked at me. "Why have you come here? What do you want?"

I told him, "Chani and I are in mortal danger if you tell anyone in Berlin that she's not Heidi Mueller from Danzig, but a Jewish girl from Warsaw, and I'm her Jewish husband. I can't emphasize enough how serious our situation would be if that information got into the wrong hands."

Kaplansky stood up. He said, "Bah, you don't understand! I've known the Machinski family all my life. I would never put any of them in danger… ever! You can count on me!"

I knew he was sincere. There was nothing more I could say. I shook his hand and thanked him. But I made a mental note to keep a close watch on him, and we left.

I said to Chani, "Let's be optimistic about Kaplansky and get started for Lodz, Lublin, or wherever you want us to go." I hired a car and we made it to the first event before dinner.

Our hosts showered us with kindness, showed us around their town and introduced us to more kinfolk and community leaders. Of course I knew if I lived to be a hundred, I would never remember all those names. Even so, it was an unforgettable honeymoon.

Then summer was over in Warsaw. It was time to get back to

Berlin. I'd already said goodbye to everyone else. The last one was Bertha Kessler. I stopped by to pick up a few things I'd left with her.

With tears streaming down her wrinkled face she said, "Come and visit me again sometime. I'm always good for some potato soup and a few cookies."

"I know." I said with a smile, and waved goodbye to her as I made my way to the railway station. I caught the night train.

We soon pulled into the Anhalter Banhof (the Berlin train station). I'd written to Hugo asking him to meet me there and I was glad to see him standing next to my old black Mercedes. I tossed my bag on the back seat and slid behind the wheel. The engine purred nicely and I thanked him for taking such good care of the car over the summer.

"I hate to give it back," he said. As we arrived at his apartment, he added, "Let me know if you need me for anything."

I said, "I will," as I took off. I had mixed emotions about being back in Berlin... apprehension, excitement, anxiety... everything all at once. I pulled up to my apartment and looked around, just from force of habit. No one except Hugo and the Lowenthals knew I was here. I didn't see anything suspicious.

I got unpacked and peeked into the kitchen. I had to laugh. Mrs. Lowenthal had labeled every drawer and cupboard with M for meat and D for dairy. She left me a note advising that everything had been properly koshered, including the pots and pans. She'd even filled the refrigerator with kosher food.

I called the Lownenthals and told them how grateful I was for all their help. Then I said, "Because of our difficult situation, Chani and I will be together only during the week. Can she still spend the Sabbath with you just as she did before we were married?"

"Certainly," the Rabbi said. "But what about you?"

"Unfortunately, I can't be with you. You understand."

"Be careful," he answered.

After that I phoned Karl. He was surprised… amazed… that I was back in town. "Why didn't you let me know?" he said.

"Well… it's complicated. But I'll explain everything as soon as I see you. I'm on my way now!" I hung up, hopped in my car and headed for the theater.

As soon as I got there I met Karl and Gretchen. I told them everything that happened over the summer… my conversion… my marriage to Chani and how happy we were. They couldn't believe it. They were astonished! They wished us all the best.

I thanked them and continued. "We're apprehensive. Because of my father we're in a perilous position here in Berlin, so I'm asking for your help." I told them about my plan… I told them about Kaplansky and then I asked Gretchen if she would be willing to bring and take Chani as needed. "I know it will take a lot of your time, but you're the only one I can trust in this situation."

She answered with a big smile and a shrug. "It's no bother… it's no problem. I'm glad to help in any way I can." Then she turned serious. "But you know you're playing with fire. It's a dangerous game in today's Germany."

I nodded. "I know. And I want you both to know that at the first hint of danger, Chani and I will drop everything and leave Germany immediately." They understood. But they looked worried. I worried too.

Then Gretchen went to get us some coffee and pastry while Karl and I got down to business.

"I've been working on our repertory for the coming Season," Karl said. "In October we'll open with AIDA. It'll be a big production; in November we'll do RIGOLETTO; in December, for the Holiday Season, it's TOSCA. January is always a slow month. I thought we'd do LA BOHEME again. It's so popular… such a crowd-pleaser. In February CARMEN, March PAGLIACCI, April FIDELIO, and we'll end the Season with THE BARBER OF SEVILLE.

So, we have a lot of work to do. We have to start ordering sets and costumes. We'll need to arrange delivery dates and calculate costs. Please work on a budget for each production. Gretchen and I will arrange the rehearsal schedules and advise the cast, crew, and musicians."

It was a long day. By the time it ended I was exhausted, but I'd phoned Hermann Maas and I went to see him. I wanted to tell him all that happened and to thank him for connecting me with Rabbi Lowenthal who played such an important part in my Conversion, my marriage and in our lives here in Berlin.

When I got back to my apartment I made myself a little dinner and waited for Chani. I knew she wouldn't get here until the next morning, but tired as I was, I couldn't fall asleep without her.

The next day, after she arrived and I had her back in my arms again, everything went as planned. As soon as rehearsals started I checked up on Kaplansky. For the entire week he was always prompt and in his orchestra seat well before rehearsal began.

On Opening Night my father arrived with Cosima Wagner this time, along with several Brownshirts. I turned cold, as I always did, at the sight of my father. He said, "Well... well... I'm glad to see you're back. Why didn't you call me?"

"I'm sorry about that," I lied. "But I had a lot of business to take care of." And I turned my attention to Cosima. "Welcome. I hope you enjoy our production."

She looked at me coldly. "Why don't you ever present German Operas? My husband wrote many excellent ones."

I said, "I'm sure we'll schedule some in the future and I hope you'll attend to enjoy them."

My father added, "It's difficult for them to stage Wagner Opera. They have this slip of a girl... this soprano performing here... and it takes a big voice to sing Wagner!"

Then he looked at me. "Want to join us for a drink later?"

I shook my head. "You've asked me that before and I've told you, I have too much to do here."

"You never have time for me, do you?" he snarled. "But maybe that will change soon." Then all of them went to their seats, leaving me shaking and wondering what the hell he meant by that.

The following day I noticed I was being followed by that same silver Mercedes, but of course the driver wasn't Josef anymore. Now I didn't know who it was, and maybe it didn't matter. I knew I'd be followed an allowed for it. I felt confident my plan was working. Things were running smoothly. Then in November, when we started rehearsals for RIGOLETTO, Chani began to feel sick. She had stomach pains that persisted. I asked Gretchen to take her to a suitable doctor and we soon got the good news. Chani was pregnant!

Bubbling with excitement, she said, "The doctor told me we'll have our baby in May! Isn't that perfect? That's when the Opera Season ends." Then she got pensive. "Do you think I'll be able to sing when I'm out to there?"

I said, "Who knows? Maybe you'll be able to sing Wagner! And I chuckled.

"What's so funny?"

I just shrugged. Some things can't be explained.

The next morning the door was open as I was shaving and Chani popped her head in. "Listen, we can wait until our baby is a few months old and then the three of us can go to Jerusalem. That way Fannie will get to see our new addition to the family."

"Okay," I said. And she disappeared. A few minutes later she was back, this time with a serious face.

She said, "I have a question. Do you care if it's a boy or a girl?"

"No... we don't have any, so what difference does it make?"

She smiled. "That's right!" she exclaimed. "If we have a girl now, later we can have a boy, then another girl, and another boy...

"Wait a minute... wait a minute! How many babies do you think we're going to have?"

"Well... I don't know," she answered with a smirk. "How many can you make?"

"How many can I... ouch!" I nicked my chin. "Lots!" I said as I wiped off the speck of blood and the lather. "I can make lots of babies!"

"Then that's how many we'll have," she announced. "And it's so wonderful!" She ran a delicate finger around my ear. "Just think, you and me and HA SHEM (G-d) are creating a new person... a brand new human being... that'll just be ours!" She whispered, "I love you." I kissed her, held her tight and moved her towards the bedroom.

"No... no... we can't make love now! We'll be late for rehearsals and Karl will be mad!"

"Listen, I'm a partner. We can be late sometimes."

Of course when I got to the theater, smoke was coming out of Karl's ears. "Where the hell have you been?" he screamed, as he slammed into my office. "And where is Chani? The orchestra is sitting there waiting for her!" I didn't answer. I just smiled.

He closed one eye and squinted at me with the other. He folded his arms across his chest and leaned against the door jamb. "So tell me," he said, "what'd you have for breakfast this morning?"

I laughed and told him. "Sometimes that's how it is with newlyweds."

Then Chani showed up. She threw a fearful glance at Karl. "I'm so sorry," she murmured as she dashed on stage to start rehearsal.

December blew into Berlin with gale winds and heavy snow. So we didn't expect much of a crowd for TOSCA. But Opening Night my father showed up as usual. This time he brought Julius Streicher as his guest. The minute I saw him I clenched my fists and every muscle in my body tensed. As the editor of the weekly newspaper, DER SHTURMER (The Attacker), Streicher filled his paper with ugly caricatures of vile-looking Jewish men seducing young, beautiful blonde German girls. He printed endless, hideous lies about the Jewish people. And now I was supposed to be civil to this anti-Semitic son-of-a-bitch!

Suddenly I remembered an old joke about an elderly Jewish man walking on the street. The man saw that he would have to pass a big, burly Nazi swinging a club. As the two passed, the Nazi yelled, "Shvinehund!" The old Jew tipped his hat and said, "Weisburg" and kept on going.

Well… that was me now. So I smiled at the bastard and said, "Enjoy the performance and give us a good review, won't you?"

As I hurried to the back of the theater, my father yelled, "I want to talk to you after the show, Erich."

I joined Karl just as the curtain went up. "Did you hear what my father said?" He nodded. "Can you stick around when I talk to him?"

He said, "Sure."

When the applause and bravos died down, my father came to find me. Streicher waited for him at the door. "Great production," my father said. "You have a talented group here. But I want to talk to you about the Holidays. You'll get an invitation, of course, but I wanted you to know I'm having my usual Christmas Dinner and fundraiser for the Nazi Party on Sunday night, the 20th. Come around seven o'clock. And don't be late this time. You know there's an election coming up in the spring. I'm raising money for the campaign. We think Hindenburg is going to run for re-election, even if he is old and sick. Hitler hasn't committed yet. He knows he can't win against Hindenburg, but there's always the possibility that he could gain. He'll speak to that issue at the dinner.

Then on Christmas Eve we'll have our usual dinner together and gift exchange. Come around six o'clock. We'll have a few drinks first."

My mouth went dry. I'd been so happy in my new life, I'd almost forgotten about the old one. I was stammering as I told him, "I'm... I'm sorry. I've made other plans for the Holidays. We have the last performance of Tosca on the 20th. And after that I'm going skiing with Karl and his wife." Karl played along. He nodded.

My father's face turned red. His eyes narrowed to black slits. "What do you mean?" he growled. "That's been our tradition for years. Christmas is family time and I'm your family!"

I said, "But everything's changed now. I used to visit you twice a year at school breaks or a pause in my travel. Now I live here... work here... see you often. No... I've been working hard and I'm taking a little vacation. I'll be back after the first of the year."

He was spitting now... and furious! "It's not right!" he shouted. And he left, leaving me shaking.

Gretchen took Chani to the Lowenthals' for the weekend first. Then the three of us, Karl, Gretchen and I, headed for the Swiss border. We didn't stay long. We had to get back to start rehearsals for

LA BOHEME.

January in Berlin was mid-winter... cold, snowy, and dark. Still, LA BOHEME was a good choice for us because Chani's role as Mimi had her dressed mostly in rags which easily hid her condition. All went well until Opening Night. Suddenly we had a grim problem. Kaplansky didn't show up!

Karl was in a lather. We were fifteen minutes until Curtain and no violinist. He called all the Jewish agencies to get a substitute in a hurry. They were best because they had the most unemployed musicians.

I was horrified. I asked when Kaplansky was last seen. No one knew. I was beginning to feel sick. Then Karl got off the phone. He told me a substitute violinist was on the way. He was relieved. I wasn't. I told him, "As soon as the performance is over, Chani and I are leaving Germany!"

He said, "What do you mean? It may be nothing. Kaplansky could just be drunk somewhere."

"I can't take a chance. He knows that Chani and I are married. He knows everything and now he's missing. You'll have to use the Understudy for the rest of the Season. Chani and I are going back to the apartment, packing everything into the car and heading back to Warsaw tonight!"

The violinist arrived and took Kaplansky's seat. The orchestra played the Overture and the curtain went up. The first Act began. I calmed down and joined Karl at the back of the theater. Everything seemed to be alright. Then Chani made her appearance. Rudolfo introduced himself to her in a beautiful aria, "I'm a poet! What's my employment? Writing! Is that a living? Hardly! I've wit... tho wealth be wanting; ladies of rank and fashion... all inspire me with passion. In dreams and fond illusions, or castles in the air... richer is none on earth than I!"

Then Chani began her aria, "They call me Mimi, I don't know why. My name is Lucia. Then she turned toward the audience and sang, "My story is a short one... fine satin and silk I embroider..." A shot rang out! She fell to the floor. Karl and I ran forward, but we couldn't get to her. The crowd was screaming and scattering in all directions... coming right towards us. I had to push them aside until I could get close enough to leap on stage. She lay in a pool of blood. I knelt next to her. Her eyes were open. I yelled her name. "Chani! Chani!" I shook her. I tried to lift her up... there was no response. She was dead!

CHAPTER 28 – DEATH

"No!... no!... no! You can't be dead! Wake up!... Wake up!" Tears ran down my face. I knew she would never wake up again. I screamed, "Who did this? Who did this to you? I'll kill him!"

Karl grabbed me. "Erich, the police are here. They want to talk to you." I looked at the policeman. He said, "Did she have any enemies that you know of?"

I couldn't speak. I didn't know what they were talking about. My mind was black with rage. "Where's Kaplansky?" I shouted. No one answered.

An ambulance came. They were taking my Chani away. "Stop!" I yelled. "Where are you taking her?"

One of them answered, "To the nearest hospital."

I told him, "I'm coming with you."

There at the hospital my beloved Chani was officially pronounced dead. I was sweating and shivering. The hospital people asked me where to take her. I didn't understand what they were talking about. "What cemetery?" they insisted.

I whispered, The Weissenssee Jewish Cemetery." They covered
her up with a sheet before they placed her back in the ambulance. I
climbed in back with her and turned down the sheet so I could look
at her. As the ambulance made its way to the funeral home, I held her
cold, tiny hand and murmured, "I have to tell your father what
happened to you. I have to confess that I failed. My plan failed.
That's why we lost you."

By the time we got to the funeral home it was the middle of the
night. The women in charge of such tasks told me they were going to
wash Chani's body, wrap her in a shroud and place her in a plain pine
casket. Then they would bring her back to this room. But someone
must always be with her until burial. I told them I would stay with
her. I asked, "Do you have a telephone I could use?"

I was directed to a nearby office, but advised that only local calls
could be made. I wiped my face with my sleeve and stared at the
phone. I knew that bad news can never wait until morning. My hands
were trembling as I called Rabbi Lowenthal.

Between sobs I told him all that had happened. I could hear him
gasp as he repeated, "She's dead? Chani has been killed?" He began
mumbling in Hebrew and in Yiddish, and moaning. Finally I asked
him to phone Reb Saul and tell him the tragic news.

I stammered, I'm at the Weissensee Cemetery now. I plan to stay
here until the early morning when I'll be bringing Chani back to
Warsaw on the six o'clock train. We should arrive by four o'clock
tomorrow afternoon. Please ask Reb Saul to make all the necessary
arrangements."

Rabbi Lowenthal said, "I'm going with you. I'll meet you at the train station." There was a long pause. Then he choked up as he said, "I don't know how I'm going to tell Reb Saul what happened to his beautiful Chani. I'm overwhelmed with grief myself." And he hung up.

The burial society women wheeled the coffin back into the anteroom and left. Chani and I were alone together. Her eyes were closed now. Her long dark eyelashes rested on sallow cheeks. I stared at that lovely face. I wanted to believe she was only asleep, yet I knew her long black silken hair would never again catch a gleam of sunlight.

I closed my eyes as I remembered those hot summer days in Warsaw when we walked through the cool woods down to the shimmering river. I recalled every word she said to me there. I whispered, "Chani, don't leave me here. Take me with you!"

Only silence echoed off the yellow brick walls. Suddenly the door flew open with a bang! I jumped! Karl and Gretchen barged in, along with an icy blast of air.

"Oh my god," Gretchen cried. "We've been looking for you for hours. We searched everywhere... looked in every bar and saloon we could think of..."

Karl said, "It's three o'clock in the morning. What are you doing here?"

"I want to be with my wife as long as possible. I'm taking her back to Warsaw on the morning train." Tears burned my eyes. "I'm going to take her home. I have to give her back to her father."

Gretchen got tears in her eyes too. She gave me a hug. "Karl and I will stay with you until it's time for you to go. "We all stood there together looking at Chani for the last time.

Karl said, "We can't be there for the funeral. We'll drive to Warsaw during the week of mourning. I can't leave now. The police investigation requires that I give them a report."

I glanced at Karl and asked, "The same kind of investigation they had for Dr. Liebman?"

"No... not this time. There were a number of witnesses and the man's been arrested."

"Arrested!" I shouted. Who'd they get? One of my father's Brownshirts? Did anyone ever find Kaplansky?"

Karl seemed uneasy. His eyes were downcast. He shuffled his feet. Finally he looked at me. "The man who pulled the trigger was identified as Otto Von Bruener. He's now in jail awaiting trial for Capital Murder."

I stared at Karl in shocked silence. I shook my head. "No... no... it's not possible, Karl. Why would he stand up in the middle of a crowded theater and commit this murder, knowing there were many witnesses? It's insane!"

A loud bell rang out! We were all startled. The funeral people rushed in and opened the door for the hearse driver who swept inside with a gust of freezing air. "It's time to go," he said. They started to close the coffin.

I shouted, "Wait! Wait! Not yet." I kissed Chani's forehead one more time and murmered, "Goodbye, beloved." They closed the coffin and hoisted it inside the hearse.

It was late afternoon when the train arrived in Warsaw. Dark storm clouds filled the sky as the casket was transferred to a waiting hearse. Reb Saul met me at the station with a red, tear-stained face. He was trembling as he told me, "We're going to the Okopowa Street Jewish Cemetery. That's where we'll bury my beautiful daughter... next to her mother."

Okopowa Street Jewish Cemetery

My eyes filled with tears as I hugged him and whispered, "It all happened so fast. I'm sorry... sorry for your loss and mine."

When we got to the Jewish Cemetery the big black iron gates were open and a huge crowd of people was already assembled.

A blanket of grief covered every mourner as they lowered young, beautiful Chani Machinski into the frozen ground and recited the Kaddish... that ancient, defiant prayer that declares no matter what savage events unfold in this world, we still believe in Ha Shem, our nameless God, now and forever.

All the traditions of mourning were observed and endless numbers of people snaked up the three flights of stairs to the Machinski apartment. They offered sympathy to Reb Saul and the family. By now everyone knew what happened to Chani in Berlin. Some tried to hide their feelings, but I felt many piercing looks… as if to say, if she hadn't married you, she'd still be alive.

That was true! But she wanted to marry me. She wanted to sing for the Berlin Opera Company. Nevertheless, it was brutally painful.

Reb Saul saw how tortured I was. He told me, "Don't blame yourself. It's my fault. I knew it was wrong for her to sing in public, but I couldn't stop her. It was what she wanted.

Then Bubbe came and said, "No. It was my fault. I'm the one who took her to the audition. Tears rolled down her face. "I did it to save MY daughter. And I failed. Look what's happened."

I thought, why are we at fault? How is it nobody curses the Nazis and the anti-Semites like my father? Why isn't it their fault!

CHAPTER 29 — THE TRIAL

When the seven days of the Shiva (mourning period) were over, Reb Saul handed me a package. He whispered, "Don't open it for at least thirty days. I wondered what might be in it, but I didn't ask any questions. To me, Reb Saul always tried to do what was right. I said goodbye to him and the family. Then I headed back to Berlin. My father's trial was scheduled to start.

As soon as I got to my apartment I received a notice to appear in Court as a witness for the Defense! Now what the hell was this? I called Karl. He told me he was also called as a witness for the Defense.

The trial opened for the District of Berlin in a spacious room of the Court House. There were the Presiding Senior Judge and two Associated Judges at the head of the room. To the right was the Gallery, now crowded with journalists from newspapers throughout Europe. The case was so sensational. I heard different languages spoken, English, French, Spanish, Italian, Polish, and others. As many people as possible were jammed in with them. I caught sight of

Hermann Maas and other friends who had managed to squeeze in, Martin Neimoller, Frau Reinhardt, and even Hugo.

Directly across from the Gallery were the witness box and a dais for testimony. Karl and I found ourselves seated in the witness box with five others, two women and three men.

At the back of the courtroom was the highly guarded door to the jail. In front of that prison door were two large tables separated from each other. One was for the Prosecutor and the other for the Defense. My father was seated at the Defendant's table with two advisors. Both were in SS uniforms.

All of this was strange to me. I was accustomed to English Law and a trial by a jury of one's peers, but this was Germany.

The Senior Judge called the Court to order and read the charge. "Otto Von Bruener of Berlin, you are charged with the murder of Heidi Mueller of Danzig, on Sunday, January 10th, 1932 in Berlin. Herr Von Bruener, please stand. Are you guilty or innocent of the charge against you?"

My father answered, "Innocent." Karl and I looked at each other in disbelief. The Senior Judge then said, "Prosecutor, you may begin."

The Prosecutor said, "If it please the Court, I will bring five eyewitnesses to the stand to testify about what they saw on January 10th, 1932 at the Berlin Opera." He then produced the witnesses, each of whom testified under oath that when Heidi Mueller appeared on stage, they saw Otto Von Bruener stand up and shoot her. The Prosecutor said he could provide more witnesses if the court deemed it necessary, then rested his case.

The Judge then called on the Defense. My father stood up. "I will defend myself," he told the Court. "I call as witness, Karl Klempner." On the stand, under oath, the testimony went as follows:

"Is your name Karl Klempner?"... "Yes."

"Are you a partner in the Berlin Opera Company?"... "Yes."

"Did you hire Heidi Mueller as your soprano?"... "Yes."

"Is Heidi Mueller from Danzig her real name and origin?"... "No."

"What is her real name and origin?"... "Chani Machinski. She was from Warsaw."

Was her name changed legally?"... "No. It was a stage name."

"Did you give her that name?"... "Yes."

"Why?"... "Well... we wanted to give her an easy name to remember."

"Aside from that, isn't it true she was a Jew and you wanted to deceive your German audience?"...

"We wanted her to be accepted for her talent and to protect her from the anti-Jewish, anti-Polish sentiment that exists here."

"Thank you. That's all."

"I now call to the stand Erich Von Bruener." There was a buzz from the gallery.

"State your name and place of birth."... "Erich Von Bruener, Berlin, Germany."

"Are you a partner in the Berlin Opera Company?"... "Yes."

"Were you baptized a Catholic and did you attend church as a boy with your parents?"... "Yes."

"You went to live in England with your Uncle. Did you attend church there?"... "Yes."

"Are you now a Christian?"... "No."

"Are you a Jew?"... "Yes." (more buzz from the gallery)

"Did you marry Chani Machinski, alias Heidi Mueller?"... "Yes." (more buzz)

"Thank you. That's all."

My father said, "If it please the Court, I'd like to sum up the case for the defense." With no objections, he continued, "I did not murder Heidi Mueller from Danzig because she didn't exist. I didn't even kill a person. Chani Machinski was a Jew from Warsaw. She only looked like a person. But she was a demon that emerged from the Polish slime... a black witch bent on evil..."

I leaped out of the witness box and grabbed him by the throat. I squeezed as hard as I could until I was struck on the back of my head.

I woke up on the floor of a jail cell with a pounding pain and blood dripping from my head. I heard voices. I couldn't make out what was being said. I looked around slowly. There was no one there. Then I realized the voices were coming from another jail cell. I heard a man say, "Otto! Why are you so crazy? If you wanted that Jew out of the way, all you had to do was tell us. We know how to make people disappear so not even a bone is found... to kill a young woman like that, in the middle of a theater full of people... all those eyewitnesses! Of course you don't have to worry. We've fixed everything up with the Judges. But it's bad for the Party... bad publicity. And we have an election coming up soon."

I heard my father say, "Don't worry. You'll see what I have to say will be good for the Party. But I need time to tell everything in Court without being attacked."

The man answered, "They had to adjourn for the day. But we'll be back in Court tomorrow and your son will be shackled and gagged for the proceedings. I'll make sure of that. But, Otto, he doesn't have to be in Court. He can be kept here."

"No... I want him to hear what I have to say."

The following morning several guards came to get me. They strapped me to a chair on wheels, taped my mouth shut, and made sure I couldn't move, not even slightly. As they hauled me into the courtroom, I saw that the Gallery was packed again. But I couldn't make out any faces in the crowd.

The Senior Judge called on the Defense to conclude arguments. My father stood up and spoke to the Gallery as well as the Judges. "You have to understand that the Von Brueners have defended our Fatherland for generations. My two younger brothers were killed in the Great War in defense of our country. They were unmarried and had no children. I had only one child, my son Erich." And he pointed at me. "He's the last of the Von Brueners." Here he paused and faced the Judges. "As a partner in the Berlin Opera Company, my son came in contact with the soprano Chani Machinski, the Jew from Poland.

It's important that you understand the nature of the Jew. They are like mushrooms that grow wild in the forest, except that they are the poisonous, deadly kind. This young woman poisoned and bewitched my son."

Now he was shouting. "She got him to abandon his Christianity and convert to Judaism so she could marry him and mix his pure Aryan blood with hers! That way… her child, a Von Bruener, would be born a Jew! I say NO! NEVER!" Then he screamed for all to hear. "What I did was for the sake of Germany… for our Race, our Nation, and our Faith! I ask to be exonerated of all charges!"

There was a burst of applause and cheers from the Gallery. It was an outrage! A beautiful young woman and her child had been murdered and this was the reaction? I couldn't believe it. Then I thought, the Nazis had probably packed the gallery with their followers.

In the end the Judges found a way to exonerate Otto Von Bruener. They charged me with contempt of Court and disorderly conduct. I was returned to my jail cell, still shackled and gagged. I could hardly breathe. I couldn't move at all. But I was filled with rage thinking of ways I might get revenge, and knowing it couldn't happen in Germany.

Eventually Karl showed up, accompanied by a prison guard, and I was set free. I didn't say anything. As soon as we were in the car on the way to my apartment, Karl told me, "Reverend Maas spoke to the Judge about your case and persuaded them to let you go. Otherwise you'd still be in jail and they might have thrown away the key, seeing how they feel about Jews."

My head ached badly. My lips started bleeding when they ripped off the tape and they were still sore. But I was desperate. "Please thank Reverend Maas for me, because I won't have time to thank him myself. I have to get out of here. As soon as I pack up a few things, I'm leaving Germany."

Karl pulled up to my apartment. I glanced at him, the guy who always managed to save me, and groped for words. It was time to say goodbye. I told him, "I'm never coming back. But you and I will always be partners. Now I can only be a silent one. But you're more than a friend and partner... to me you're the brother I never had. I'll keep in touch. Say goodbye to Gretchen for me. And thanks for everything."

Karl said, "Cut out the flowery speeches. We have problems. A silver Mercedes followed us and it just pulled up."

CHAPTER 30 — ESCAPE

I turned to look and saw two heavyset Brownshirts approaching, each swinging a club. I felt that old familiar stab of fear in the pit of my stomach as one of them positioned himself on Karl's side of the car and the other came to my side and opened the door.

"Your father wants to see you," he said. "Come with us."

I gritted my teeth. I wasn't going anywhere with these bastards. The old fear gave way to blind anger. I stalled... trying to formulate some kind of plan. I had to find a way to separate these two thugs. I needed my weapons.

He pulled me out of the car. I stammered, "I... I... I... I can't walk very well. I was shackled for two days, you know." I concentrated on looking helpless and pathetic. "I need my cane and it's in my apartment. And I'd like to pack up a few things to take a long, if you wouldn't mind. Will you help me get my stuff?" I teetered a little and clung to the car door for support.

I was unwashed and unshaven. Dried blood matted my hair and my lips were still bleeding. His eyes narrowed. He frowned and looked me up and down. He wasn't sure what to think. But I guess I didn't look like much of a threat. He nodded.

I leaned on him heavily as I lurched up the steps. Once inside the apartment, I pretended to rummage around in the front closet, although I already had my hands on the cane.

"It's dark in here," I said. "I can't see. Would you turn on the light, please? It's over there, behind you." I pressed the mechanism on the cane, releasing the blade at the bottom. When he turned back to face me, I slashed him across the throat. He looked shocked! Blood spurted all over. He made a gurgling sound and crashed to the floor.

I listened to hear if there was any reaction to the noise. The apartment next to mine was empty, but above there were other tenants. I didn't hear anything. It was eleven o'clock in the morning and most people were at work or out looking for work. I took off my blood-spattered clothes and got washed up before putting on clean ones. I stepped carefully around his body to reach my desk drawer. I slipped the Derringer into my coat pocket.

Now I put the second part of my plan together. I wanted the other Brownshirt to open the trunk of his car and lean inside it. So I got out a small suitcase and put a few books inside. One of them was my unread autographed copy of MEIN KAMPF.

I left the apartment, pretending to limp badly, leaning on my cane as I approached the Brownshirt guarding Karl. I told him, "I have a few books I want to take along. Will you put them in the trunk of your car? The other guy is bringing my larger, heavier suitcase."

This Brownshirt also seemed suspicious. "Open it up" he snapped. When he saw there were only books inside, he went over and opened the trunk of the silver Mercedes. As I followed him, out of the corner of my eye I saw Karl quietly get out of the car.

I said, "Put it in the back of the trunk so the other suitcase will fit in the front." When he leaned into the trunk I took out the Derringer, pressed it against the back of his head and pulled the trigger. It only took a few seconds. He didn't make a sound, but the gun did. I looked around to see if anyone heard the shot. Luckily no one was nearby except Karl, who quickly came to help me shove the guy inside the trunk. I slammed the lid shut and told Karl, "I killed the other guy too. It won't be long before they're missed and the Nazis come looking for us. I'm getting out of here and if I were you, I'd grab Gretchen and head for Switzerland. You're still a citizen there, aren't you? But in case they get to you, tell them whatever they want to know. Don't worry about me! Goodbye, for now."

I ran back to my apartment. I had to get my papers, passport, car keys, bank books, and whatever cash I had around. I packed up some necessaries, my short wave radio, some clothes, shaving stuff. I started opening drawers. I found my moustache and beard disguise and took that, just in case. I made room for the package that Reb Saul had given me, still unopened. Then I spotted the box of family pictures that was Chani's prized possession. I couldn't leave that in Berlin. I squeezed that in too. I opened another drawer and ran my fingers over one of Chani's silk nightgowns. Inside the bedroom closet I saw her clothes... her shoes... still waiting for her. I glanced, just for a moment, at her side of the bed. I swallowed hard. I couldn't think about that now. I whispered, "Goodbye." Then I snapped the suitcase shut and locked the apartment door on my way out. When I reached my car, I tossed the cane and suitcase in the back seat, slid behind the wheel and headed for the British Embassy.

It was snowing heavily now and I was glad because it would hinder identification of my car. Even so, I parked behind the Embassy building, so the car wouldn't be seen from the street.

Several guards were stationed at the back entrance. They became alert as I approached them with cane and suitcase in hand. I spoke to them in English and told them I was a British citizen. I asked to speak to Ambassador Rumbold immediately. "This is an emergency," I told them.

"What name shall I give?" they asked.

I didn't want them to know my name, in case they were questioned later. "Just say a friend of Tony Ambrose." I knew the Ambassador and my uncle had been classmates at Oxford and still remained friends.

One of the guards rang the Ambassador's office on the intercom and told him, "There's a gentleman here, says he's a British citizen and insists on seeing you, won't give his name. Says he's a friend of Tony Ambrose and his business with you is urgent. What shall I tell him, sir?"

"I'll be right there."

Ambassador Horace Rumbold of England

When the Ambassador showed up, I saw a man in his late fifties… early sixties with graying hair and a moustache to match. He was of medium build and dignified-looking in a dark blue suit. As soon as he saw me, he told the guards it was all right and motioned for me to follow him. Once inside his office I introduced myself. "I'm Erich Von Bruener."

He said, "I know who you are. I was at the Opera when your wife was killed. I heard the details of your father's trial… sorry about all of it… terrible tragedy. Have a seat and tell me how I can help you."

"I must leave Germany immediately. I need to get back to England."

He nodded. "I see. Well… I don't know what kind of trouble you're in. And I don't have to know. At this time of the year there are no cruise ships coming to either Hamburg or Bremen. There are only freighters and cargo ships. But they also take on some passengers. They bring trade from England and then return, though not always directly. I'll have my secretary check on what is available. Meanwhile, I can issue special travel papers for you. But it would be best, under these circumstances, if you used another name."

"Yes… yes… let me write it down for you."

The secretary soon buzzed. "There's a British freighter in Hamburg called the Tilbury leaves for Liverpool first thing in the morning. They take on up to ten passengers."

The Ambassador looked at me. I nodded. Then he asked the secretary to purchase passage in the name of… and here he read, "Daniel Benavrum." And he spelled it for her. "Have them charge it to the Embassy."

He mentioned that Hamburg was quite a distance from Berlin. "You'd best get there in an Embassy Staff Car. We have a good driver, Tom McGinty. He'll get you to the ship, but you must get started at once."

"Thank you so much, Sir Horace. I'm overwhelmed by your kindness to me."

He smiled. "I'll have those transport papers ready for you in a few minutes."

While he worked on that, I put my car keys on his desk and went into my suitcase for the Title to my Mercedes. I told him the car was parked behind the building. "I won't be needing it anymore. So I'll turn ownership over to the Embassy."

He thanked me and said, "Behind the building, you say? We'd better get your care inside our garage. The authorities may be looking for it." He got on the phone to Tom McGinty and called him into his office.

As soon as Tom showed up, he gave him those instructions, along with the car keys. Then Miss Collins, the secretary, buzzed and announced that my ticket would be waiting for me at the dock. Everything was in order now. I shook hands with Ambassador Rumbold and thanked him again. He gave me an envelope. "Give this to the ship's Captain as soon as you're onboard.

Miss Collins buzzed again and in a strained voice said, "Sir Horace, there are two men at the front gate to see you. They're from the SS and they said it's very important."

I panicked when I heard that. The Ambassador raised an eyebrow and looked at me. Then he calmly replied, "Have them come in and ask them to take a seat, Miss Collins. I'll be with them shortly." He hung up and said, "Get started!"

Tom and I ran down the back stairs. I climbed into the Embassy Staff Car with my cane and suitcase while he pulled my Mercedes into the Embassy garage. Then he slid into the driver's seat and we took off for Hamburg. Meanwhile I wondered how the ambassador would take the news that I'd killed two Brownshirts. Would the Nazis be able to question Miss Collins and the guards? Or can the Ambassador prevent any questioning of his staff? I was filled with fear.

It was dark outside now and still snowing. We were speeding

along when Tom began to slow down. There was a line of cars ahead that had stopped.

"What's the matter?" I asked. "An accident?"

"No… it looks like the police are searching for someone. But it shouldn't be a problem. Usually they let an Embassy car go right through."

I thought, Maybe… maybe not. I watched as the police flashed lights into each car. They were looking for me and evidently they had a good description or a photo to guide them. I opened my suitcase and took out that old disguise. I put it on, along with the eyeglasses. I was sorry I didn't have a hat too. I fingered the Derringer in my pocket with one hand and clutched the cane with the other. If I was arrested, I wasn't going quietly.

CHAPTER 31 — THE JOURNEY

I held my breath as the police flashed their lights into our car. Then I endured a few moments of scrutiny. I started breathing again when they waved us through. I wondered if we'd be stopped again, so I waited a few hours before I took off my disguise and slipped it back into my suitcase.

As we drove through the dark, blustery winter night toward the Hamburg docks, much as I wanted to stay alert and awake, the ride was so smooth and the car so warm and dark, I soon fell into an exhausted sleep.

Tom woke me when we arrived. I glanced at my watch. It was ten o'clock and he was in a hurry. It was a long drive back to the Embassy. I thanked him quickly and gave him a generous tip. Then I picked up my ticket and got onboard the ship.

The first thing I did was go to see the Captain. I introduced myself as Daniel Benavrum and gave him the envelope from Ambassador Rumbold.

"I'm Captain Fleming," he said as we shook hands. "Have a seat while I read this." It didn't take him long. He asked for my ticket and transport papers. "Everything seems to be in order" he told me. "The Ambassador says you're a British citizen and asks that I get you safely to Liverpool. That right?"

I nodded, but began to feel uneasy. The Captain, fortyish with graying dark hair, leaned back in his chair and eyed me coldly. "Something isn't right here," he said. "This ship is scheduled to leave here at first light tomorrow. The Port Authority has already inspected us. But now I'm told the police, along with the SS, insist on searching every ship before it leaves this port." He leaned forward. "They're looking for someone. Did you get yourself in a bit of a fix? Is it you they're looking for?"

My heart raced. I could feel it pounding in my chest. I said, "Yes! They killed my wife and baby. Then they sent a couple of Brownshirts to get me. I killed them both!"

His pale eyes widened. He looked at me differently now. Did I see a shadow of a smile? He said, "It takes a long time to search a ship. There are so many places a man could hide. And I understand the SS are quite efficient and effective. But we know a trick or two ourselves. It won't be comfortable and you may have to be hidden for a long time, but we can hide you where they won't find you. Meanwhile, I suggest you go to the Mess Hall and get something to eat while there's still time. I have lookouts to warn us when they get close."

I gladly took his advice. I was starving and it wasn't hard to find the Mess Hall. They were baking bread. I just had to follow my nose.

The ship's cook, a short, stout middle-aged man, took one look at me and handed me a cup of hot black coffee. "Cream and sugar?"

"No... thanks. But how about a little whiskey? Got some you can spare?"

"Hah! A man after me own 'eart! Sure thing!" And he poured some into my cup. I took a few sips and it warmed me down to my shoes.

"Me name's Charlie. What's up, mate? It's late and you're looking bad!"

I smiled. "I usually look a lot better. I'm just hungry, that's all. Can you fix me some eggs fast? I don't have a lot of time."

"Comin' right up," he said. But what's the rush? You're the only passenger on this trip, which is amazing... nobody gets on a freighter in the dead of winter!" And he soon put a big plate of scrambled eggs in front of me, along with some of that fresh bread... right out of the oven.

"I need to get to England," I told him. "When will we get to Liverpool?"

"Ohhh... not for a while. We'll be stopping in Antwerp first and Rotterdam next, before we get to Liverpool." He handed me another cup of hot coffee. But before I could drink it, Captain Fleming showed up.

"They'll get around to us soon. Come with me. I'll show you where to hide. Stay there until we give you the all-clear. And Charlie... we don't have any passengers... in case you're asked. Tell that to the rest of the crew."

I took my cane and suitcase with me as I followed him below deck. There, I was lowered into their fresh water tank. It wasn't yet completely filled. I found myself in ice-cold water up to my waist. I leaned against the steel wall of the tank, still clutching my suitcase and cane to keep them from getting wet. It was black in there and I was shaking from the cold water. I couldn't see anything. But I could hear the crew piling up boxes of provisions to make the water tank less accessible.

It wasn't long before I heard the clomp of heavy boots and heard the German Police demanding to see every inch of the ship. It wasn't just the cold water. I was frozen with fear. What if they find me? I heard them questioning the crew, promising a substantial reward for any information leading to the arrest of Erich Von Bruener who'd already killed two mean and was armed and dangerous.

I closed my eyes and listened in terrified silence to hear if anyone would speak up. No one said a word. Then I heard dogs barking. Oh my god, I thought. They brought dogs onboard to find me. Images of Sonja, screaming as she was devoured by dogs, stuck in my brain. I started shaking.

I heard the Police ask the crew to remove the boxes from around the water tank. They wanted to see if there was water inside. I became paralyzed with fear. They let out some of the water. Inside the tank the water level dropped down to my knees. I bit my lips. Then I heard them tramp up to the deck with the dogs still barking. Apparently they were satisfied. I started to breathe again. But there was no all-clear. I didn't move. My whole body ached. I stayed that way, knee-deep in icy water, for what seemed like hours. Finally some crewmen gave me the all-clear and hauled me up and over the edge of the tank.

Dripping wet, I made my way up to the deck. A high wind was blowing sleet against me as I sloshed my way behind one of the crew, who took me to my cabin. Once inside, I stripped off my wet clothes and shoes, dried myself as best I could, and dived under the heavy covers on the bed. Somehow I just couldn't get warm. I tossed and turned until I was a cocoon of heavy blankets... still I shivered and shook. My throat closed. I could hardly swallow. Exhausted as I was, I couldn't fall asleep. Ghostly images floated in my mind... Dr. Liebman smiled at me and asked, "Are you alright? Are you alright?" Then I saw frightened, trembling Sonja, before she knew her fate. Josef floated by. He was telling me something, but no words came out. Chani, in her long pink Shabbos dress, came and kissed me. I asked, "Are you taking me with you now?" She smiled. "No... you have lots of things to do." I said, "What things? Tell me what things I have to do?" But she faded away.

I felt the ship begin to move. I wrestled myself out of the covers and looked out the porthole. It was 'tomorrow at first light' and we were gliding slowly out of the harbor on the gray water of the North Sea. I fell back on my bed. Thank god! Thank god! We were leaving Germany.

CHAPTER 32 — ENGLAND

I couldn't sleep. I was too cold. I tossed and turned. My aching head was filled with Brownshirts, Police, Nazis chasing me, and I was running and hiding. I can't let them get me… Then suddenly I went from cold to hot. I began to perspire. I have to get away from them! I can't let them find me!

I heard voices. I opened my eyes a little. Everything was blurry. One guy said, "It's influenza." The other one said, "I think it's pneumonia." After that I fell into a dreamless sleep.

I don't know how long I slept, but I woke up hot and dry. I moaned… "Water!" And then some guy hauled me up and began to wrap my chest in some foul-smelling greasy cloths. I said, "No… What the hell's happening? Leave me alone… Leave me alone… What are you doing?" I was dizzy and unfocused.

One of them said, "Drink this. You'll feel better." And he gave me a horrible drink of scalded milk with butter in it! Aaargh! Finally they let me lie down, covered me up and put cold compresses on my forehead, on my eyes, on my parched lips, and on my throat. That

251

felt good. I lapsed back into sleep.

When I woke up there were still two crewmen sitting there. I didn't know if they were the same ones, but they were watching me. One sailor said, "Hey... look! He's awake." And they grabbed me and pulled me out of bed.

"Wait! Who are you? What are you doing?" They didn't answer. They just unwound all the smelly cloths from my chest and one of them pulled me into the bathroom and scrubbed me up from head to toe. He shaved my itchy, stubble of a beard while I saw the other guy strip the bed and put clean linens on it.

I was so weak and groggy. My legs were shaking. I could hardly stand. But they managed to get me into some warm pajamas and propped me up on a chair. "Drink this," one of them said. "You'll feel better."

"Feel better than what? Better than dead? No... I'm not drinking any more of that shit!"

"It's just hot tea," he said. "Take a sip. You'll like it." He was right. It was hot tea, and it had some lemon in it... maybe some honey... and something else... something heavier... rum! It was great. It made me terribly hot after I drank it. But I asked for more. They both laughed and got me back in bed.

Before I conked out I asked, "Did we get to Antwerp yet?"

My eyes were already closed, but I heard one of them say, "We left Antwerp. We're on our way to Rotterdam."

The next time I woke up two different crewmen were in my room. I guess they all looked after me in shifts. I felt stronger now. I was hungry. They brought me some kind of broth. Later I was able to get out of bed and get washed up and dressed without any help. They brought me more food, although I couldn't eat much of it.

"Did we get to Rotterdam?"

"Oh... yeah... we're on our way to Liverpool now. Should be in port by dawn tomorrow."

I whispered to myself... "We'll be in Liverpool. Tomorrow I'll be in England."

Now I was too excited to sleep. I got up while it was still dark. I was weak and shaky, but I got myself together somehow. The guys weren't there to help me now, so I had to manage to get washed, shaved and dressed by myself. My clothes hung on me. I'd lost a lot of weight.

As soon as I felt the ship was moored, with cane and suitcase in hand, I went to say goodbye to gutsy Captain Fleming. I found him on deck and shook his hand.

"Count me among your admirers. You saved my life. I can't tell you how much I appreciate all you did for me. If I'd been found, you'd be arrested and detained for who knows how long. There would have been penalties for you and I don't know what they would have done with me. Thanks again. And thank your crew for all their care."

He nodded. "Good luck."

I stumbled down the gangway. I was in England and the sun was trying to peek out on this frosty-cold morning. I pulled up my coat collar and looked around for a place to phone Uncle Tony. I was surprised to see him and Aunt Jane standing on the pier waiting for me. I was so glad to see them because I didn't know how I was going to get to Doncaster. I was still so weak. When I got closer, my aunt burst into tears. I guess I looked pretty bad. Uncle Tony put an arm around my shoulders.

"We're so glad you made it home. Ambassador Rumbold cabled me to expect a 'special package'."

I said, "I guess that's me. And as you can see, I've been sick. But I'm lucky. I not only recovered from my illness, I survived the treatment!"

They both laughed and we got started on the long ride home. It was then that I told them everything that had happened in Berlin. They just listened... at least I think they listened. They didn't make any comments. But once we got home and were sitting in front of a blazing fire with a glass of wine in our hands, they toasted my homecoming and Uncle Tony asked, "What are your plans now?"

I couldn't answer. I didn't have any plans, except that it was important that no one know I'm in England. That's what I told him.

He said, "Your father sent me a cable inquiring about you. He claimed it was important that you return to Germany immediately or an extradition request would be made to the British Government."

I felt as if the blood drained right out of me. "Are there extradition agreements between England and Germany?"

"I don't know. I could only respond by cabling your father that I had no idea where you were." My uncle looked at me. "You're a fugitive now. But you needn't worry about me or your aunt. You'll always be safe with us."

I stood up. My eyes filled with tears. "I'm grateful that I have you and Aunt Jane. Everyone else is gone... Chani... Karl... Gretchen... all my friends in Berlin... Chani's family in Warsaw... I can't contact any of them. And there's the Berlin Opera Company... I can't find out anything about that either. I'm completely disconnected and I don't know what to do or where to go."

Aunt Jane said, "No one is rushing you. Stay with us."

I nodded and kissed them goodnight. I went up to my old bedroom. It was late now and I was worn out. But I decided to get unpacked... just the necessaries. When I got to the bottom of the suitcase, I spotted the package from Reb Saul. I remembered he said to wait thirty days before opening it. I decided it was time.

I ripped the string and wrapping paper off and got a jolt! No... no... oh my G-d! He'd given me our wedding pictures. There was Chani... smiling... dazzling in her white satin gown... so young... so alive. I clutched it to my heart and fell across the bed... My bride... my beautiful bride.

I stayed like that for a while. Later, I looked at the other two photos. All of them were framed with a narrow silver band. The second picture was of the two of us... the newlyweds... smiling at the prospect of a happy future together. My eyes began to burn. Tears slid down my face as I looked at the third one. It was of the family. Reb Saul was seated on the left. Bubbe sat on the right with little Avi, almost two, on her lap. Sarah stood on her right, leaning on her. Chani and I stood behind them, with Natan next to Chani and the twins standing next to me.

I wiped my tears away. But nothing could wipe away the memory of that magical summer in Warsaw when we spent every Sabbath together. They were my family now. I had told Reb Saul that I'd be coming back to Warsaw someday. I didn't know when. But I promised I'd be back.

I put the two pictures on my dresser. Chani's photo went to sleep with me, that night and every night.

Over the next few weeks I began to realize that I couldn't stay with my aunt and uncle. They were wonderful as always. They hadn't changed. I had. I wasn't the same person anymore. I was a Jewish man now and I needed a Jewish life.

I wasn't sure how to start or where to go. I'd regained my health somewhat. I'd taken many long walks. During the day I listened to my shortwave radio for news from Germany. I never heard any mention of the murder of those two Brownshirts, or that I was a man wanted by the Police. I guessed that the excitement of the upcoming elections was far more important. Hitler had decided to run against Hindenburg and it was announced that he was campaigning more vigorously than before. He had chartered a Junkers passenger plane and was flying from one end of Germany to the other, addressing three or four big rallies in different cities every day.* On top of that, he had changed his approach. Instead of harping on the present government and its inability to improve the German economy, he now promised that if elected he would create jobs for workers, more business for businessmen, and a big army for the military. He stood for a happy, prosperous future for all Germans. I wondered if the people would go for it.

The elections were scheduled for early April. Meanwhile the weather began to turn warm and after careful consideration I decided to phone Rabbi Shaposhnik in London. He had been very kind to me when I was undergoing Conversion. I asked if I could come to visit him. To my surprise, he seemed reluctant. But we did set a time and date.

When I met with him I told him I wanted to return to the Yeshiva here in London. He nodded but I could see something was bothering him. He quietly asked, "Do you want to talk about your wife?"

I didn't answer. Somehow I hadn't expected that question. Finally I said, "It's very painful for me to talk about Chani. What is it that you want to know?"

The Rabbi looked at me with great sadness in his eyes. "Many Jewish communities all over the world know what happened to Chani Machinski. She was the victim of the most brutal Nazi propaganda. Here in London we got details of your father's trial and his explanation of why he killed her. His rantings about blood... that she wanted to mingle her Jewish blood with your pure Aryan blood are so outrageous! It didn't seem possible that any intelligent person would accept it, particularly those in the medical profession! Yet many in Germany and elsewhere believed that ugly Nazi propaganda! It has no basis in medical fact. There is no such thing as Aryan blood or Jewish blood. Blood is blood! No matter the color of your skin, your religion, gender, or country of origin. There are only blood types: A, B, O, or AB, positive and negative. And that's all.

What is most ominous is that your father's statement declares that German is a race... the Aryan Race, and that Germany is no longer a nation of resident citizens. It is a nation only for Germans, and many agree with that too. As for our people, the Jews in Germany are so assimilated they believe they are Germans first and Jews second, if at all. This is a fearful development."

I said, "I agree with you. But what has all this to do with my admission to the Yeshiva?"

The Rabbi continued, "We also heard that you killed two Nazis. I don't know if the British government has extradition agreements with Germany. But if it's discovered that you are enrolled here, in a Jewish institution, it will look as if we harbor criminals. And I can only guess what will be made of that!"

"I had to kill them!" I shouted. "They came to get me and I wasn't going with them!" I stood up to leave.

The Rabbi said, "Sit down please. I was only pointing out the danger of having you in Yeshiva. I didn't say we would refuse you. We can never turn away a Jew in trouble. But we have to be extremely careful. You can't contact any of your friends for fear that the German Police may be watching them for information on your location.

You have a Jewish name now. Use it to get a new passport. There may be inquiries about you in the future.

CHAPTER 33 — ANOTHER BEGINNING

I went back to Doncaster to pack up my few things before I entered the Yeshiva. I listened to my shortwave radio that night and heard the results of the National Election. Hindenburg received 49.6% of the vote; Hitler received 30.1%; the other Communist candidate, Ernest Thaelmann, received 13.2%; and Duesterberg, the Nationalists' candidate, received only 6.8%. Since an absolute majority was necessary, another election was scheduled for April 10, 1932. But it was frightening that the Nazi vote increased by 86%.

Again there was no mention of the murdered Brownshirts. But I worried about Karl and Gretchen. Did they make it to Switzerland? There was no way for me to find out.

I said goodbye to my Aunt and Uncle, promising to come back whenever possible.

At the Yeshiva the Rabbi had arranged a small apartment for me, without a roommate, which was what I preferred. The other students were much younger and much different. Still, on Friday nights the local families invited Yeshiva students to their homes for Shabbos. It was a wonderful custom and their kind hospitality helped soothe my dark depression.

I would be spending another summer in a Yeshiva. But this wasn't Warsaw. There was no Bertha Kessler and her friendly impoverished home, no Sabbath with Chani and her family. On those long Saturday afternoons, Chani and I used to walk down to the Vistula River. Now I walked down to a different river, the Thames… alone, accompanied only by memories. I'll go back to Warsaw someday, I told myself. It won't be the same. But I'll go back.

Here during the day I spent all my time on my classes. I planned to get a PhD in Biblical Studies. At night I listened to the news from Germany. In the April Elections it was reported that 53% were for Hindenburg and the Republic, 36.8 for Hitler and the Nazi Party, and 10.2% for Thaelmann and the Communist Party.

Finally I was proud of the German people. Despite everything, the burden of the Versailles Treaty and the terrible poverty of the Great Depression, they didn't choose the rightwing Nazis or the leftwing Communists. They chose the Republic! Now maybe the new government would bring my father and men like him to justice for their barbaric crimes. That was my hope.

But it didn't happen. The political situation quickly became turbulent. President Hindenburg appointed Franz Von Papen as the new Chancellor of Germany and I was shocked to hear that he immediately dissolved the Reichstag. Maybe it was because they weren't functioning. In any event, he called for new elections to the Parliament on July 31st. Another election?!

The following nights the news centered on waves of political violence and murder in the streets so intense that Martial Law was declared in Berlin. It was reported that Von Papen used this situation to suspend the Constitution in favor of Authoritarian rule for the sake of law and order. President Hindenburg approved.

I was stunned. I had no idea the German Government could suspend their Constitution for any reason. What did this mean?

I tried to concentrate on my studies. Why should I care what happens in Germany now? But I did care. I had friends there.

The weather turned warm. London was filled with sunlight and bright flowers in every window box. It lifted my spirits until I heard the results of the July elections. It amounted to a huge victory for the Nazi Party. They won 230 seats in the Reichstag*, making them the largest party in the new Parliament. Worst of all, I was certain my father occupied one of those seats. As a contributor and fundraiser for Hitler, that had been his goal all along. Now he was a big success. Shit! I started reading the British newspapers to see if others felt as I did. There was little concern in England. Nobody gave a rat's ass.

The summer slid by. I got rid of my old disguise and grew my own beard and moustache. I tried to fit in with the other students as much as possible. But then January 10, 1933 rolled around. It was the first anniversary of Chani's death and I was like Job... alone... alienated... and suffering.

My Uncle called. He said he had a surprise for me and asked me to come home right away. A surprise! It was more of a shock! Karl was standing there! I gave him a bear hug.

I said, "I can't tell you how glad I am to see you! But how did you find me? And where is Gretchen?"

He shrugged. "I cabled your Uncle to ask if you were here. He said no. But I didn't know of any other place you would go, so I came to see for myself. I told your Uncle it was most important that I speak to you."

Aunt Jane interrupted to announce dinner. So we socialized, had some after-dinner drinks and then asked to be excused. We slipped upstairs to my bedroom. I stoked the fire in the fireplace as the wind howled outside. January in England was always a mean month. We sat down to another glass of wine and Karl explained.

"Gretchen and I made it safely to Switzerland. We now have an apartment in Basel. But since we had to leave Berlin in such a hurry, we left a lot of unfinished business behind. You're still my partner. Together we own the Berlin Opera Company building, which we renovated, plus our company's bank accounts. What we have to do now is sell our building in Berlin, take care of all unpaid bills and close our German bank accounts.

"Yeah... sure... but how can we do that? Neither of us can go back there. We'd be arrested!"

"That's the point," he said. "Gretchen can handle all of our business in Berlin. She hasn't committed any crime. She's innocent. The Police may question her. But it's okay for her to tell them what she knows... that I'm in Basel, Switzerland and she doesn't know where you are. I didn't tell her I was coming to England to look for you, so she doesn't know I'm here. Right now she's in Berlin, staying with Hermann Mass and his family."

I smiled, remembering the time I spent with them. I said, "They're such kind folks. They take in strays, you know."

Karl smiled back. "Listen... in order for Gretchen to sell our building and take care of all our business, we have to make her a partner in our Opera Company. That can only be done by a solicitor and both our signatures will be necessary. That's why I'm here."

I stood up, alarmed. "Karl, I agree with everything that needs to be done. But it can't be done in England. That will give away my location and cause problems for the Yeshiva. And more... if there is an extradition agreement between Germany and Britain, I can be sent back to face charges!"

"I know... I know... Sit down and let's think about how it can be done."

I mumbled... "And even if we are able to get our investments out of Berlin, what do you want to do with them?"

"I want to go back into business. We'll have the funds to open a new opera company... somewhere in Europe, or in America or Canada. Someplace that's safe for us."

I shook my head. "No! Karl, I can't. I don't even listen to music anymore. You want me to hear all those arias Chani used to sing? And bring back all those memories? I can't do it!"

Karl yelled, "Oh, shut up, goddammit! You don't want to listen to music anymore? You don't have to! You can stick to the financial end of the business... budgets, salaries, bills. But we have to continue our opera production. What else is there to do? What do you want to be?

Some kind of Jewish monk?"

I didn't answer. I got up, stoked the fire again and refilled our glasses with wine. Then I sat down to think.

Finally I said, "It's complicated. But here's an idea. Come with me to London. Rabbi Shaposhnik, the head of the Yeshiva, has lots of connections. He might have one in Paris. Maybe we can go to France for legal advice on how to make Gretchen a partner, sign the necessary papers and send them to her in Berlin. I want to live in England. If we're successful, I think this is where our new opera company should be."

"Well, you know there are lots of places to consider for relocating. Biarritz is a very nice location… and then there's always Vienna. But if you're adamant about staying in England, then that's where we should look when we start putting our project together."

The following day we left for London. On the way I explained to Karl that Rabbi Shaposhnik knew everything that happened in Berlin. So at this time we should discuss our future project with him. It's a long way off. But he needs to know.

We met with the Rabbi in his study and explained what we wanted to do and asked if he could help us in obtaining our Berlin assets without disclosing my location. He agreed to see what he could do.

After we left him I told Karl I could put him up at my apartment. It was small, just a sitting room, bedroom and bath, but he could sleep on the couch. We walked through the snow and cold to my place. It was nearby. There I got a fire started and as soon as we warmed up, I turned on my shortwave radio for the news from

Germany.

We heard a solemn voice report that at 5:00pm on this day, January 30, 1933, President Hindenburg had sworn in Adolf Hitler as the new Chancellor of Germany.

Karl and I looked at each other in shock. We both knew this was a catastrophe and I said so.

"Well… wait a minute," Karl said. "Maybe not. Remember there are still Conservatives, the Catholic Party, and others in the Parliament who will want to find a way to control Hitler and his Storm trooper thugs. Let's wait and see how things go."

For the next few days as we waited to hear from Rabbi Shaposhnik, we went forward with plans to establish a new opera company somewhere in Britain. We traveled to Southampton and Plymouth trying to find out if the local population could support an opera company. In both cities we looked for a good location for a theater, but nothing was conclusive. We decided to change our plans a little and search for a location in the big cities of Scotland. Before we could take a look at that situation, we heard from the Rabbi. He told us he had contacted a friend of his in Paris, Rabbi Josef Wolff, who recommended several lawyers in Le Havre, the closest French port to England. We were pleased because it would enable us to conclude our business quickly.

We chose an attorney called Rene Lassalle because his name sounded French and the least Jewish. Rabbi Shaposhnik told us Rabbi Wolff would arrange an appointment for us. And in a couple of weeks we were on our way.

Rene Lassalle was a stout, balding, middle-aged man with piercing brown eyes. He spoke to us in a clipped German. Karl explained that we wanted to include his wife, Gretchen Klempner, as a partner in our Berlin Opera Company so that she could liquidate our assets in Berlin, as we planned to establish our company elsewhere. We asked that he provide the necessary forms, which we would both sign, and forward those papers to an address in Berlin which we would provide. Then we requested he forward any of our mail coming through his office for us to Rabbi Wolff in Paris, as we were now involved in finding a suitable location for the new opera company and were frequently on the move. For a small fee, he agreed.

As soon as we returned from Le Havre, we wrote to Rabbi Wolff and asked him to forward all mail addressed to either one of us to Rabbi Shaposhnik at the Yeshiva. Now that we'd accomplished everything we needed to, I was beginning to feel a little excited about this project.

Back at my apartment, as usual, I turned on the radio. We sat there stunned to hear that the Reichstag had been set on fire and burned to the ground. The reporter continued, "It is felt that this is a Communist plot to overthrow the new duly elected government. The arsonist, Marinus van der Lubbe, has been found and arrested. He is a Communist and a Dutch National. But other Communists have been implicated and will soon be arrested to face trial."

I turned the radio off and looked at Karl. His face was ashen. He whispered, "Germany is descending into chaos and my Gretchen is there."

The following night the news was worse. Hitler had prevailed on President Hindenburg to sign a decree 'For the Protection of the People and the State' suspending the seven sections of the Constitution which guarantee individual civil liberties. I asked Karl what this meant.

He said, "I'm not sure. But it sounds like the Nazis can arrest anyone for any reason."

I stood up and started pacing the floor. I was afraid for my friends. "Do you think they'd arrest Hermann Mass, Niemoeller, Von Ossietzky or Bonhoeffer? They've always been opposed to the Nazis."

"I don't know... I don't know!" he shouted. "I only know my Gretchen is there and it's a violent place now. He covered his face with his hands. When he looked at me I saw fear in his eyes. "I don't think we'll be able to relocate our opera company. Gretchen may be able to close our bank accounts but she'll need a real estate agent to sell our building. And with the atmosphere so explosive, who would buy it? I'm going to write to her and tell her to forget everything and go back to Switzerland. We'll have to wait and see how things develop in Berlin."

We stayed glued to the radio every night. Very quickly the trial of Marinus van der Lubbe was reported. He was found guilty, of course, and immediately beheaded. We now heard that other Communists and opposition leaders had also been arrested. No names were mentioned.

A few days later, through our French connection to Rabbi

Shaposhnik, we received a letter from Hermann Maas. He wrote, "Gretchen has been arrested by the Gestapo."

CHAPTER 34 — TEMPORARY FUTURE

Karl leaped up, grabbed his suitcase and began to toss his belongings into it.

I said, "Wait a minute... wait a minute! Listen to the rest of this letter."

The Gestapo has been investigating Gretchen and concluded that she has Jewish grandparents on her mother's side, and is therefore a Jew. Jews are prohibited from sending money out of the country or being partners with Aryan Germans in any enterprise. In addition, they claim she is involved with two men who are wanted for murder. Questioned on this last issue, the Gestapo says her answers proved to be lies.

This is what I've been told time and time again when I try to explain to them that she is a member of my church. She is a Christian woman and although her husband may be accused of a crime, she is innocent of anything illegal. I told them that she hasn't lied about anything. She simply doesn't know the answers.

I have begged for her release, but been refused. The latest word is that she's been sent to a Concentration Camp. But they won't tell me where! I'm frantic to find out so I can visit her and I intend to continue to press for her release. I'll keep you informed.

Best regards,

Rev. H. Maas

I handed the letter to Karl. He threw it into his suitcase and snapped it shut.

"Where are you going? You can't go back to Germany! You'll be arrested."

He gave me a grim look of determination and yelled, "She was safe in Switzerland. I sent her to Berlin and look what happened! I don't know where I'm going or how I'm going to do it. I only know I have to get my wife back! I'll keep in touch with you somehow." And he slammed out the door.

I just stood there, filled with dread… the Gestapo! I started shaking and stumbled into the nearest chair. Would he ever find Gretchen? The room grew cold and dark. I didn't move. Karl was gone and I didn't know what to do to help him.

There was a knock at the door. I jumped! When I opened it I saw Rabbi Shaposhnik standing there. He looked around and said, "What's wrong? Why are you sitting in the dark?" He switched on the light. I blinked a few times. He came in and stoked the fire until the room began to warm. Then he sat down on the sofa and waited to hear what was on my mind. I tried to pull myself together and finally told him…

"Things are bad in Germany. Karl's wife has been arrested by the

Gestapo and Karl left to try to get her safely back to Switzerland somehow."

I got up and started pacing the floor. "It doesn't seem to matter that Gretchen was raised a Lutheran and is a devoted member of the Confessing Church." I was shouting now, I was so agitated. "The Gestapo found out that her grandparents were Jewish and that makes her a Jew. Of course, her grandparents died before she was born, but that doesn't count. The Nazis found a reason to arrest her and send her to a Concentration Camp!"

I glanced at the Rabbi. His eyes were filled with tears. He whispered, "She was young and pretty, wasn't she?"

His words hit me like a bullet. I stood there for a few moments and then crumbled into a chair. I sank my head in my hands as I thought about Gretchen, with her red curls and bright brown eyes, freckles on her nose and a dimple in her cheek when she smiled. No... no... I couldn't bear to think of her in the hands of the Gestapo.

Rabbi Shaposhnik wiped his eyes and shook his head. "When the power of the government is used against you, it's time to go. I've urged all the Jews I know in Germany to leave. But they think that this anti-Semitism is just a passing phase caused by the Great Depression and everything will soon go back to how it was before." He shrugged. "They think that way because it's so hard to leave everything you know... everything you have... your home, your business, your family... and go to some other land where you don't know the language... you don't know a street... you don't know a soul!"

I got up and turned off the light. The two of us sat in the semi-darkness, listening to the crackle of the logs in the fireplace. I don't know how long we sat there in silence. Finally he said, "So there's no future in relocating your opera company?"

I murmured, "We're in the middle of a Shakespearean tragedy... 'The time is out of Joint'... I don't know if I'll ever be in business with Karl again. I don't even know when I'll see him again. And he's one of the most important people in my life! My only hope is that he can rescue Gretchen from the claws of the Gestapo and get her safely to Switzerland. Then... to hell with whatever we left in Berlin. We can start again... together. Do you think that's realistic?"

Out of the darkness the Rabbi spoke. "No... not at this time. But hope is always the last to die. Right now you're in a good place, here in the Yeshiva. You're safe and you can work if you want to. I can assign classes for you to teach – in mathematics, German or secular studies. That may not be the career you have in mind. But who knows what the future will bring."

I looked at this kind and decent man. The fire lit up part of his face and I could see a tear that still glistened, lodged in his gray beard.

I said, "Thank you. Yes. I'd like to do that."

The Rabbi got me teaching assignments right away and that helped by occupying my time, which somewhat distracted me from my deep concern for Karl and Gretchen.

Months went by and in all that time I hadn't heard one word from Karl. I had no idea what was happening and no one I could contact for information. I was frustrated and anxious. It didn't help that those families that continued to invite me for the Sabbath insisted on introducing me to marriageable women. I'd already told them that I wasn't interested. But they paid no attention... apparently the consensus was that I should consider re-marriage. So, I advised them that I hadn't yet done my duty. "I need to set a stone on my wife's grave," I told them. "But it's in Warsaw and I'm unable to go there now." That slowed them down.

Then spring came round again with sunny skies and red and purple flowers, followed by an amazing announcement. The BBC reported that on May 16th, the United States' President Roosevelt had sent a message to the chiefs of State of forty-four nations outlining plans for disarmament and peace, calling for the abolition of all offensive weapons... bombers, tanks, and mobile artillery.

The following day, German Radio stated that Hitler replied and that Germany was prepared to agree to this method of maintaining peace and was ready to renounce all offensive weapons if the armed nations on their side would destroy their offensive weapons. And more.... Germany was prepared to agree to any solemn pact of non-aggression. Germany didn't want war... etc. etc. etc.

I clicked off the radio. It was all such a crock! But the London newspapers were filled with praise for Hitler. Even the Conservative weekly, THE SPECTATOR OF LONDON, concluded that this gesture provided new hope for a tormented world.

Of course, somehow they missed his one warning. He demanded equality of treatment for Germany with all the other nations, especially in armaments, and threatened if this didn't happen, Germany would withdraw from the Disarmament Conference as well as the League of Nations.

I knew that Hitler's real goal was to get the other nations to disarm. Germany had been secretly re-arming since the 20's. Von Ossietzky had published that fact in his journals years ago and was supposed to go on trial for revealing State secrets. I didn't know what happened to him. I figured he must be in prison by now. I had really admired him from the moment I met him. He stood up for what he thought was right, no matter what! He was one tough guy!

There was a knock at my door. I opened it to find Rabbi Shaposhnik standing there once again.

"This letter just came for you," he said.

As soon as he left, I tore it open. It was from Hermann Maas. It read:

Dear Erich,

Karl wrote to me from Switzerland. He's asked the Swiss authorities to help him secure Gretchen's release from Germany and asked me to help as much as I could. But things have gone badly. The Nazi authorities, desperate to get their hands on Karl, immediately requested that he be extradited to Germany in regard to a murder case in Berlin. The Swiss government responded that they do not have an extradition agreement with Germany, however, Karl Klempner, a Swiss citizen, would voluntarily return to Berlin as soon as his wife Gretchen was released from custody and safely returned to Switzerland.

It was a simple request. The Nazis really didn't have any legitimate reason to keep her in a Concentration Camp. But they became belligerent... threatening... They replied that if Karl Klempner did not return to Berlin immediately, he would never see his wife again.

Karl was willing to do anything. But I advised against it and the Swiss government restrained him. They didn't understand why the German government wouldn't comply and release her. Of course there can only be one answer. They couldn't comply because Gretchen was already dead...

The letter fell from my shaking hands.

CHAPTER 35 — TERRIBLE TIMES

I was so despondent over what happened to Gretchen, it was dawn by the time I picked up the letter to read the rest of it. Maas wrote:

The Swiss government questioned Karl about the alleged double murder in Berlin. Karl confessed that he was there at the time but he didn't kill anyone. Neither did he report it to the police. Frightened by the prospect of being prosecuted, he and his wife fled the country.

All this was reported to the Nazi Government, but I doubt that it satisfied them. Your father has grown more powerful since Hitler was appointed Chancellor and he's angry that you were able to leave the country. He wants you back! And he probably put a lot of pressure on the Gestapo to make that happen. If you're in a safe place, stay there. I'm still free but I expect to be arrested, as well as Neimoller, Bonhoeffer, and other Nazi opponents. These are terrible times. I can only hope that we'll have a glass of wine together again one day.

Rev. H. Maas

The sun was coming up now. I made myself a cup of black coffee, poured a little whisky in it and read the letter again and again until I saw more clearly what was happening. Nazi Germany was a cauldron of evil that was being poured over the more liberal, moral segments of German society to transform it into Hitler's idea of the "Uber-Mensch" (the Master Race)... those that felt entitled to everything that belonged to others.

They had to be stopped! But who could do it? I was overwhelmed by my own helplessness here in England. But so too were Reverend Maas and the others in Germany opposed to Hitler. I was safe, but they were waiting to be arrested!

I listened anxiously to every scrap of news from Germany and read the British newspapers. The Nazis were gaining more power and there was no attempt to stop them. I was ready to fight! I was waiting to join the opposition... any opposition. But there was none.

I began to keep a diary of events in Germany. My first entry was:

January 20, 1934:

Nazi Concordant signed with the Vatican, guaranteeing the right to Church self-regulation if they did not protest Nazi authority. This lent Hitler's government much needed prestige and eliminated any Catholic protests.

January 26, 1934:

Hitler announced the signing of a ten-year non-aggression pact between Germany and Poland. What a bad joke! The vast majority of Germans despised the Poles. Germany was furious over the loss of Danzig and Silesia, and they would kill to get them back.

Meanwhile, Rabbi Shaposhnik had assigned a number of secular study classes for me to teach: Business & Finance, Accounting, and German language for those who requested it. That kept me busy. More than a year went by.

September 15, 1935: The Nuremberg Laws were enacted by the Nazi Government, effectively depriving the German Jews of their citizenship and all civil rights. There was no mention of any protests.

I met with Rabbi Shaposhnik to discuss the situation. He said, "This is nothing new. It's an old method of stealing. First the Jews are demonized. This allows the Nazis to seize Jewish property, businesses and assets of the Jews and use them for their own purposes. I'm planning to get together with other Rabbis so that as a group we can meet with British immigration authorities to see if they are willing to grant visas to Jewish families in Germany."

March 7, 1936: Germany occupies the Rhineland in defiance of the Versailles Treaty. France, Britain and the League of Nations do nothing! I'm disgusted!

I made another notation in my diary on August 1936: The Olympic Games are being held in Berlin and it seems they were so spectacularly organized and foreign journalists so lavishly entertained that they heaped praise on Hitler's new Germany.

Then in October, 1936: I was thrilled to read in the London newspapers that von Ossietzky had won the Nobel Peace Prize. I asked Rabbi Shaposhnik if I could cancel my classes because I wanted to go to Oslo for the ceremony. I could hardly wait to shake the hand of this rugged hero. But the Nazi Government refused to allow him to receive the Prize. This was followed by an international outcry and, as a result, the Nazis declared that von Ossietzky, though ill, was free to go to Norway to accept the Prize as soon as he was well enough to travel. At this time he was hospitalized. Journalists reported that they were unable to interview him.

Carl von Ossietzky

July, 1937: The BBC reported that Dr. Martin Niemoeller, the highly regarded Protestant Minister, was arrested by the SS and placed in "Protective Custody." No other details were available, but it looked to me like the Nazis were trying to eliminate any opposition to their regime.

On March 13, 1938: I wrote what all the newspapers were shouting… that Germany had annexed Austria in what was called the

"Anschluss." This union was welcomed by the people of Austria. I didn't know why, but it was reported that Hitler was seen as a hero. Church bells rang and Nazi flags were everywhere, as seen in the latest news reels.

Sad news... on <u>May 4, 1938</u>: The BBC reported that von Ossietzky died. He was never able to claim his Nobel Peace Prize. The Nazis made sure of that!

Then came the great turning point. On <u>September 30, 1938</u> Hitler demanded the Sudentenland for the "Protection" of the German minority living there. Chamberlain for Britain and his French counterpart agreed to Hitler's demands. Chamberlain declared, "peace for our time." This kind, educated humanitarian, who had witnessed the savagery of the Great War, was determined to avoid another war at all cost. But I knew, and so did others, that another war was coming.

I went to see the Rabbi and told him that in the event of war with Germany, I would join the armed forces and fight against the Nazis. I said, "As Jews, we have to fight against evil ourselves. But in warfare there won't be any kosher food, no Sabbath, no synagogue for prayers. So what advice can you give me?"

The Rabbi's eyes filled with tears. "You know, our life here at the Yeshiva centers around Torah study and learning. Our needs are so simple... a roof overhead, a warm bed, enough food, and to be left alone in peace. But the world won't let us. It's like Shakespeare said, 'Whether 'tis nobler in the minds of men to suffer the slings and arrows of outrageous fortune, or to take up arms against a sea of troubles and by opposing, end them.'

And so, King Saul fought against the enemy. King David fought, Sampson fought. And if you have to fight, my advice to you is to choose life. The Creator's greatest gift to you is your existence. Do whatever is necessary to persevere and survive."

He didn't wipe away his tears. They slid down his face into his beard.

November 9, 1938: Kristallnacht was a massive Nazi coordinated attack on Jews and Jewish property throughout Germany. This event, called "The Night of Broken Glass," began the pogrom against the Jews, many of whom were arrested and sent to Concentration Camps. The world was shocked by this wanton destruction. But no action was taken.

On August 23, 1939, I wrote in my diary that Nazi Germany and the Soviet Union signed a non-aggression pact. Another bad joke! Hitler hated the Russians.

And then the end. On September 1, 1939, Hitler invaded Poland. Three days later Britain and France declared War on Germany. Finally! Finally! It was MY turn.

I ran to Rabbi Shaposhnik to express my enormous gratitude for the years he sheltered me… educated me… employed me. And to say goodbye. I shaved off my beard and moustache and rushed to join the RAF.

I was angry when they rejected me. They said I was over age. They were looking for nineteen and twenty-year-olds. They claimed men my age didn't have the razor sharp reflexes necessary for this kind of fighting.

Meanwhile, I learned that the Nazis had completely destroyed the Polish Air Force on the ground. Pilots were in short supply. So I managed to hook up with the Polish flyers who had escaped to England.* These were tough guys. They called themselves the Kosciuszko Squadron and were the largest contingent of foreign pilots in the RAF, although there were also men from New Zealand, South Africa, Canada, and a handful of Americans.

I was thrilled with the Polish Contingent. I spoke a little Polish from my days in Warsaw and they spoke a little English. Their combat reputation was superb, rooted in experience and reckless courage. They wanted revenge and so did I. When I saw that Swastika on those Messerschmitts, my brain snapped into place. I had to get them! I had to... for Chani... for Gretchen... for all of them!

This was the battle for Britain! And even if we were all worn out from scrambling two, three, and sometimes four times a day, we were all alone in this fight and we had to win it!

Our Spitfires were our magic carpets into the sky. I think every pilot fell in love with his aircraft. But we received scarcely any training in air fighting. The Germans were much better at it. We had to learn by experience. And we did.

Even so, the Germans were getting the best of it. But for some unknown reason, they suddenly shifted their attack away from military objectives and began bombing London and other major cities... targeting the civilian population. Night after night they sent their bombers in what was call the Blitz! This change in German strategy gave us a chance to produce more airplanes, more defensive weapons, and then... at last... in 1942, the United States joined the fight.

CHAPTER 36 — EUROPE

We all knew of the terrible destruction in London and other areas of England, but focused as we were on our mission, none of us knew the full extent of the Nazi atrocities until the end of the war. Then came the shock of the Holocaust, the death camps and all the horrors committed by the Nazi regime.

The world was outraged and the Nuremburg Trials tried to put a civilized face on what was impossible to describe or acknowledge. On top of that, Europe was in complete chaos. Concentration Camp survivors were freed, along with thousands of men and women who had been used as slave labor in mines and factories. The roads were clogged with refugees. Displaced Persons Camps were set up in many locations. The newspapers and radio reported on all that was happening. It looked like everyone wanted out... except me.

As soon as the war was over and I was discharged, I gathered my things together at my Uncle's place. I took my wedding pictures as well as Chani's family photos. I didn't know if I would ever return to England. After a tearful goodbye to Uncle Tony and Aunt Jane, I set out for the Continent. Transportation was impossible. I wore my RAF uniform, hoping it would be helpful. As a precaution against the unknown, I kept the Derringer in my pocket and extra ammo in my suitcase.

With much difficulty and long delays, I finally managed to arrive in Switzerland. I wanted to find Karl. When I looked for him at his apartment in Basel, I was told that he'd picked up his things and left as soon as the war ended. I had a hunch he'd gone back to Berlin to look for Gretchen.

Since Switzerland was neutral during the war, their railways hadn't been bombed and I was able to take the night train to Berlin. When I got there the following morning, I couldn't believe my eyes. Destruction was everywhere. Rubble filled the streets and the street signs were gone. I wasn't sure which way to go. I hiked to what looked like Kurferstandam, where our old Opera Company building stood. It was gone.

All of Berlin was a wasteland filled with crowds of desperate pitiful people... hungry and needing medical attention. The allies, along with the Red Cross, appeared to be doing their best to help as many as they could. I looked the crowds over carefully. I suspected that plenty of Nazis were hiding among the displaced survivors. I wondered if my father was among them. I kept a sharp eye out for him. I intended to kill him as soon as I found him. But I didn't see him and there was no one to ask.

I hitched a ride with some G.I.'s to Karl's old Berlin apartment and although it was damaged, it was still standing and people were living there. I asked them about Karl and Gretchen from many years ago, but they didn't know what happened to them. Someone else was now living in their apartment and using their old furnishings. As I stood there I remembered their Christmas Open House, back in 1930. My broken ankle was in a cast and I was on crutches when I met von Ossietzky, Neimoeller and Hermann Maas. Von Ossietzky was dead now and Niemoeller had been arrested. I wondered what happened to the others who opposed the Nazis, even back then. But there was no time to wonder. The day was wearing on and I had a lot of ground to cover.

It was hot now, as I found my way to Dahlem. I looked for the magnificent home that once was mine. It wasn't there. All I found was a huge mound of rubble. The pond in front was still there. People were bathing in it... drinking it.

Most of the pine trees that had lined the driveway now lay dead on the ground. Only a few were left standing. As I looked at this rotten mess, knowing everything that was buried in it, I hoped that one day someone would dig down in that heap, perhaps to build another house. I wondered if they'd find the painting of my beautiful mother standing beside her favorite steed. Then I turned away!

I looked for the old pink brick building that was once the home of the Confessing Church. I knew it was nearby. I was afraid it would be gone too. But then I spotted it. As I came closer, I saw that it was badly damaged. The door had been blown off and most of the windows were shattered. But I thought I saw someone moving around inside.

I walked through the open doorway and found a gaunt old man with a wisp of white hair sweeping up debris. He had his back to me but I would know him anywhere.

"Hermann Maas," I called out. He turned and stared at me wide-eyed.

"Erich! Erich is that you?" We hugged and marveled at the miracle of finding each other in all this destruction.

There weren't any chairs. We went outside and sat on the stoop. I said, "Tell me what happened to you and the others."

Tears came to his eyes. "You know that Ossieztky died?" I nodded. Hermann Maas wiped his tears away on his tattered sleeve. "He never got the Peace Prize, you know. And the money award was stolen from him," he said in disgust. "Martin Niemoeller was arrested by the SS and sent to Sachsenhousen Concentration Camp. Later I heard he was sent to Dachau, but I've been told that he survived and I'm hopeful he'll come back to Berlin. He was such an outspoken opponent of Adolf Hitler and his Nazis. In one of his sermons he said:

'FIRST THEY CAME FOR THE COMMUNISTS, AND I DIDN'T SPEAK OUT BECAUSE I WASN'T A COMMUNIST.

THEN THEY CAME FOR THE TRADE UNIONISTS, AND I DIDN'T SPEAK OUT BECAUSE I WASN'T A TRADE UNIONIST.

THEN THEY CAME FOR THE JEWS, AND I DIDN'T SPEAK OUT BECAUSE I WASN'T A JEW.

THEN THEY CAME FOR ME... AND THERE WAS NO

ONE LEFT TO SPEAK FOR ME.'

Dietrich Bonhoeffer

Ach... what a wonderful man he is. As for Dietrich Bonhoeffer..." Hermann Maas paused again, shook his head and sighed deeply. "In case you haven't heard, Bonheoffer was involved in a plot to kill Hitler. It failed and he was caught and sentenced to death. The war was over! The Russians were fighting door to door. But that didn't matter to Adolf Hitler! On a cold April morning, young, brilliant Bonhoeffer was first humiliated by being marched naked through the courtyard at Flossenburg Concentration Camp where he was hanged with a thin wire, so it would take the longest time for him to die. That's what Hitler ordered for him! Dietrich Bonhoeffer was a true Christian martyr."

I closed my eyes and nodded in agreement. The two of us sat there in silence, mourning for all those brutalized and murdered by the Nazis. After a while I asked, "What happened to you? You've grown so thin."

"Ach... that doesn't matter. You know I had so many Jewish friends. I will never forget the frequent visits from those poor persecuted and tormented people... hounded by the Nuremburg Laws day and night. I helped as many as I could, using the connections I had, to get them visas to other countries. The Nazis arrested me and I was sent to a forced labor camp in France. Thankfully my family was spared and I was liberated by the Americans when they pushed through in 1945. But enough about me. I'm surprised you came back to Berlin. I never expected to see you again."

"I came to find Karl. He's looking for Gretchen and this is where she was."

"Karl was here," Maas said. "He doesn't believe that Gretchen is dead. He went to several Concentration Camps and someone told him that she was sent to Auschwitz. So he went to Poland to look for her. But that was months ago. I don't know where his is now."

I shrugged. "It doesn't look like I'll be able to find him. But I want to go to Poland anyway. I have many photographs of Chani's family and I want to return them. I'm going to Warsaw to see if I can find any of the Machinski family who may still be there."

We both stood up. It was time to say goodbye. We knew we might never meet again. Sadly we shook hands and promised each other to keep in touch somehow. I turned and waved as I started on the long road to Poland.

Trains weren't running. I'd have to hitch a ride or walk. I did both. But these were strange times. There were different armies going in different directions... British, American, French, and, as I got closer to Poland, a lot of Russians. It took more than a week. Roadway signs were destroyed and I got all turned around. I didn't intend to go to Auschwitz. By mistake I found myself standing in front of the twisted, open gate. There was a terrible stench. An overwhelming odor of death.

I'd heard that this was the place where the Nazis had gassed hundreds of thousands of Jewish men, women, children... even babies. They burned their bodies and reduced them all to smoke and ashes. Nothing of them remained!

It was eerie, but I went inside. The place was huge. I saw miles of heavy barbed wire and raised guard towers. It was quiet and ghostly. There were no bodies... no prisoners... no survivors. It seemed empty except for a mountain of shoes... men's, women's, children's... I stared at one little shoe. It was the kind Sarah wore. The sight of it made me want to throw up. Then I spotted piles of eyeglasses... each maybe twenty feet high. My mouth went dry. I couldn't swallow. Many of them were like Reb Saul's reading glasses. I turned away, but out of the corner of my eye I saw something else. Something hidden in the darkness. I couldn't make out what it was until I came closer. It was hair! Piles and piles of human hair! Filled with horror, I ran out of there. I ran as fast as I could until I felt a piercing pain in my side. I fell to the ground and waited for the pain to subside.

Eventually some soldiers came to help me. They were Russians. They stood me up and dusted me off, all the while asking me something. I didn't understand them. I said in English, "Warsaw... Warsaw." They pointed me in the right direction and I started walking.

There were many stops and starts along the way, and a few redirects. It took me about two weeks to get there. Auschwitz was with me every foot of the way. It was a relic of what Germany had become... a dark, sinister power that had abandoned its proud cultural heritage and sunk to a level of barbarity unknown in the whole history of civilization.

On the way to Warsaw I saw crowds of people coming towards me. They were leaving the area. I figured they must be on the way to a nearby refugee camp where they could find food and shelter. I shouted to them in Yiddish... "The Machinski family? Anyone from the Machinski family?" As the crowd filed by I repeated it again and again. No one looked at me. I went farther down from these, slowly shuffling by and repeated it... louder and louder. Finally I heard a voice yell back, "They're dead!" I didn't want to believe it. I went towards him. He came closer and repeated, "They're all dead!"

The man was half alive himself... a scraggly guy who was little more than a bag of bones. He came right up to me and with fire in his eye he said, "All except one. Fannie Machinski lives in Jerusalem!"

CHAPTER 37 — RESURRECTION

"They're all dead!" I repeated. Were they all gassed and burned with all the others at Auschwitz? I asked myself. No I couldn't accept it. I saw them all in my mind as I trudged along the road to Warsaw. I remembered everything. All the Sabbaths we spent together. I could almost smell the chicken soup. I saw the candles on the table, shining brightly as the children lined up for their father's blessing. Those memories stayed with me.

I wanted to get to Warsaw to visit Chani's grave. I hadn't put up a stone for her yet. And in all this chaos, I probably couldn't do it now. But I had to go the cemetery anyway, just to be with her again.

A few weeks later I stumbled onto a place that was once called Warsaw. I didn't believe what I saw. The front of the old Europjeski Hotel was still there. But that was the only wall left standing. The rest of the building was debris.

The area all around that wall was filled with Russian soldiers and their armored vehicles. The soldiers, seeing my RAF uniform, were kind enough to share some of their food and water with me. But the city… the entire city had been destroyed.

The majestic mansions of the ancient Saxon Kings were gone. The magnificent Grand Theatre, where Chani had auditioned for us years ago, was rubble. There were no trees standing, so I could glimpse what was once the shimmering Vistula River. Now it looked like a mud hole.

Palaces of the Saxon Kings

I knew all this devastation wasn't for any military purpose. It was the Nazi effort to erase the pride and history of the Polish people. A symbol of German hatred.

Ruins of The Great Synagogue of Warsaw

The Great Synagogue of Warsaw, where Chani and I were married, was now a charred ruin. The entire Jewish quarter of the city had been obliterated. That's where I stayed with Bertha Kessler, where the Machinkskis lived, where the Yeshiva stood, and where, I'd heard, the Warsaw Ghetto Uprising occurred. It was led by Mordechai Aniliewitz, who fought with hardly any weapons against the deadly Nazi war machine. He and a small group of desperate Jews held out longer than the whole Polish army back in 1943. I hoped Reb Saul and his boys fought alongside them.

Mordechai Aniliewitz

There were no streets or street signs so I started walking in the direction I thought I'd find the old Jewish Cemetery. I looked for the heavy black iron gates, but they must have been blown off. It took me a long time to locate the place. It was growing dark and I was broken-hearted when I found it. The entire Jewish Cemetery had been desecrated. Grave stones had been broken up or removed. I couldn't find Chani's grave. By the time night fell, I was exhausted. I found a spot where the old gates used to be. I whispered to Chani... "This is the last time we get to sleep together." Then I curled up and fell asleep, dreaming of her in my arms.

The next morning I spoke to Chani again. I said, "I promised when the Opera Season was over we'd go to Jerusalem to visit your sister Fannie." I wiped my eyes on my sleeve. "I'm going to visit your sister, just as we planned." Then I turned and walked away. I knew I would never come back to Warsaw.

Later I found out it wouldn't be easy to get to Jerusalem. Thousands of survivors wanted to go to Palestine. The Arabs were absolutely against it. The British, who had a mandate for Palestine that would soon expire, sided with the Arabs, probably for their oil interests, and prevented Jews from entering the country. It was a terrible time… filled with turbulence and violence. I couldn't get there!

I had to go to different countries to get to Palestine and it took months and months of effort. Finally I made it, just in time to celebrate the United Nations establishment of the Jewish State of Israel in 1948. But I barely got to celebrate before the new Israel was invaded by half a dozen Arab armies. I had to fight again!

I went looking for the Israeli Air Force. There wasn't any! I hooked up with some pilots from different countries, mostly from the U.S., and I got to be part of what we laughingly called the Israeli Air Force. Of course because of the British boycott of arms to Israel, we were forced to get our planes from Czechoslovakia. Ironically, they were German Messershmitts! The planes had to be taken apart, shipped to Israel and then re-assembled. We didn't get much time for training because we were involved in combat sessions immediately. We lost a lot of good men and it tore us up. But we were desperate and somehow we managed to be effective. Israel was saved, at least for now.

Not much later the Israelis began to put together their commercial airline, El Al. I was hired to fly for them and also to train new pilots.

I loved to fly. These were mostly overnight flights. We landed back in Israel early in the morning.

I lived in Tel Aviv and loved living in Israel. All the food was Kosher, everything shut down for the Sabbath, and strangers in the street greeted each other with "Shabbat Shalom." On top of that, every morning I sat in an outdoor café with the warm sun on my back as I read the daily newspaper and enjoyed black coffee and a danish.

One day a group of musicians were in the middle of Dizengoff Street playing excerpts from Mendelssohn to advertise the Israeli Philharmonic which would be performing in the city for the next several days.

They were great! All the musicians were dressed in Arab garb, flowing robes like the Bedouins wore. When they finished playing the conductor turned and smiled at us then took a bow. Somehow he looked familiar. He was dark-eyed with a black beard. But he had the whitest teeth I'd ever seen... a handsome guy.

I went over and introduced myself. I said, "I think I know you from somewhere. I used to be with the Berlin Opera Company. Back then my name was Erich Von Bruener." Before I could say another word, he screamed and fell to the ground. People gathered around and looked at me accusingly. I didn't know what happened! I shrugged and bent down to him. "What the hell's the matter? What's wrong with you?"

He looked at me with terror-filled eyes and sobbed. "I'm Michal Kaplansky. I didn't mean to betray her. The SS arrested me. They beat me and tortured me. But I wouldn't tell them anything. Then they put my right hand in a vise and told me they would cut it off if I didn't tell them about Heidi Mueller. I'm a violinist! I need my hand! I told them what they wanted to know… that she was really Chani Machinski, a Jew from Warsaw… and they cut off my hand anyway!" and he screamed and showed everyone the stump of his right hand. "Then they threw me out in the snow. The snow and ice froze my arm and stopped the bleeding until someone came and saved me. But Chani! They killed her, didn't they? Forgive me. Please forgive me."

I said, "Yes," as I helped him to his feet. What else could I say? I patted him on the back in sympathy and walked away, black with despair. Even after all these years, the cutting pain of losing Chani was still there. I went back to my apartment, closed off the sunlight and sat in the dark as I tried to come to grips with myself.

Kaplansky had brought everything into focus. Had I forgotten why I came to Israel in the first place, almost five years ago? Yeah… sure… the war got in the way, other things too. But that didn't make it right. I promised Chani I would visit her sister and I had to do it.

Within the next few weeks I gave up my position with El Al and moved to Jerusalem. The old King David Hotel had been blown up during the War for Independence. It was rebuilt now and I rented a residential room there. As soon as possible I found my way to Hadassah Hospital to search for Fannie Machinski.

Once there I asked the nursing staff about her. None of them could remember anyone by that name.

I said, "What! Listen! I know she came here as a young girl from

Poland in 1931. She wanted to finish her education in nursing right here at Hadassah Hospital and work in this facility."

I was advised to go to Personnel. And when I did, I got the same answer. But I insisted that she'd come here. "Speak to one of the older nurses," I was told. Sure enough, one of them smiled when I mentioned Fannie Machinski. She told me she remembered Fannie very well, but that Fannie had married years ago and her name was now Fannie Liebman. "I'll find her address and telephone number for you," she said. Fannie doesn't work much anymore. She's busy with her family."

As soon as I had Fannie's telephone number I went back to my place to rehearse what I would say to her. Finally I phoned her.

"I'm your brother-in-law, Erich Von Bruener, now called Daniel Benavrum," I said. "I'd like very much to visit with you. I have photographs of the family I'd like to show you."

There was a long pause. Then in a cold voice she told me I could see her the following Tuesday afternoon at 2:30.

When I arrived she showed me into a beautiful, spacious apartment. She motioned for me to sit on the sofa while she sat opposite me in a lounge chair. She didn't look at me. Instead she stared at her hands folded neatly in her lap. I studied her face. She had aged, of course. But she hadn't changed that much. She was still slim with dark hair and eyes like her father... an attractive woman in her forties.

She didn't speak. And in this awkward silence I didn't know what to expect. Finally she looked at me and said, "I hated you for many years because I thought my beautiful, talented sister was murdered because she married you! I loved her so much… she was so dear to me." And she burst into tears.

My right leg began to shake uncontrollably. She wiped her eyes and continued. "Later… much later, I realized that if she'd married a man Papa picked for her… a banker or an industrialist, she would have been in Warsaw when the Nazis came. And they would have squeezed her into one of those cattle cars and taken her to Auschwitz where they'd shave off her gorgeous black hair and gas her and burn her like all the others!" Fannie began to sob. I closed my eyes to block out that dreadful image.

A door slammed! I looked up to see a young man, tall, slim, suntanned, with dark hair and eyes. He wore an Israeli Army uniform. "Hey!" he said. What's going on here? What's wrong Ma?" He threw me an angry look.

She wiped her eyes again and murmured, "This is your Uncle Daniel. He was married to my sister Chani. We were just remembering some things." Then she introduced him. "This is my oldest son Max," she said with a look of pride.

A bell rang somewhere in my mind. I said, "Your son's name is Max Liebman?"

She said, "Yes. I married Emile Liebman. He's also a doctor like his father who was a physician in Berlin years ago.

Although it's a mother's privilege to name her firstborn child, my husband begged me to name this one for his beloved father who was murdered by the Nazis."

My throat closed. I began to cough as I remembered that scene once again... Dr. Liebman covered in bandages like a mummy with only his mouth and one eye exposed. I told the young man, "I knew your grandfather. Sometime I'll tell you what a great man he was and how important he was to me."

Now another boy came in, bouncing a soccer ball. He was about fourteen years old with dark hair like his older brother, but with pale blue eyes. He gave me a quick look then told his mother, "I'm starving! Is there anything for me to eat in that refrigerator?"

She smiled. "How come you're always hungry? Go take a look. I'm sure you'll find something."

He punched his big brother on the shoulder gently. "Hey, Let's see what there is." And the two of them left for the kitchen.

Fannie said, "That was Saul. I named him for my father."

"Reb Saul," I murmured, as scenes of my summer in Warsaw flashed in my mind. Those study classes with the Yeshiva guys... our private sessions. "I loved your father," I said.

"Everyone did. He was a wonderful man."

"Are the boys your only kids?"

"Oh no, I have five children. I didn't intend to have such a large family, but..." her voice trailed off... "we lost so many."

"Yes... we lost so many..." and I handed her the package I'd brought. She looked at me. I told her, "These are the wedding pictures." She tore the package open and saw Chani, smiling, glowing in her white satin gown. Fannie clutched the photo to her heart as tears ran down her face again. Her voice cracked and she gave me a doleful look.

"You know I missed the wedding." Then she glanced only briefly at the picture of Chani and me. But then she saw the family photo with Reb Saul on the left and Bubbe on the right holding little Avi, with Sarah leaning on her. Chani and I were standing behind them with Natan on one side of us and the twins on the other. Fannie began to sob again. But she quickly wiped her tears away when we heard the noise of someone coming in. "It's the children," Fannie said. "School just let out."

A beautiful blond, blue-eyed little girl about ten years old came in holding her little brother's hand. He was about five or six. He jumped onto his mother's lap for a hug and a kiss while the little girl kissed her mother's cheek.

"This is Bayla," Fannie said. "She's named for my mother and she looks like her too. And this little guy..." She ran her fingers through his brown curls... "this is Natan. Children, this is your Uncle Daniel." Bayla gave me a shy smile. Natan turned to look at me with soft brown eyes that broke my heart as I remembered the Natan he was named for. The gentle big brother who soothed his sister Sarah with endless stories he read to her. I thought, what did the Nazis do with them? Will we ever know? Then I said to myself, that kind of thinking will only lead to despair. I'm in Israel now! THIS is the ancient homeland of the Jewish people and they are the ones who invented Resurrection! And here it is! This is it!

I was startled to hear a baby cry. Fannie got up, with Bayla and Natan both clinging to her. Soon she came back carrying a little girl, not yet a year old, with pale blond hair and big blue-green eyes. She was rubbing her little nose. Then she saw me and smiled, showing off two pearl-like teeth. Fannie said, "This is Chani."

"Chani?" I mumbled. "This is Chani?" I was shaking but I didn't want to scare the baby. I wanted to hold her and kiss her. I felt as if she were mine! I forced myself to smile and wink at her. She got shy and snuggled into her mother's neck. I whispered, "She's so beautiful!" Fannie nodded and smiled.

This visit had been so intensely emotional, I couldn't stay any longer. I said, "I'd like to come back again. It would mean a lot to me to meet with your husband. I haven't seen Emile since his father's funeral, so many years ago. And I have more family pictures for you."

"Come for Shabbat dinner," she said. "Five o'clock. And thank you so much for bringing the wedding pictures. It meant everything to me to see them."

I gave her my address and phone number, in case she wanted to reach me. And although I couldn't take my eyes off the baby, I said a grateful goodbye. Then I left... still trembling, overcome by Fannie's family and all the memories that came with them... especially the baby... Chani.

When Friday night rolled around, I brought flowers and wine, along with the Machinski family pictures. Again, there was a lot of emotion and tears. Fannie tried to explain to her children about Uncle Moshe, Tanta Esther and all the other aunts, uncles and cousins. She told them about the close family life she had with them when she was growing up in Poland. And that now it was over. All of them were gone. The kids didn't understand why the Germans killed them. They asked a lot of difficult questions. I didn't say anything. To me it was clear... just as Rabbi Shaposhnik had said, demonize a people so you can steal their homes, their businesses and everything they own, right down to the gold in their teeth. But the Nazis killed more than a million children. What did they gain from that? Except to be labeled as more beastly than any beast!

I turned to Emile to ask about his mother and brother.

"They're both in Toronto and doing well. Stephan is a physician there and looks after our mother. We hope they'll come to visit us again soon."

Then I spoke about the tragedy of his father's death and how my deep remorse caused me to examine my own life and go forward in a whole new direction.

Later I spoke to Fannie and offered to babysit whenever she wanted to get away. Before long I was invited for every Shabbat dinner and the kids called me Uncle Danny. For the first time since my summer in Warsaw, I felt like I belonged. This was my family now.

CHAPTER 38 — HOPE

Some months later, on an ordinary sunny morning as I was having breakfast at my usual spot, the outdoor café at the King David Hotel, a shadow fell across the newspaper I was reading. I looked up and got the shock of my life!

"Karl!" I screamed. "Karl, is that you?" I leaped up and gave him a bear hug. I started babbling... "What happened to you? I looked everywhere! Where the hell have you been? How did you find me? What are you doing here?"

He smiled. "I've brought the Berlin Opera Company to Jerusalem. But before I made this trip I contacted your uncle and he told me where I might find you."

"Why didn't you write me?"

Karl laughed. "I wanted to surprise you." We sat down and stared at each other. So many years had gone by and we'd been through so much together. He ordered coffee and after a few sips he said, "Gretchen was killed at Auschwitz, you know." I nodded. He went on, "The war was over and I didn't know where to go or what to do after that. Eventually I made my way back to England to look for you. But it was too late. You were gone. Anyway, I stayed in London, got a job with the London Symphony Orchestra, and I remarried. My wife and I have two boys."

"Two boys…" I whispered.

"Yes. The oldest, Richard, is a fantastic violinist. He's going to be a star. And he's only seven. Our little one is three. We named him Erich Victor. He's a curly-haired, beautiful, wild kid. I don't know what we're going to do with him. Anyway… when Germany finally pulled itself together, years after the war, I went back to Berlin and took my family with me. I got in touch with the proper authorities there concerning our old company's assets. I made a settlement with the present government on our behalf, with the provision that I rebuild our theater on Kurfurstendam. It's much smaller, of course. But you're still my partner and you own half of it. I didn't try to reach you sooner because for years I couldn't make a go of it. I couldn't find musicians or suitable talent. All our former contacts for costumes and scenery were gone. It's only recently that I've turned a corner. Erich, the whole world has changed. Germany is a different country now. How about coming back to Berlin and being an active partner again?"

I didn't answer his question. I had questions of my own. "So you've been in Berlin for quite a while now. Have you heard anything about my father? Was he killed in the war?"

Karl hesitated for a few moments. "I don't know for sure. I've been contacted by the Israeli Secret Service (Mossad). They're checking to see if he's still somewhere in Europe. But there seems to be a rumor that he's in Argentina."

"Argentina?" I repeated. "So he gets away with everything."

"Maybe," Karl said. "We have to wait and see. Now how about it? How about coming back to Berlin?"

I shook my head. "Oh… god, no! You're right. The world has changed, and I have a new life now. I came to Jerusalem to find Chani's sister, Fannie. And I found her. She's the only member of the Machinski family that survived. She's now married to Emile Liebman, Dr. Liebman's son. You remember him?"

Karl's eyes widened. "Emile Liebman is here in Jerusalem? Of course I remember him. Listen, I'm only going to be here for a few days. I'd like to see him. Can you arrange it?"

"I'll try. But now they have five children, including a beautiful baby girl named Chani. She's starting to walk and she's teething. She drools on everything! I'd like to lick it! I see her often. She's so gorgeous… she has blond hair like mine and blue-green eyes like Chani. I think of her as mine… the baby we never had."

Karl nodded and whispered, "I'd like to have a little girl too. One with red curly hair, bright brown eyes and a few freckles on her nose." The two of us sat there in silence letting the pain of loss wash over us. It would never go away. Not for us or millions like us.

Finally Karl said, "If you're planning to stay a silent partner, we have accounts to settle. Come to our performance tonight. It starts at eight o'clock. We're doing Tosca. We can take care of business afterwards."

I didn't want to go. It always tore me up to hear those arias that Chani used to sing. But Karl would only be here for such a short time. I agreed to attend.

I got there a little early and stood with Karl at the back of the theater as we had so many times before. As the first Act unfolded, I closed my eyes as the soprano sang a beautiful aria. In my mind it was Chani singing. But on stage it was another soprano with a silver voice. I opened my eyes to see a beautiful woman, Spanish-looking, with long silky black hair and large dark eyes.

At Intermission Karl said, "Isn't she terrific? I got her through an agency. Her name is Anna Kozlen and she's originally from Riga. She's a widow now. Her husband was killed by the Nazis."

I nodded. It was a familiar story. "She's great!" I said. "Does she have any children?"

"Not anymore. The Nazis killed them too." He paused for a few moments. Then he said, "Would you like to meet her?"

I said, "Yes."

Made in the USA
San Bernardino, CA
20 November 2016